The Best of
Marion Zimmer Bradley's
Fantasy Magazine

Edited by
Marion Zimmer Bradley
and Elisabeth Waters
With an Introduction by Marion Zimmer Bradley

WARNER BOOKS

A Time Warner Company

WARNER BOOKS EDITION

Copyright © 1995 by Marion Zimmer Bradley and Elisabeth Waters
All rights reserved.

Cover design by Don Puckey
Cover illustration by Steve Youll
Hand lettering by Carl Dellacroce

Aspect is a registered trademark of Warner Books, Inc.

Warner Books, Inc.
1271 Avenue of the Americas
New York, NY 10020

W A Time Warner Company

Printed in the United States of America

First Printing: November, 1995

10 9 8 7 6 5 4 3 2 1

A RICH FEAST
OF ENCHANTMENTS AND DELIGHTS

"What a Wizard Does" by Hugo Award winner and Nebula Award nominee Janet Kagan: Faced with a cloud of gloomy children and a swarm of sniggets, a wizard and her cat must conjure a special magic . . .

▲ ▼ ▲

"Satanic, Versus" by Mercedes Lackey: Sorceress sleuth Diana Tregarde is stuck at a romance writers' reception where a witchy wannabe's love spell works too well . . .

▲ ▼ ▲

"Arakney's Web" by Jo Clayton: Arakney the Story Spinner must weave a spell to save a village of besieged were-folk from her ancient enemies . . .

▲ ▼ ▲

"Kill Dance" by Mary A. Turzillo: In a society of flight, and nests, and hatchlings, one twin imposes an ancient ritual on her sister—a duel to the death.

MARION ZIMMER BRADLEY'S
FANTASY MAGAZINE, VOL. II

Fifteen Tales of Magic and Adventure

ALSO BY MARION ZIMMER BRADLEY

The Best of Marion Zimmer Bradley's Fantasy Magazine

Published by
WARNER BOOKS

For my late father, Leslie R. Zimmer, Sr., whom I never appreciated when he was still alive.

—MZB

CONTENTS

INTRODUCTION

For the second anthology from *MZB's FM*, as I call my magazine, I wanted to explain that when I speak of us as MZB Limited, we really are. Some of the letters I get speak of us as if we were a gigantic corporation with almost unlimited resources and dozens of employees. Nothing wrong with that—except it's not true.

There are six of us; me and my secretary Elisabeth, who makes out payroll checks and is also the author of some of the finest stories in my anthologies. In fact, her story "The Keeper's Price" was what convinced me to edit my first Darkover anthology. At signing parties when people ask me to sign a lunch bag, a T-shirt, or something, I say, "I'll sign anything but a blank check." Well, for Lisa, I'll sign even that.

Or for our bookkeeper. Raul is an ex-policeman who is really—so we tease him—our token male to lift anything that's too heavy for us not-so-helpless females on the magazine—like the incoming mail. Raul handles all incoming manuscripts; he goes to the post office and hauls them home, then logs them in. He is empowered to reject immediately (in the interest of saving my eyesight) the handwritten manuscripts and anything he can't read, such as anything printed on a dot matrix printer. He also handles the magazine's bookkeeping.

Our most recent employee is a young trainee named Stephanie; a fine young writer, being trained to do anything any of the others can do.

Our subscription department is called Heather; she sends out renewal notices and handles new subscribers. She's a fine musician and song writer and has just sold a story to me for *Sword & Sorceress 12.*

Last, but emphatically not least, is our managing editor, Rachel Holmen. She's the only one of us who—as far as I know—has never tried to write fiction. For all I know, she might cherish the ambition to produce the next Pulitzer Prize novel, but she's never discussed it with me. Together she and I decide what goes in the magazine—our policy is that either can reject, but it takes both of us to accept. (For anyone who wants to brave my slush pile, send a #10 SASE—Self-Addressed Stamped Envelope—to me at P.O. Box 249, Berkeley CA 94701, for guidelines. This is also the address for subscription information.)

Rachel also handles the artwork, all of it. She goes around to conventions and finds new artists. If she finds work she likes, she commissions artwork for us by sending a photocopy of the story to be illustrated to the artist. So far I've agreed with her choices. I am sure that if I really disliked any artwork, she'd concede; but so far we've been in agreement. As the old saying goes, I don't know anything about art—I don't even know what I like. She does, and I give her a free hand.

But I do know what I like in fiction, and furthermore I am perfectly willing to defend what I like. I like the stories I've chosen for this anthology; here you'll find the cream of the cream.

Enjoy!

About Brad Strickland and "Miracle at Roodwell"

This story was originally printed in issue 4, back in 1989 (and it seems like only yesterday that I started the magazine). It takes a somewhat unorthodox view of miracles, and I've always liked stories that shed light on their subject from a different angle. It is certainly possible that a miracle may be as much curse as blessing.

Brad Strickland has been writing fantasy, as well as horror and science fiction, since 1982, and his short stories have appeared twice in *The Year's Best Horror Stories*. He is also an associate professor at Gainesville College and lives in Oakwood, Georgia, with his wife Barbara and children Amy and Jonathan.

Miracle at Roodwell

Brad Strickland

The city of Roodwell, swollen to many times its normal size, bustled with pilgrims rich and poor, credulous and cynical, noble-born and common; for on this day, the feast day of high spring, a miracle that could occur but once in a human lifetime might come to pass. Blind Mat and his wife Elowyn had done a good business in the begging way since early morning, as the milling pilgrims seemed to feel that a small display of charity might improve their chances of receiving the miracle-to-be.

Mat now worked the crowd in the southern part of the churchyard, not far from the stone-rimmed well that had drawn so many to Roodwell this day. Here the crush was greatest, with mailed shoulder jostling rag-clad arm, and the rose perfume of court ladies joining the sweaty rankness of farmers. The raucous bray of donkeys punctuated the continuous buzz and hum of conversation, and through it all the small high voice of a middle-aged priest struggled to be heard.

"Six times," the priest cried, waving his bony arm, "six

times the water of this well has healed. One helpless and hopeless person healed each time. Always on the anniversary day of the very first healing. That healing was of the blessed Saint himself, and that miraculous blessing allowed the Saint to live to see the cornerstone laid for his church, and the Lord has blessed the water and, in memory of the Saint, has permitted the healing to continue, even to these latter days. Come and try the water, you afflicted. Which one of you might the Lord smile on today?"

"Penny for a blind man," Mat sang out. "Penny for a poor man whose eyes are dark in his head. Take pity, take pity." Coins clanked in his tin cup, a quick rattling hailstorm of charity. "Thank ye, thank ye," Mat said, nodding at the black world, while inwardly weighing the cup and calculating the best time to remove the take and pass it to Elowyn, who trailed him at an inconspicuous distance. It was not good for a beggar to have too many pennies in his cup, for a full cup dried the wellsprings of brotherly love.

"Let's see your 'blind' eyes," a gruff masculine voice said.

Mat recognized the officious tone of a town warden. "Aye, sir," he said, and lifted a hand to push up the faded blue scarf shielding his eyes from the world. "Here they be."

He heard a few people nearby gasp. His eyes he knew were bad. The rough voice, softer now, said, "Faith, man, how did it happen?"

"A fire, long ago," Mat said, settling the scarf back into place. "I was just a lad."

"Here." The owner of the gruff voice plinked a coin into the cup, and others followed.

"Bless ye, bless ye," Mat said. He felt his way a little farther along, shook his cup, and cried out, "Alone, alone, in a dark, wide world!"

Quick on her cue, Elowyn was there. "Ah, Mat," she said admiringly, "you've done wonders today."

"Can you help me, love?"

"Aye. Nobody's looking. There's a lame man not far off, about to drink of the water, and he has all eyes. Here, Mat."

Her cool, soft hands touched his callused ones. He felt the burden of the cup eased, felt it lighten as Elowyn slipped most of the coins into their purse. "You are lovely," he told her.

"Mat. Not now." But her shy voice was pleased.

"Your hair is fairer than spun gold," Mat crooned to her, softly, confidentially. "Your eyes are the blue of Heaven's very dome. Your skin is white as milk, and you've two roses in your cheeks."

"Go on with you," she said, but her hand caressed his seamed cheek for just an instant.

"You're my eyes and my treasure," Mat said. "Elowyn, I love you."

"Then go beg enough to buy us a proper bed for one night," she told him, but love warmed her words. "Go on with you now, Mat. I'll be at hand."

Mat turned and began to nudge his way back into the crowd, toward the priest's high, fluting voice: "Come, come, all you who suffer. Come and taste the holy water of Roodwell. Come and try its virtue—"

"Damn the water!" screamed someone just ahead of Mat.

"Penny for a blind man?"

"Who's that? Who's that? The lame fellow?"

"The water failed him. Look out for him—'ware of the crutch!"

"Pity for the blind man?"

"Hold him back—hold him!"

"Out of the way, you blind fool!"

"Penny for the—"

Agony cracked Mat's shins, lighting swirls of red and yellow in his dark universe. He heard his tin cup clatter to the cobblestones, spilling his hard-begged pennies. Then the crutch hit him again, this time in the chest, knocking the wind out of him. So crowded was the marketplace that his fall was slow, cushioned by hands, thighs, and calves. His scarf slipped loose and was gone.

"Blind, eh?" The tip of the crutch thumped again into his chest. Mat gasped for breath but could not reply. "Here, blind man. Take this. Take the damned healing water of Roodwell."

Cold, cold, flowing over his face, running into his ruined eyes, spilling across his cheeks. He snorted, choked on a spume of water, and coughed.

"Get him away, get him away. Don't let him—"

"Here, old man, bring your crutch here—"

"Let me through! Let me through!"

"Here, what is all this, what is—"

"Father, a crippled man knocked this fellow down—"

"He's gone, now—"

"This man's blind—"

The priest, a young man, not the one who had been preaching at the rim of the stone well, leaned over Mat. "Are you hurt, old man?"

Mat blinked. "I—"

Faces surrounded him. Faces. He could not put a name to any of the thousand colors around him.

The priest frowned. "Did you hear me?"

"I—"

Oh, the sun was bright. He had forgotten the sun.

"I can see!"

The murmur around him rose to a shout. A multitude of hands pulled him upright. The priest yelled something in his ear.

Mat said again, wonderingly, "I can see!"

He was lifted, held up for all to look upon. "Healed!" someone shouted. "The miracle! This man was healed!"

Wildly, Mat's renewed eyes gazed about at the crowd. Hands reached out to touch him, startling as reared serpents, and he shrank from them. Afflicted faces turned toward him. He tried to look away from their stares of anger, their accusation and cheated desire.

"Elowyn!" he cried. "Elowyn, where are you?"

But his voice was utterly lost in the jubilant chaos of the churchyard, and nowhere did he hear the answering voice of Elowyn.

More than two weeks before, they had come out of the hills, Elowyn and he. In the high country, Elowyn had said, spring was still a gold-green promise, wrapped tight in the buds of willow and ash. But in the farmlands, where the road uncoiled itself at last to run between gently rolling fields and pastures, the season had already come. Elowyn had picked flowers and named them to him, her hands full of fragrant spring: violets, lady's-smocks, daisies, even early brier roses. "A good warm day," she told him as they rested against a grassy bank. Overhead, birds sang, and behind him somewhere, a cow clanked her brass bell.

"Lots of crowds in Roodwell, the travelers say," Mat murmured. Their purse was already swollen with donations from passersby and pilgrims. "Should be well fixed for weeks after the festival."

"And don't we deserve it, after the winter we've had?" Elowyn's voice lilted with indignation. "Thrown on the charity of the priests and separated, as if we were not man and wife!"

"Aye. Me in the parish house, and you in the nunnery. My poor Elowyn. It hurts me to think of your hardship there."

" 'Twas nothing, Mat. Only the being parted from you hurt. The washing of the clothes and the mending—that was nothing. But still I was glad to show that niggardly prioress the back of my heels."

Out of his private darkness, Mat reached and found her hand. He brought it close enough to kiss. "You should never have come with me, all those years ago. You should have stayed with your father."

Elowyn always laughed at this. "And by now he'd have married me off to a farmer, belike. Or even worse, a coachman. An innkeeper's daughter has poor prospects, Mat. That day when you came to beg and my father turned you away—well, that was the day something in me let go of my father at last." Her hand squeezed his. "And the next priest we came to married us, and if you say you regret it, Mat Macrone, then you just go on your way alone. A girl like me can have her choice of the next bonny fellow to come down the high road."

"But you love me." After seven years, there was still wonder in the statement.

"You spindle-shanked rascal," she said, but the warmth in her voice belied the words.

Mat smiled and leaned back on his elbows in the warm, soft grass. "Tell me again what you look like."

"Faith, are you not a-weary of that fairy tale?"

"Tell me, Elowyn."

With a sigh, she began. "My hair is long and soft—that you can feel for yourself—"

"And the color of it is gold."

"If you're going to take the tale from my mouth, then tell it yourself."

"No, no, Elowyn. I won't stop you again."

"It is gold, like—oh, like the morning sun on the water, with sparkles in it, gold like a bright fire, gleaming on the face of the night. Gold, like money new-minted, and it falls below my shoulders when I let it down."

"And your face," Mat prompted.

"They tell me I am very comely. My forehead is smooth and white, and in my cheeks are two lovely pink roses. My eyes—all the visitors at my father's inn told me I had bonny eyes—my eyes are blue, the deepest sky blue you can imagine, the blue of the halo 'round the moon. The blue of the edge of evening, rising to overtake the day. My nose is small, as a woman's should be, and delicate. My mouth is a wide mouth, but a good one, with full lips as red as cherries in the summer." On and on she spoke, not with vanity in her voice, as one might expect, but frankly and openly, pleased to serve as Mat's eyes, as much as when she steadied him on a foot log, or warned him of a tree root in the path.

"Am I not the luckiest fellow beneath the sun?" Mat said when she finished.

"And are you not the laziest, too?" she asked, laughing. "Up, now, and on the road, or we'll never make Roodwell today."

Geoffrey was the innkeeper's name, and a broad-faced, hulking man he was, his red face and huge belly proclaiming him fond of his own food and drink. The inn was a two-storied, dark grey wooden building called, too grandiosely, the Saracen's Arms. Geoffrey, like his building, was grey, scabrous, and by no means overly clean.

"High summer is coming," he grunted grudgingly. "Suppose I could use some extra hands, to serve the customers and tidy up the place. But times are hard."

"Yes," said Elowyn, not believing him. The inn was full to bursting with pilgrims, excitedly chattering about the miracle of the day: a blind man, miraculously healed, then hailed into the inner recesses of the chapter house. The church services this year would have an added attraction indeed, a man touched by divinity itself. In celebration of that, the pilgrims were already getting drunk.

Geoffrey rubbed a hand over stubbled jowls. "Give you a bed and meals," he said. "And you keep what the customers give you. Can't ask for fairer."

Elowyn stood in the steamy kitchen of the inn, and Geoffrey sat at the pegged table. Around them bustled a cook and her two helpers, preparing the evening meal. Over Geoffrey's shoulder, the cook scowled and shook her head. "Thank you," Elowyn said. "But perhaps one of the other inns—"

The frown did not improve Geoffrey's looks. "Wait a bit, wait a bit. Not too hasty. Maybe I can pay a bit. Just a bit, mind you. Barmaids're plentiful, and you're, well, nothing special."

"No."

Geoffrey shifted his considerable bulk, and his breath

rattled deep in his throat. "Maybe one shilling a month, if you're competent."

"Maybe two?"

The cook turned and shook her head slightly. Geoffrey sighed. "I can't ruin myself for a vagabond," he said. "A shilling and sixpence." Behind him, the cook turned back to her stew.

"Done," Elowyn said. "Should I begin right now?"

Geoffrey rose ponderously to his feet. "No time like the present, I guess. Aprons are in the pantry behind you. Start at the bar."

Lord, how easily and unwelcomely it came back to her: serving the ale and the stronger drink, bantering with every vile-tongued, leering rascal with the price of a cup, and pretending to like it; avoiding (when she was lucky) the quick, insidious grope of dirty hands, reaching to squeeze her breast through her clothing, or, worse, sweeping up beneath her skirts to graze her naked leg. Before the night had dwindled to the inevitable six or seven maudlin or stupefied drunks, the old ache in her back returned, growing up from her heels, up the backs of her legs, like an evil vine, to bear its tiresome fruit just above her hips.

So tired was she at the end of the day that she unwisely allowed Geoffrey to show her to the little cubicle where her pallet and blanket were spread on the floor. So despairing was she that she was not really surprised when Geoffrey pulled her against him. When she pushed him away, he put his hands on her again. They struggled, and that was when Geoffrey found the money pouch. "That's mine!" she cried as he ripped it away.

He hefted it in the dark. She heard the clinking of coins. "Thieves about," he said. "I'll just keep it safe for you. Now—"

"No," she told him. "Take the purse, but—"

His hands were at her. She scratched and pushed. Finally, wheezing, he growled, "I'll have the money anyway, vixen. Fool, you'll make nothing extra like that. Customers're willing to pay summat extra for a bit of fun, even with a plain-looking slut. But you—pfah! I'd sooner lie with old Teresa." He pushed himself away and out the door, but the stench of his sweat lingered, with the prickling memory of his stubbled jowls against her throat and cheek.

She drew the ratty blanket up to her neck and clutched it there. "Oh, Mat," she moaned. In the dark, tears stung her eyes, overflowed, and ran first warm, then cold, down her temples and into her grey-streaked, mousy hair.

Brother Xavier—that was the young monk's name—brought Mat his supper of broth, bread, and peas. He said before he was asked, "Not yet, Mat. We haven't found her yet."

"It's been seventeen days!" Mat protested.

"I know, I know. Here, please, eat."

Mat gnawed the dark bread and sipped at the broth. "My wife," he said. "Something's happened to her."

"We are still seeking her," Brother Xavier said.

Mat looked around. The business of looking, of seeing, was still new to him; it seemed that the little cell broke new on his sight each morning, born wondrously out of the black night. It was plain enough, three high narrow windows let in bars of sunlight. A simple chest, a bedstead that held a straw mattress, two straight chairs, and high on the wall facing the bed, a wooden crucifix. Mat found delight in it all still. He marveled at the texture of the stones that made up the wall, the cunning fit of one among its fellows, at the different ways the dark wood of the cross looked, with the hazy glow of morning on it, or the deep shadow of noon, or the warm gleam of the setting sun. His eyes were as hungry as his stomach.

"Father Berien has spoken to the Duke of Welford about you," said Brother Xavier. "Would you like to meet the young duke?"

"I'd like to find my wife," Mat said. He finished the broth and rubbed the back of his hand across his mouth. His beard bristled. Elowyn always kept him clean-shaven.

When Brother Xavier had confessed him and shriven him, on the day of the miracle, the cup of ritual wine had been borne on a salver of polished silver; in it, Mat had seen his face for the first time in forty years: seamed, red, and rough, the eyes dark under hanging brows, the cheeks lined with care and travel. Since that first shocking glance, Mat had shaved himself only infrequently, not caring to see that countenance again in any mirror.

Brother Xavier now bowed his head, as if in silent prayer. His tonsure was startlingly white in the dark nest of his hair. "We are trying to find her," he said, finally. "But no one recalls a woman such as you describe. And she has not come to the church, though everyone knows you are here."

Mat reached for a flagon he kept on the chest. The brothers made their own wine, very good though a bit thin for Mat's taste. "It's me," Mat said. "I'm so damned ugly."

"Brother Mat, that's not so. You're a man, like other men."

"But next to her, I tell you, next to her, I'm like—like a jackass next to a prize mare. Like a crow next to a dove. How could she love me, she that could see me?"

"And yet she married you, you say, seven years ago. And she's been beside you ever since." Brother Xavier sighed. "I know little of women or of their hearts, Brother Mat, but this I do know: a woman who has given you seven years of her life will not desert you. She will turn up, never fear. But of this visit to the young Duke of Welford—"

Folk thronged all summer to the place where miracles happened. The inn seemed always full of hungry, thirsty men. Elowyn grew to live with the dull ache in her bones; she did well enough as a barmaid—though she did without the "summat extra," she fended off the leering proposals of the inn patrons with forced smiles and false wit. Soon, as she became more used to the place and to her new master, she put a decisive end to Geoffrey's visits to her room. He roared and grumbled, but went off instead to the cubicle of a more willing servant and after a day or two seemed to have forgotten all about Elowyn.

One day dragged into the next, and through them all, Elowyn saw no more of the world than she could see through the dim windows and open front door of the Saracen's Arms, and most of what she saw was an endless procession of pilgrims, seeking entertainment, enlightenment, or a blessing from the healed blind man of Roodwell.

Geoffrey welcomed all, not believing in miracles himself, as he said, but well content to take more money in, more, always more; Elowyn knew, as indeed she had known from the beginning, that she probably would never see Mat's purse again. Geoffrey kept it, she supposed, with the rest of his hoard, behind a loose stone in the fireplace of his own bedroom. It mattered little, for she felt no need of the money. She felt only the familiar ache of despair.

On the other hand, she was hidden away, safe in the bustle of the crowds. So she worked for well over a month, until one evening when she served wine to a loud table dominated by a young man come to town for the first time.

"I don't believe that beggar ever was blind," he declared as Elowyn set a cup before him. "How could a beggar afford such a healing?"

Elowyn's hand froze.

A steady customer slapped the table and said, "I saw it, I tell you. He had no eyes. Heard that melted silver splashed in his face when he was younger, apprentice to a silversmith. Aye, just pits, that's all, burnt out and the color of raw liver. And the water is free to all, I tell you— that's the way of the monks, you know."

"Pour, wench," the young man ordered. She did so, stiff with listening. "Priests aren't like that. Toll for this, tax for that—probably he was a mummer, a fraud, meant just to draw people and donations into the church. Miracle!" He raised the cup again and drained it at a gulp. "Don't talk to me about such nonsense as miracles!"

Another young fellow, holding his cup to be filled, said, "You can ask the man yourself, you know. He's working up at the stables now."

The man who had seen Mat's burned eyes said, "I never heard that."

"Truth! The monks offered him bed and bread for as long as he wanted, but he said he had to get out of the cloister. So Brother Xavier—don't know if you know him, he's all right, for a monk, better than most of them— anyway, last week Brother Xavier got him a job, working for old Hubert at the stables, pitching hay and wiping down horses. We can see him if you want—"

"Wench! Over here!"

The voice pulled Elowyn away. She served wine to two other tables, then went back to the first. The group had gone, leaving behind three copper pennies. She took them with numb fingers, her eyes far away.

Next morning, when old Teresa, the cook, went to haggle for the purchase and delivery meat, Elowyn went with her.

Roodwell was a confusion of stone and wooden buildings, some grand, some plain, some wretched, and now it was a sea of faces. Elowyn broke away from the old woman and made her way around the fringes of crowds, skirting street acrobats and jugglers, walking through clouds of spice-fragrant but alien cooking smells, at last seeing in the distance the stables.

Many stables stood there, managed by different men, but she discovered the one she wanted soon enough: it was owned by the man named Hubert, and, oddly, it reminded her of the inn, a splintering grey structure that promised the barest of comforts to its animal guests. Hubert himself, an old man with the broad shoulders of a former blacksmith, stood there, and Mat cowered, beside him.

"Blind!" Hubert roared, his chest working like a bellows. "Stone blind, and Roodwell's water healed him! Come talk to the blind man, only a penny!"

Elowyn dared not get close. She watched from a distance, as several men and women stepped up, paid their pennies— all the coppers went into Hubert's pocket, she noted, none into Mat's—and they spoke for a moment with Mat. She saw her husband nod, his head bowed, his gaze in the dust, she caught just the sound, not the words, of his mumbled replies to their inquiries. She heard derisive laughter, saw once the haunted look in his new, clear eyes, and felt her heart twist within her.

A stableboy led some horses into the stalls behind Hubert and Mat. When he came out again, Elowyn beckoned him and pressed a penny into his hand. "Where does the blind man sleep?"

The boy seemed dull, but the penny brightened his wits. "Up in t'loft," he said. "Among t'hay. Old Hubert's too cheap to spare a room for him in t'house."

Elowyn pushed away and plodded back to the inn.

Mat lay in the scratchy straw, above the dung reek of the stable. *I can stand no more*, he told himself. Long had it been since he had called any man "master," and Hubert insisted on that title for himself. But worse, blind as he had been, Mat had never felt himself more a beggar than now. The center of a circle of eyes, he was the butt of a thousand jokes, a show given to a doubting and jeering audience—and alone all the while, so alone.

Soon it would be night, and with night came a chance of escape. If only this time his nerve did not fail him. If only he could get away.

As evening came to Roodwell, Hubert, as usual, had gone to seek wine and revelry. From the inns in the next street came distant sounds of music, brawling, and laughter. Through the open loft window drifted the dusk light that preceded nightfall. When at last Mat sat up to pull on his boots, he started and realized that he was not alone. A skinny, dull-looking drudge stood hesitant in the dim light from the open door.

"Run away, Mat Macrone," she said in the softest of voices. "You were never born to be a show and a servant. Run away!"

Mat's breath caught in his throat. Before he even knew he was about to move, he had burst out of the hay and swung down from the loft, dropping not three steps from the woman. She cried out, in fright or anger, and turned from him—

"Elowyn," he said, catching her by the elbows.

The woman shook her head. "No," she said roughly.

"You can never fool my hands or my ears," he said. "Elowyn, turn and look at me."

"No. Go away." Anguish brimmed in her voice.

"Elowyn . . . my love."

A noise from the street—as if someone were raising a cry of "Thief!"—jerked her head around. Her face was haggard and drawn in the half-light. "Go or they'll catch you," she said.

It was as if he had not heard. Mat reached to pull Elowyn to him, and again she twisted away. "Can't ye see I'm ashamed, you fool?" she wailed.

"Ashamed—of me?" Mat asked, his voice appalled.

"No, no. You don't understand."

"Elowyn, I understand you are my wife. If you no longer want to be my wife, I—I no longer want to live."

"Don't. Such words are a sin."

"I don't care. Damn Roodwell! Damn its healing waters. It's brought me nothing but grief. I was happier blind."

"Because then you could not see me."

He could only look in bafflement at the averted figure. "No," he said, at last. "Because it's made me something I never was and never wanted to be. I've seen my own face. A bad face it is, and I cannot blame you if—"

She whirled on him then, anger hot in her eyes. "You've a kind face and a decent one, and I'll hear no more of that, Mat Macrone! Look at me! Damn it, look at me! What do you see?"

Mat's face broke into a smile, a smile like all the sunrises of spring rolled into one. "Faith," he said, his voice trembling a little, "I see hair like soft gold, and a skin as white as milk, and two lovely roses in your cheeks—"

"Don't mock me!" Elowyn buried her face in her hands. "I'm plain! I'm homely! My hair is brown as a mouse, and my skin is dark with wind and the sun. I told you all those lies—"

The cry of "Thief" had subsided, but all of a sudden they burst through the door: Geoffrey, bushy-haired and wild-eyed in the light of a torch, two stolid wardens, and a young, troubled-looking monk.

"There she is!" roared Geoffrey. "She's the one who took my money!"

Mat stepped in front of Elowyn, shielding her. "Brother Xavier, what is this?" he demanded.

The young monk shook his tonsured head. "Mat, this is an innkeeper who swears that this woman robbed him."

"She did! She stole a purse with silver and copper in it from me." To Elowyn, he hissed, "You'll give it back, whore. And then I'll take you to bed and teach you manners, ugly as you are."

"Mat," she whispered, "it's our money, our purse."

"This is my wife," Mat said, and his voice had never rung as it did now.

"Give Brother Xavier the purse." He closed his eyes tight.

"It is leather, studded with eight smooth brads," Mat said, eyes still shut. "There is a nick on the inside of the flap, just to the right of the bend. You will find an embossed circle, with a line through it—the sign of Carradon, the maker, who gave it to me."

"It is his purse," the monk said.

Mat opened his eyes.

The wardens were looking at Geoffrey and not in a friendly way.

"I believe a thief has no right to cry 'thief' on another," Elowyn said.

"Indeed not," the monk replied. "Geoffrey, I see a long penance and a hard one for the wrongs you have done."

Whatever protest Geoffrey began to make was stopped in his mouth by Mat's fist, sudden and incontestable. Geoffrey simply collapsed backward, between the stolid wardens. One did stoop, prudently enough, to pick up the burning torch the innkeeper had dropped. Behind them the barn doorway was beginning to fill with spectators. Geoffrey gurgled and moaned, finally forcing himself up on his elbows.

In the torchlight, Mat looked at Elowyn in undisguised wonder. "You are even more beautiful than you said," he murmured.

Forgetting the monk, the wardens, and the onlookers, Elowyn wailed, "But I'm plain! I told you lies, Mat—all lies!"

"No." He put his hand under her chin and lifted her face to his. "If gold is not the color of your hair, it is gold that lies, not you. If milk is not the color of your forehead, why milk is the falsehood. Oh, Elowyn, don't you know I measure all beauty by you? I could always see you, Elowyn. Not with my eyes, but with my heart. No splash of water is going to change that."

A derisive guffaw choked off short in some male throat. For as the others looked from Mat's adoring face to her, astonishment came to them, and awe.

From the ground, Geoffrey growled through bloody teeth, "They're in it together! I tell you the money is mine! Anything this bitch has is mine—"

Elowyn whirled on him, but before the angry words could leap from her tongue, the innkeeper fell back, stammering in confusion: "Mine! *Yours.* I mean, of course, yours, all yours, my—my lady."

And then the wonder of the true miracle fell upon her. *I am beautiful,* she thought; and with the thought came the reality. She could not say for certain that any thing about her had changed. But as they walked from the stable, the crowd melted away before them, murmuring, falling silent as they caught sight of her, and men looked after her passage with yearning, women with envy, all with fascination.

They left Roodwell behind them that night. In all their ways and wanderings that were to follow, Mat and Elowyn never met another miracle, but then, neither wanted to. As Mat always said afterward, two miracles are enough for anyone but a knave or a fool.

About Deborah Wheeler and "Under the Skin"

Deborah has been one of "my" writers for over a decade now, so I was delighted to get a story from her for my magazine. I was not, of course, at all delighted about the real-life circumstances that inspired this story.

Shortly after Deborah's second daughter was born—and, as I recall, it was an unusually difficult pregnancy, requiring her to spend months in bed—Deborah's mother was raped and murdered by a teenage neighbor. The guy finally wound up in San Quentin, but it was a very difficult time for everyone involved, and with his first parole hearing coming up this year, we're all remembering it. And many writers deal with trauma in their lives by writing about it, which is less likely to land you in jail than acting on your feelings about the creep who brutally murdered your mother.

Deborah says that "Under the Skin" came to her at a time when she felt overwhelmed by her own pain and anger. The opening scene draws from fantasies of revenge, coupled with twenty years' experience in the martial arts, and she used these as a springboard to explore "the seductive nature of hatred." Agatha Christie said in one of her murder mysteries that if you invite evil into your heart, it will make its home there. Deborah adds, "Understanding that hatred, even in a righteous cause, can devour from within is a crucial step in healing."

Under the Skin

Deborah Wheeler

It could have been a mugging, or some kid on dope roughing up a wino, but when she paused before the darkened alley on the humid July night, something in her guts went *zing*! and Jodie Marshall knew another woman was in trouble and needed her help. She stepped beyond the Hollywood streetlights and saw two bodies wrestling between the trash cans. Without thinking of the danger she might be putting herself in, Jodie dropped her sweat-soaked karate *gi* rolled in its black belt and sprinted toward them.

She could not see much more of the man than his back and a thatch of hair, but she did not need to in order to know what was going on. He hunched over his victim, pinning her legs apart with his knees. The woman beneath him moaned, a hoarse, almost animal sound. Her white thighs shone in the darkness.

Jodie's first kick, a sweeping roundhouse with all the power her *kiai* could generate, caught the man across the back of his kidneys. Breath burst from him as his spine arched reflexively. His neck snapped back to meet her knife hand at the base of his skull.

The man's head thwacked against the cracked pavement, bounced, and then lolled from a limp body. Jodie clung to him like a limpet as he fell, and then slid her fingers around to the front of his neck, digging through the layers of muscle for his carotid arteries. The pulse under her fingers felt strong and vital. She wondered what it would be like to press just a little harder. . . .

It would be so easy, wouldn't it? No one would ever know it hadn't happened accidentally during the fight. Just a little more pressure, and the elastic walls of the blood vessels would bend inward, bend and finally collapse . . .

Temptation swept through Jodie like a wave of sexual heat. She sweated with wanting it.

The heart itself, now so arrogant in life, would begin to falter, beat by beat growing slower and less regular. Then stillness, blessed peace, one less monster to prowl the darkness, giving women nightmares they would carry for the rest of their lives. His brain might cry out as it squandered the last of its precious oxygen supply, but it would be a silent cry. She would never hear it, not even in her dreams. Now she had the chance she'd longed for these past ten years, the chance to get back for what those bastards did to Sherry.

Just a few more moments . . .

The woman on the ground moaned again. She pushed herself up on her elbows, her face hidden beneath a tangle of darkness.

"C'mon, we've got to get out of here." Jodie lifted the other woman by one slender wrist. The skin was marble cool under Jodie's fingers, the bones light and fragile as a bird's.

"I'll take you to the hospital—you might be hurt and not realize it. Adrenaline does that to you—" Jodie hurried her out of the alley, pausing only to scoop up her *gi*.

"No hospital. No police," the woman said in a low, heavily accented voice. She sounded Russian or Polish, not Hispanic, but Jodie could not place her origin.

"You can't let that creep walk away, not after what he

tried to do. The next woman he jumps might not be so lucky—she might end up dead."

Jodie realized that she was talking too fast and her fingertips ached from pressing against the woman's arm. With an effort, she released her grip. It wasn't the woman's fault that she had been brainwashed into taking whatever shit this sexist society dumped on her. Or maybe there was another reason.

"You don't want the authorities to know about you? Are you an illegal or something?"

The woman's face glimmered in the artificial light— huge shadowed eyes, pointed chin, wine-dark lips. "I need only a place to rest."

"I can't just leave you here." Jodie pointed to her battered Honda at the curbside. "You can stay with me for a few days."

The woman slid into the front passenger seat. "I shall not overstay my welcome. A few days, as you say."

Jodie unlocked both locks to her one-bedroom apartment. "C'mon in, sit anywhere. What's your name, by the way?"

"Mary Smith."

"Look, I don't care who you really are or why you want to stay hidden—" Jodie flicked on the lights. "And if you're dealing, I don't want to know about it, but we've got to call the cops on this."

Mary Smith sat on the battered sofa covered with an old chenille bedspread. "What good would that do?"

"For one thing, the creep could still be lying there and they'll pick him up. Even if you don't press charges, he'll spend the night locked up instead of assaulting the next woman he comes across. Also for the record, so the cops start believing us about the frequency of rape around here. Every unreported attack puts us that much further from decent protection."

"As you wish, but it will do no good."

She was right. The duty officer sniggered, "You did

what to him and left him *how*?" and refused to take the report without Jodie's name.

Christ, another bozo who doesn't believe women can fight back, Jodie thought as she hung up.

The next morning Mary Smith was gone. After Jodie dressed for work at the women's bookstore, she headed for her favorite coffee shop. She was low on funds, as usual, but after last night she deserved a meal she didn't have to cook herself.

"Hi, Stell." Jodie slid onto a stool at the counter and picked up the copy of the *Los Angeles Times* that the last customer had abandoned. "How's life in the old roach coach?"

"And to you too, Jo. The usual?"

"Yeah, and the coffee up front, please. I had the strangest night— Holy shit."

The waitress craned her neck around to read the page Jodie laid flat on the counter.

"Some creep got bumped off in an alley. Since when is that news in Hollywood? They figure he was a rapist because his dong was out. Serves the bastard right."

But he was alive when I left him. I swear he was! Maybe some doper rolled him for his wallet and it had nothing to do with me. But if I hadn't left him there . . .

Christ, Jodie, he had it coming. One less macho shit pig in the universe.

He deserved prison, he didn't deserve to die. . . .

Jodie bent over her coffee, feeling the warmth seep through fingers grown suddenly cold. She had wanted him dead in the height of her fury. But she had stopped herself from acting on it.

Or had she?

Jodie set down one of the two bags of groceries she carried, unlocked the door to her apartment, and pushed the bag inside with one foot. The reading light over the one comfortable chair was on and Mary Smith sat beneath it, her legs tucked underneath her. Instead of the torn clothing of the night before, she wore a creamy blouse, obviously silk, and black velvet pants. Two expensive-looking suitcases lay in the corner beside the orange-crate bookshelves.

Mary looked up from the book she was reading. "My friend! How glad I am to see you!" she exclaimed.

"Can you give me a hand with these groceries?" Jodie mumbled. "I'm sorry, I've only shopped for one."

Mary got up from the chair in a movement that would stir envy in a dancer. As she took the bag, Jodie smelled her perfume, a dry spicy scent, unfamiliar and disturbing. Mary laughed. "I did not expect you to feed me too! I will put these things away for you—no, let me do just this little thing. You have done so much for me already."

In the bathroom Jodie pulled off her clothes and stepped into the shower. The hot water beating on her shoulders helped relax the iron tension of the day. She lost track of time, for when she had dried and dressed, she found the living room empty. She wolfed down a frozen dinner, flipped the TV on and off a few times, and finally tumbled into bed.

The dream began as an ordinary residue of the day's events, but soon Jodie found herself walking down a deserted hallway, peering into one doorway after another. As the light faded into shadow, colors took on a strange new richness and all her senses grew sharper. The cold air brought her waves of intoxicating scents; her own heartbeat and the gentle whisper of air in her lungs seemed more compelling than an ocean storm. Finally she reached the last doorway and stopped. She looked down at her hands, to find them spattered with fresh blood. But instead of being horrified, the sight and smell filled her with an almost orgasmic ecstasy, a pleasure so deep that it sent her reeling into terror and she woke up in a cold sweat.

* * *

The next day Jodie awakened feeling as if she'd been on a three-day drunk, her body sodden and unresponsive as she lurched out of bed. She ran cold water down the back of her neck and scrubbed her teeth while she stared into the mirror. *You did kill him*, she thought despondently. *That's what your subconscious was trying to tell you last night. What are you going to do now? How are you going to live with this?*

Jodie decided to make the morning karate workout even if it meant losing a few hours of work. Her boss wouldn't object, and she badly needed the mind-clearing exercise. She dug out a fresh *gi* and her belt. The stitched black fabric had gone gray with wear along the sides.

We are taught to revere life, never to use our art for aggression, but only the preservation of that life. But how could I have turned away from everything I believe in for one moment of insanity?

The class was small, and Jodie was the only woman present. Normally this didn't bother her, although she had gotten some harsh comments from friends who felt that a woman of her rank owed it to her sisters to work out only with other women. Some of the men had an ego problem about a woman who was their rank superior, and she'd had to "accidentally" bloody a few noses during sparring. As *sensei* led them through the solo exercises, Jodie worked out next to a barrel-chested man named Steve Azusa. Although he smiled hello as usual, white teeth shining in his dark-complected face, she did not return his greeting with her usual glare, *What do you think I am, some second-class plaything?* She remembered he was a cop, a detective sergeant with the LAPD.

There's no scarlet letter on your forehead, no token of what you've done, Jodie told herself, clinging desperately to her concentration. *It's only your own conscience that says he can see right through you. And why should you care what he thinks? He's probably an arrogant s.o.b. like the rest of them.*

Jodie finished the workout with a long round of sparring with Steve Azusa. She forgot her doubts, forgot the misery of not knowing if she was really a killer. All she saw was his face, as closed and set as her own, but with a hint of good nature in the lift of his eyebrows. With a mind like ice she blocked his moves, spinning to counterattack. Her hands and feet were not bone and flesh, but hammers, knives, claws, as bereft of emotion as the tools they resembled. Finally *sensei* drew the class together for closing meditation. Jodie sat on her knees, *seiza*, and felt her heartbeat calm, her thoughts grow still. *Sensei* clapped three times to end the class.

Got to air this place out, Jodie thought as she unlocked the door. She'd worked late that night to make up for the morning's karate practice. The air in the apartment tasted flat, as if all the life had gone out of it.

Mary Smith sat on the sofa in a pool of light from the reading lamp. "Ah, my friend, you are so late tonight. You work too hard. I shall treat you to a concert—Holly Near, at the Pavilion—that would please you?"

Jodie shook her head with genuine regret. "I'd love to, but I'm so grubby, and it's too late for dinner—"

"Not a problem. You dress, and I'll make you something you can eat on the way. Please let me do this for you, it's the least I can offer in return for the refuge you've given me."

They sat in the best orchestra seats, waiting for the concert hall lights to dim. Jodie said uncomfortably, "You're spending rather a lot of money—"

"I would rather not speak of it. Do you intend to tell me—"

"No, I'm just used to paying my own way, usually the cheapest." *I wonder if she uses her money for dope too. That would explain why she bounced back so quickly after that first night—maybe the new designer crack* ... "I don't understand why you don't have a place to stay," she continued, somewhat snappishly. "Surely you can afford a hotel."

"Do you understand that I would rather not be identifiable by the authorities?"

"You're an illegal alien, then?" *And not a dealer?*

"Something like that."

"You should be getting legal help through the Sanctuary movement or the ACLU—"

Mary sighed and laid one hand on Jodie's. She lowered her voice to a disturbing intimacy. "I have found through the years that there is a certain loyalty which only one woman can give to another."

"Are you making a pass at me?" asked Jodie, suddenly skittish. She wasn't turned on by other women, but there was something about Mary . . .

Mary smiled and withdrew her hand. "I speak of sisterhood, not sexual bonding. Why else would you risk yourself to save a strange woman? Why else do you run a women's bookstore for a pittance when your skills could bring you much more from a corporation?"

"I didn't run down that alley because of some politically correct concept of sisterhood," Jodie answered hotly. "I knew in my guts what was happening, and then I *had* to help you. I've never had the chance to jump a rapist before, but I can't tell you how many times I've wished I did. Not enough to take stupid chances, hoping something would happen, but ever since I was sixteen and my very best friend was gang-raped—"

"My dear, you don't have to tell me this."

Jodie said through her sudden tears, "I want you to know, to understand why saving you was so important to me. She fought back—and they took after her with chains—and she died. Those incredible bastards—I saw what they did to her—

"Thinking about it—I don't believe I'll ever be free of it. I had nightmares for years, that it was *me* being raped and murdered, me instead of Sherry. That's how I got into karate, to stay sane. I would have given anything to save her, but there wasn't a damned thing I could do. But this time—this time—"

"Hush. More than you can know, I understand the passion of your anger. It is a mirror to my own. Once I was as you, struggling with the brutality of what men had done to the women I loved. My hatred was all that kept me alive.

"See, the lights grow dim. Day's judgments fade into shadow and the truth emerges, pure as the virgin moon."

Jodie turned to stare at her companion before the concert made further conversation impossible. Whatever else she might be, this woman she had saved from rape had an extraordinary and disturbing presence.

Put the whole thing behind you now, she told herself. Mary is safe, there's one for Sherry, and that's the end to it.

For the next month she believed it. Then came another dream of hunting down a darkened corridor, a dream in which the blood on her hands touched a chord of hunger within her. Restlessly she paced the hallway, always stopping before the final door. There was the same smell in the air, the perfume of fear. She drank it in, and it mixed with the smell of the blood and flooded through her, searing her with pleasure.

I'm going crazy, Jodie thought, staring at the newspaper story. How could I kill a second time, and without any conscious memory of it? The first one I could put down to the fury of the moment, getting carried away— It was an accident. But this time—Mary and I were at the ballet— ABT at the Shrine—we came home—I went to bed, I got up this morning—I don't remember anything in between! Could I have walked—and killed—in my sleep?

Even the tough evening karate class brought Jodie only a parody of calm. One moment she remained convinced of her own guilt, the next she knew with equal certainty that she had not, could not have done such a thing. After the workout, she wiped the sweat from her face with the towel that she kept by the drinking fountain and leaned against the wall, delaying the trip home.

"How about a cup of coffee, on me?"

Jodie scowled reflexively and started to snap back that she didn't date men, but Steve Azusa continued quickly, "This isn't a pass, you just look like you could use a friend."

I can't keep on like this, she thought. Hiding and lying, I have to find out the truth, and it might as well be from someone I already know.

Over coffee, amplified by doughnuts, Jodie blurted out her story. Steve listened intently, without interrupting her. When she finished by saying, "... and I honestly don't know if I killed them or not," he shook his head.

"It's not my case, but I can tell you this: Those men didn't die of a blow to the back of the head. I don't disbelieve you hit the first one hard enough to knock him out, but what actually killed him was some blood disease. The coroner's had to call in Public Health, and they're going nuts trying to figure it out."

Steve swallowed the last of his coffee. "But what if those guys had died from trauma? You'd have made a confession without your Miranda rights."

"And you'd have to take me in. I guess that's what I was hoping for, if I'd really done it."

"Feeling a little guilty?"

"Steve, I *wanted* to kill that first creep. I was so bone-deep angry there was nothing I would stop at. I know I'm not rational on the subject of rape, but I didn't know just how far I'd go. I still don't and that—that frightens me. I can't go back to thinking I'm a civilized person, not after the way I felt."

"I won't jolly you along with speeches about how many normal people feel that way too. A pat on the head won't make you feel any better. But it's no crime to want it, only to actually *do* it. The bottom line is that you *didn't* do it, Jo. So get off your own case. If it's any consolation, I feel the same way about rapists."

"What could you, or any man, *possibly* know about how I feel about rape?" *And why am I telling him all this? Am I so weak I have to go running to a man for reassurance . . . or confession?*

"I haven't been raped, if that's what you mean. But I've laid my life on the line to bring in some crack pusher, or a wiseass pimp that keeps his girls hooked and beats them to a pulp if they squeak back. I've seen the smirks on their faces, knowing they'd be back on the street just as soon as their bondsman can hop to it. I've thought of all the decent people they're going to hurt, and that one day they might get trigger-happy and blow my ass away. I think how much better this town would be without them. I think, *I'm the one with the gun, and there's no one else looking. . . .*"

Jodie held her breath, seized by the fire and darkness in his eyes.

"You know what I feel," he said. "Don't tell me it isn't the same. Nobody, not cops or women's libbers or nobody, has a monopoly on righteous anger. But the bottom line is—my hands are clean, and yours are too, lady. The rest is nobody's business."

Jodie could not rebut his argument, but she had yet to find a way of forgiving herself for wanting to kill, for the blood lust now that ran like an unbreakable thread through her dreams. She clung to her relationship with Mary as the one good thing that had come out of the whole incident, refusing to discuss her moving out. As the weeks passed, she became increasingly worried that she might have saved her from rape, only to lose her in another way.

"Mary, I'm going to level with you," Jodie said. "I said I didn't want to know it if you were dealing, but whatever you're using is killing you. You've got to get help."

Mary Smith lay on the sofa, her eyes flat, trapping all the light that entered them. It was two months later, three months since she had come to live with Jodie, and her once rosy skin lay over her cheekbones like parchment over driftwood.

"It is nothing. I will be better soon."

"Soon! You mean when you get your next fix! Mary, that's not *better*, it's only making you worse."

Jodie sat on the sofa and laid a firm hand on her friend's shoulder, feeling the bones as fragile as eggshells. "I see what you're doing to yourself. You look great, hyped up on super-crack or whatever you're doing, we have a good time, and then you get wasted. Two, three weeks at most, and you're a basket case. Look at you, you can barely sit up by yourself. How much longer do you think your body can handle that shit?"

"Do you want me to move out?"

"No, I just don't like what you're doing to yourself. I care about you."

"As I for you. We have much in common, two sisters in a world of hostile men."

Jodie backed off, realizing that there was nothing to be gained by further argument. Mary disappeared again while she was in the kitchen fixing dinner and she felt strangely bereft.

It's none of your business anyway, she thought as she drank her second glass of wine. *At least she's got some way to keep her going, which is more than you can say for yourself. You're a damned hypocrite, Jodie Marshall, getting so worked up about Mary's doing dope when you just bumped off two men.* Morosely, she finished the bottle. *I don't care what Steve says, I wouldn't feel this way . . . and dream this way, unless I'd done it.*

That night the dreams came again, dreams of blood and darkness, dreams of terror and hunger. The shadows welcomed her, the hallway as familiar as her childhood home. Again she halted before the last door, her hands slick with blood. Pleasure coiled around her, and she did not shrink from it. Only as she bent toward the hot red blood, almost touching her lips to it, almost feeling it slip down her throat to ignite the core of her ecstasy, did she awaken, terrified.

* * *

The morning papers carried the discovery of another partially unclothed male body, found in one of the less savory back streets of Hollywood, cause of death unknown. No longer big news, it was relegated to the second section, and Jodie saw it only because she felt so leaden it took two cups of coffee to fully wake up.

Steve agreed to meet her in his office. He'd been up most of the night, working on a child disappearance case, and his eyes were red-shot, his face ashen under the stubble of his beard. He said, by way of greeting, "You look even worse than I do."

"Don't joke, Steve. There's been another body found."

He nodded. "I saw the bulletin. Why are you so upset?"

"I don't remember what I did last night."

"So? Neither can half the city, but they don't come charging up here to tell me so."

"Steve, I don't know how, but somehow I'm tied in with those murders—"

"Not murders. Deaths."

"All right," Jodie agreed. "Maybe I didn't throttle them. But I could have killed the first guy, and on both the other nights *I can't remember what I did*. Doesn't that suggest something to you?"

"What, that you're somehow poisoning them in your sleep? They died of some weird kind of anemia, Jodie— not arsenic, not strangulation. And certainly not a bop on the head."

"Maybe I—"

"We've already had three nutcases call in, claiming to be vampires. Forget it, you had nothing to do with them."

"I want to believe that—and if I could only remember— or see those men's faces and know that I'd never seen them before—"

"You mean look at them down at the morgue?"

Jodie's stomach turned cold. "I hadn't thought—" she began. "But then I would know, wouldn't I? Steve, I swear

I'll never ask again—" *And I also swore I'd never depend on a man for anything!*

Steve brushed her words aside. "All right, I'll get you in to view the one from yesterday. Then I'll hold you to your promise. Not another word about this thing."

The room was colder than she'd expected and had a strange chemical smell. A bored-looking technician pulled the refrigerated drawer from its slot in the far wall. *It's a goddamned filing cabinet for bodies*, she thought, suppressing a shiver. Steve unzipped the thick plastic bag.

Jodie took a breath and bent over the drawer. The corpse was a Chicano in his twenties, black hair curling around the base of the skull. The body seemed to be made out of rubber instead of flesh, its expressionless face a flat uncompromising gray. The hair and eyebrows stood out like stiff, artificial bristles, and through the drawn-back lips, a fringe of yellowed teeth glinted.

I don't know this man at all, Jodie thought with some astonishment. *And somehow I'd know if I'd seen him before. Even in my dreams.* She looked up at Steve.

"You're no killer, Jodie," he said, and recovered the corpse.

I can't be—I know I'd remember a man I'd killed, she thought as they climbed the stairs back to daylight. There would be some shock of recognition, something . . . I suppose I should feel relieved.

Steve said, "I knew you hadn't done it, but I think you're using these deaths to cover up something else. You *act* as if you feel guilty, of what you don't know."

"Guilty—for how much I wanted to kill that bastard with my own hands, for how close I came to it? Maybe. Even if I didn't kill those men, I put myself on the line when I jumped that first guy. Something good did come out of it, but now . . . No wonder I can't let go of this thing, watching what's happening to her."

"Who?"

"Mary, the woman I saved."

"She's still staying with you?"

Jodie shrugged at his implied criticism. "We only run into each other a few nights a week, and she has nowhere else to go. She's using, I'm not sure what—coke or super-crack maybe. I think she's got the cash for it. I've tried to get her into a treatment program, but she won't listen."

"So you saved her from rape, only to lose her to dope? Do you know who she buys from?"

Jodie shook her head, knowing what he'd say next.

"We have to have more than that to make an arrest, especially if we want the pusher."

"I could follow her. If I saw the deal, I could identify—"

"Don't you go taking stupid risks!" he said, his voice hard. "If she won't turn him in herself, if she's not ready to get help, then kick her out and let her take her own chances. You can't save the world, Jodie. Not even the female half of it, and especially if she doesn't want your help."

"Don't patronize me!"

They paused at the top of the stairwell, Steve's hand unmoving on the knob of the door that led to the ground-floor lobby. He said, "I don't want you getting mixed up with stuff you can't handle. Leave it to the pros."

"You have no right—"

"I'd like to have the right," he said quietly, still keeping the door closed. Jodie felt his nearness in the half-lit space like a tingling all over her skin.

"I like you very much, Jodie, or I wouldn't have gotten you into the morgue. I'd like to see more of you—" He reached out to caress her cheek.

"Keep your goddamned hands to yourself! You're no better than the rest of them!" She wrestled the door open and plunged into the open space, trembling with anger and adrenaline.

The next evening Jodie lay in bed, feigning sleep, remembering other nights when Mary had "gone out." *This time I'm going to find out who she buys from and put the sucker out of business, no matter what Steve Azusa says.*

Jodie held herself rigid as she heard the sound of cloth brushing against the door frame, followed by light footsteps. She kicked off the covers, pulled on her sneakers, and slowly opened the front door. The hallway was empty. Cautiously she went downstairs and through the foyer.

Mary was halfway down the block, heading north. She walked straight, never swerving, without any apparent suspicion that she might be followed. It was easy to follow her through the garishly lit streets.

Gradually Mary slowed, losing the directedness of her walk. She seemed by degrees lost and vulnerable. A couple of men stopped, obviously looking for a trick. Mary shook her head, her dark hair rippling about her face like a child's mop. She made her way farther from the main streets to others less brilliantly lit, less traveled.

This is a hell of a neighborhood to get lost in, Jodie thought, seeing the gun poorly hidden in the jacket of the pusher's lookout on the corner. *You go wandering around, looking like you don't know what you're doing, you're going to get jumped, or worse.*

With a sudden chill, she remembered the alley where she had first met Mary. *Damn that woman, she's asking for it—* And then she realized, *She's been here before, she knows what it's like. If she comes here regularly for dope, she should know how to walk to get left alone. But she's an open invitation. . . .*

Jodie stepped back into the shadow of a phone booth and watched as Mary waited by herself at the bus stop. A man strolled up, wearing jeans and a workshirt. Jodie could read menace in his every movement. Mary nodded and hugged her hands to her sides, a perfect victim. The man moved in closer and she shrank from him but did not move away, even when he put one arm around her shoulder.

It was all Jodie could do to force herself to stay hidden. Mary was breaking every rule in the self-defense book. It was only the knowledge that whatever Mary's game, she had played it many times before, that kept Jodie from interfering.

The man leaned closer, edging Mary away from the bus

stop and toward the darkness of a side street. Mary made no sound as he shoved her back along the deserted side street. There was no point in calling out for help here, not in this neighborhood.

Jodie found herself at the edge of a boarded-up building, clearly the haunt of more than one illicit operation. She heard scuffling, and approached with caution. Light from a passing car reflected off one crumbling wall.

It was like a flashback to the first time she had seen Mary, pinned underneath the first rapist. The arch of this man's back was the same, and the pale gleam of Mary's thighs underneath her rucked-up skirt. *Why doesn't she cry out? Why is she doing this to herself?*

Jodie's hands tightened into claws. *This time I won't stop,* she thought, and stepped soundlessly toward the writhing pair.

The man was heaving back and forth, but not, as Jodie had first thought, in the reflexive thrusts of rape. Again and again, each time weaker than the last, he threw himself backward ... *away* from his victim. With a gasp he collapsed, rolling to one side. Mary rolled with him as if they were glued together, her mouth pressed to the side of his neck.

"Mary ...?" Jodie realized that it was not the shadows that made her lips look so dark, but the blood that glistened on them.

Mary sat up, shifting into the light so that Jodie could not miss the radiance blooming in her skin.

"... is he—"

"He's still alive," Mary said with an odd lisp.

"What are you?"

Mary pushed the body to one side and got to her feet, walking toward Jodie with her arms outstretched. The blood spattered on her hands was in the exact pattern from Jodie's first dream.

"Join with me now," Mary whispered. "Together we can put an end to this creature's miserable existence— together feast, together live. For the sake of justice, for the sake of all women. All the women he's already destroyed, all the women who will be safe from him now. It's what you've longed for all these years. . . ."

She drew Jodie to her in a lover's embrace. Her perfume enhanced the smell of the blood, that dry spicy scent that was like no other. Jodie reeled with it, felt it flood her veins with fire.

"It's simple, really. A sip of my blood and you are one with me. You can have anything you want, forever, *be* anything you want. An avenging angel, slowly cleansing Mother Earth. Long have I searched for a companion to share this holy work, long—"

"But to kill—" Jodie blurted, her voice a harsh parody of Mary's silken whisper. "To kill is wrong."

"Wrong? Oh, my dear, these creatures are not worthy of your compassion. No honorable man need fear us, only those who have of their own free will chosen the bloody path. We merely complete what they have created for themselves."

"I don't believe that—prison, yes, but—" *Weak, too weak compared to the ringing power in Mary's voice, to the memories that rose up in Jodie's mind.*

"Let us not speak lies to one another, lies about beliefs and political correctness. You know what I am and why I have come to you. In the silken darkness of the night I heard you call to me, even as I called out so many years ago. The fires that burn your soul were my beacon. It was *your* anger that drew me to you, *your* thirst for vengeance. I am what you've dreamed of, a woman's weapon aimed against all mankind. And now, you will be too."

Jodie shook her head helplessly. Whatever kept her from that last doorway in her dream kept her back now, and she clung to it for her very soul.

"Do you still deny the truth, my friend, my mirror? In everything but this single last step, we are already one."

No wonder the body at the morgue confused me, Jodie thought in anguish. *It was my hatred, not my hands, that killed him.*

A flickering movement behind Mary brought Jodie from

torment into panic. "No!" she screamed and thrust her to one side.

Mary whirled with the sinuous power of a leopard, but the man was too close, the jagged wooden splinter that he thrust at her too fast. She staggered under the impact as he stumbled to his knees. Jodie caught her in her arms and they both fell heavily into the dust.

The blood that spurted from where the length of wood protruded from Mary's chest was thick and black, rank with the scent of her perfume. The man heaved himself to his feet and staggered from the building.

"I'm going for help," Jodie began.

A pale slender hand waved briefly. "A stake . . . through the heart . . . too late . . ."

"There must be something I can do."

"Remember . . ." came a gossamer whisper, and then there was silence, deep and final.

Slowly the form of the woman who called herself Mary Smith collapsed in on itself. Without her artificially sustained life, gravity pulled the graceful structure into dust. Her perfume swirled in Jodie's nostrils, a last moment of sweetness before it faded forever.

In Jodie's mind, the last door began to swing slowly shut. She knew that if she could hold on another moment, the dreams would vanish along with the woman in her arms. She had only to keep still, and the nightmare of guilt and recrimination would fade.

No, she realized, it was more than that. Another Mary would come into her life, drawn to what Jodie had made of herself. And then more dreams of blood, more deaths, the choice recurring again and again until she finally decided—to become fully what she was, or to give up her hatred forever.

The last motes of dust clung to Jodie's fingers. She wiped them off on her jeans, got to her feet, and headed back to her apartment, walking a little unsteadily. For in that final instant she had touched her lips to the dark unnatural blood, and already she could feel the chill fires of the grave creeping toward her human heart.

About Mary A. Turzillo and "Kill Dance"

I met Mary Turzillo when I led a writers' workshop in Harrisburg, Pennsylvania, in 1987. She sold the story she started there, and went on to sell to a variety of markets, in addition to teaching English at three different colleges, playing a witch in *Macbeth*, designing theatrical costumes, and leading tours to the Grand Canyon, London, and Alaska.

She says that the inspiration for "Kill Dance" goes back to "a crazy, mixed-up bald eagle named Martha," who led her to an interest in golden eagles, who actually do try to kill each other as hatchlings. She lives in a small town in Ohio with her teenage son, who does not have a sibling hatchling. And she is working on a novel.

Kill Dance

Mary A. Turzillo

Hunt danced beautifully—high as a star, quick as electricity. But Silver's answer was still no.

"Why?" His eyes shone bright, almost the color of flame, and the flesh above his beak was red, an accent to his regal profile.

"You know why," said Silver, drawing her taloned writing hand into her breast feathers. She would not wear the silver jess bells he had sent her from the north.

"A dance is not an egg." He bated angrily, nearly losing his grip on the ledge.

"With you, Hunt, a dance may well end in an egg. And I won't be wanting eggs until I've settled this matter of honor."

"Silver," he said, very quiet, "the love months are halfway gone. They'll be over by the time you find Golden and defend your honor." His gaze flicked away. "You're beautiful. Even your devotion to honor is beautiful. But there are women in the sky today without lovers. I'm not blind."

She extended her wings, bated a powerful downstroke,

folded them again. "I told you not to call me Silver. My name is Jessless."

Jessless was a common given name among the Sky-breaker Gathering. It meant "with no master but the Sky-breaker." A year ago, Hunt had joined the Gathering as Silver's pupil. His own twin had died in the egg, so he was not obliged to settle old debts of honor by challenging the "Usurper," as Skybreaker Gatherers called their twins. They believed their world, Aeyrrhi, was growing overpopu-lated, that population should be controlled naturally by allowing the elder of two twins to kill the other in the nest, as happened with the lower species and with backward families in prehistory. Through Silver, Hunt had learned these doctrines. But his faith had ebbed. Yes, there were too many of his kind. Sport and work facilities often drove lower species into the high mountains. But Hunt shrank from the thought of watching his own two children (if he and Silver ever had any) tear each other to shreds.

"Perhaps," he said levelly, "Jessless only means 'unciv-ilized.'"

"I knew you didn't believe," she said, jerking her head away. "You've only been humoring me. You're no different from the silly, soft glovewearers."

Hunt knew she wanted him to protest his fidelity to the Gathering. It seemed more important to her than his faith-ful, frustrated courtship. He raised his hand before her. He was wearing a flying glove, a soft, new one. His family had been sensible people, who had always seen that he had the best food, comfortable ledges, the best Mentor, and, yes, the best flying glove. And what would have happened if his twin had hatched and tried to kill him? They would have put one brother up for adoption. His experiences with this lovely fanatic girl began to make that look like sense.

He bated again, lofting into the air and tightening the flying glove. Silver extended her own unclipped, ungloved hand. It was too much. "You're right," he screamed. "Tell the Gathering! I am apostate. And now I'm going to find myself a real wife!" He beat upward, high above her, then swooped past the ledge again.

"With jesses!" he yelled.

She tucked a jessless wrist into her breast feathers and watched him wheel northerly, out of her family sky, until he was less than a speck.

Silver was stunned. They had played this game before, but she always thought that his faith, though less than hers, was firm, that he believed because she did, that he would stay with her until she had settled this matter of Blood Trial. Eventually, she would wear his silly jess bells. And if they had eggs, anything could happen. She would hate seeing a Blood Trial, a full-scale battle between two razor-beaked babies, especially if they were her own, but maybe something would happen. Maybe she would only have one egg the first time. Maybe one egg would accidentally roll out of the nest. She might even help it a little.

The real problem was her own, real, grown-up sister.

Dance's family sky was blinding with spring loveliness this afternoon. As a child, she had imagined the day when she would return, a woman, to survey the family sky from this vantage. It was her favorite nest. And Scan had improved the nest so, with plumbing, storm shutters, a lightweight roof of wooden struts, leaves, and fabric, and his great hobby, electricity for heat and light. It was shady inside the nest; she had rolled the awning forward so that she could drowse, too sleepy to read or write letters.

For a child adopted by an elderly, barren couple, Dance had done well. Her career as a Comforter had gone well; Catch Vixen, her patient for the last two years, had improved so much and had gifted her with rings, jesses, and glove ornaments, plus gaming rights in her family sky. In a letter Catch Vixen had hinted that she might also be a wife this season. Dance's Mentor, Praise, had been so pleased that she had sent Dance home early for the love months. And her old friend Scan had also grown the light-colored, mature feathers. She had prophesied right when in childhood she had thought they might be lovers. He was a lusty, graceful dancer, full of humor, surprises, passion. And now she brooded two creamy speckled eggs.

But she was lonely right now. Business was supposed to stop when the love months were this far along, but Scan had volunteered to steer a dirigible north, where lumber was needed to repair an ancient nest that, after years and years of occupancy by a venerable family, had collapsed of its own weight.

Dance drowsed. She dreamed of the day of her marriage. Scan had rested the day before on an open mountain, preened and adorned with jess trinkets. He had come at evening to hunt. He had observed where the family ground turkeys nested, stalking them quietly, picking one out for the wedding feast. She saw him there in her family sky, though he floated silently on thermals, never opening his throat.

In the dream, as in her memory, she waited all the next morning for him. Tradition was that he would come when least expected. She oiled her glove and waxed the gauntlet, twisting greenery around its wrist. From her talon wrist dangled a gold jess with ornate bells and rainbow ribbons. Occasionally she would slip off the ledge and wheel slow circles, then light and rest again on the highest point on the floor of her sky, riffling her wings, spreading them to cool them or to bask in the late winter sun.

Then she saw the far speck. She whipped her head about, alert, scanning the whole sky. The sky-born dot was vales away, a mote to rodent or simian eyes, when she recognized the streaks in the fair belly feathers, the characteristic flight gestures.

As the dream went on (she knew she was dreaming, but settled in luxury to finish the dream), she screamed welcome, crouched, and launched into the air. Scan screamed back his love and folded his wings, plunging down and down and down before he pulled out of his first display. She cried out a strong, gay laugh for his aerial skip, and again as he climbed, rolling, flaunting strength and joy. She beat harder upward and gained his height.

Together, in her dream as in her memory, they flew, wingtips almost touching, sometimes brushing. He began a dive and she followed; he began to dive and rise, dive and rise; she followed his undulating pattern, her wingtips never more than a talon from his. He threw off his flying glove and beat upward, ahead of her, luffing in the wind. She stripped off her glove and tossed it down, noticing where it landed, far, far below, on rocks, amid blue winter flowers.

She rolled, turned, and began flying on her back. Scan, now behind and above her, drew in his wings and dove toward her. She extended her talons up toward him and he locked hands with her. Together they flew, face-to-face, she upside down. Slowly Scan started a roll. She yielded her weight outward, still soaring upside down. The two began to cartwheel through the sky.

Her silk-and-beaded jess ribbons tangled in his talons. He laughed and pulled away, nearly tearing the elaborate jewelry. She rolled upright into soaring position and flaunted under him. Before she sensed his intention, he pulled in his wings and mantled her, making real love now.

They plunged through the cold sunlight, tumbling, locked in love, heedless of their airy fall. And consummated their union, only a span from the rocks of the meadow. And spread wings, beating upward, defying death with courtship and love.

Dance stirred in her dream.

The eggs under her were too warm; she balanced on her talon hand and turned them to a cool side. Scan had installed an electric incubator. Aside from the discomfort of a hot brood patch, Dance could almost have gone with Scan. But a broody sleepiness had overtaken her, along with maternal possessiveness.

Her wings felt cramped. When the eggs had first been

laid, and she was light again, knowing the eggs to be fertile, children of hers and Scan's, she felt free, empty like a leather jess wallet. She had left Scan warming the new eggs and flapped all around the canyon and far downriver. Then, suddenly protective, she had streaked back upriver and pushed him off them. Scan had been amused.

Now she extended her wings a little, pushing feathers lightly against the egg cup wall. Stretch any farther and she would break a feather. She'd have to get somebody to come up and imp it for her. Self-coddling, she preened, wishing she had some scented oil left. Maybe Scan would think to bring a jar.

The wind, she noticed, was picking up. It was northerly. It might hasten Scan back a day sooner. Fast-blown clouds dappled the sunlight; she huddled closer to the eggs. It would not snow, surely, but it would be a cloudy afternoon, and colder, too. Eyes half-closed, she dreamed again, dreams less to her liking, dreams of struggling, of combat with a lower bird. She dreamed she had gone to hunt for the babies' dinner, a small turkey hen. She had picked it out and flushed it, on it too close to back off, when it flew at her, slashed at the flesh above her beak, at her eyes. A huge hawk, frantic to kill. She closed with it, grappling it behind the head. But it turned and squeezed her own neck.

She jolted awake. The day had turned cold; the light-weight roof rattled in the wind. Turning the incubator on, she ambled toward the front of the nest.

There was a speck in the sky.

It was not Scan.

A long time Silver, who called herself Jessless, stood in the Skybreaker shrine. But for her slightly erect hackles, she seemed enraptured in meditation. Her glove hand, naked, was drawn up into the plumage of her breast; her eyes were fixed on the twin figures in the icon above. She was unadorned now, except for the two slashes of paint, one on her writing-side cheek, the mark of childhood, for she was virgin, old enough for a husband, but denying herself for the sake of her mission, her Blood Trial. She also wore a slash of paint on her talon-side cheek, red extending her eye. The meaning of that mark was holy, secret. It was called the Mark of the Elder, but Silver's was for a younger twin bent on redressing a wrong, the wrong of having been denied her trial of childhood.

After a long time, she extended her glove hand and placed it on the head of the sacrificed rabbit doe. Her talons, grown too long to write or manipulate tools of any trade, so long that she needed no flying glove to grasp perches or hunt her own food, those talons fit around the skull of the doe. She squeezed; blood ran on the shrine's floor.

Even as the Skybreaker will on the last day take the egg of Aeyrrhi in his talons and crush it like a clod of dirt, thought Silver. *He will heed me. It will surely be his will that I so crush the breast cage of the sister who should never have lived. He will surely mantle in joy over this sacrifice, over the body of the Usurper, my twin. He will grant me the victory. He will surely be pleased with me.* A small voice said, *But you were the younger. You live only by chance.* But that voice was only in her head. She paid no attention to it.

When the messenger came, Dance had been nearly awake. She realized her strange dreams came from two things: the rising wind and a tiny sound within one egg, the first callings of her firstborn. "Mama, Mama," it would call. Then it would rest. Then it would strain against the shell and call again, "Mama, Mama." It was beginning to crack a tiny hole in the shell. The entire hatching would take two days, while the baby strengthened and grew vigorous from its struggles.

But somebody was outside—not Scan—different flight gestures altogether. But somebody she knew. She found her glove and, without putting it on, crossed the crooked flooring. She spoke soothingly to the unhatched chick, then dropped from the front of the nest ledge and climbed upward. The talon blades of the glove clanked in the wind, and she drew it on and fastened it with her talon hand as she flew. It felt stiff; she hadn't worn it for almost a day.

Yes, the intruder was someone she knew: Hover, from her Mentor's sky, a Glovemaker Gatherer who waited on the blind Mentor. "Friend," Hover cried over the wind. Dance pitched forward, beating faster to meet him.

"It's Praise," he said, breathless with fighting the wind, now that they planed together, spiraling downward.

"Is she dying?" Dance cried. "Did she send to say good-bye?"

"No," Hover answered. "It isn't her. It's you. She says, 'Beware. Fight to the death, because she means death to you.'"

The wind drove Dance back. Hover tossed a parcel to her and she nearly missed it in her surprise.

"Don't try to fly to Praise," Hover screamed. "Come afterward, if you can. Be careful!" He extended his wings and beat awkwardly upward, now against the first drops of rain.

Dance labored upward, wings straining, to a familiar dead tree. She lit there, squeezing the wood with her sharp glove blades, holding the package with her talon hand, unnatural reversal. Be careful, Hover had said. He was flying gracelessly now, swiftly north again. The rain might down him, but he'd left the message. Perhaps the blind Mentor Praise was after all dying, or he'd have invoked hospitality. But no, Hover had always been proud, chaste, and alone more than the laity of the Glovemaker Gathering.

The short flight back taxed her. Rain drizzled off her feathers on the uneven flooring in the front of the nest. The roofing, flimsy though it was, kept the nest dry. Dance took off her glove, closed the shutters, and returned to the eggs. They were warm, slowly turning. Scan had made a good incubator. The elder egg was quiet, the chick resting between calls.

The sodden parcel Hover had brought was a message, kept dry with waxed rags.

She read:

> *No time for tact. Yes, this is a blood matter. I invoke the Glovemaker's true name; you know it was Kill-near-the-Eyrie. You know the story: how he himself, in blind infant rage, killed his twin. How when he married, his own elder child killed the younger, then died of its wounds. How his wife dove onto rocks, killing herself in grief. How then he called himself Glovemaker, implying one who brings civilization. Do not forget this, Dance! Blood Trial was instinct even with the Glovemaker!*
>
> *Among the Skybreaker Gather, one woman rises as an adult to fight the Blood Trial she was denied as a child. This one is Silver, the younger sister whose older twin was given to strangers to adopt that the two might not kill one another. Silver wants now to fight that primal battle. She seeks her sister. Silver is strong, clever, and dangerous, Dance.*
>
> *Still I call you Dance. Do you not know that sometime in the naming-game, parents name twins in two consecutive throws? The names, then, come out so people know the two are twins. For your own good, the naming-game was played a second time for you by your foster parents, and you were named Dance. But the first time the game was played, by your first parents, you had a different name. I know that name, and I have kept it secret. But now, in this blood matter, I tell you your true, first name. You were called Golden.*
>
> *Silver is your younger twin. She means to kill you today or tomorrow. Do not let her. Strike first if you can. Forget your pacifism. She will make*

*no peace with you. You are nest-bound, brooding,
and cannot escape. She will die, or you will.*

*I am tired. Hover waits to carry this. A storm
is coming.*

Dance's pinions prickled. How would she know this
Silver? Her twin? Yet paint and circumstance might hide
resemblances. Better to harry off anyone who came uninvited.

Dance's brood sleepiness was upon her; she missed Scan.
Perhaps his errand was concocted by Skybreaker Gatherers.
For protection against such violence, there were ritual
peacekeepers, Glovemaker Gatherers, but in a society so
ritually territorial that there was no word for war, violence
was always personal and considered a blood matter, to be
settled within the family where it arose.

Aeyrrhi was not a violent world, but if you were determined, it was very easy to murder someone.

Back in her nest, Dance composed and sent telegrams
to her neighbors. It was not good to involve strangers in
blood matters, but she was frightened and defenseless.

She wrote to Scan. Later, she would carry the letter to
the post at the other end of her sky. Anyway, since he was
steering a lighter-than-air vehicle, the message could reach
him only by chance. The elder egg called briefly, then
seemed to fall asleep. Exhausted, Dance pulled the shutters
closed against the wind and tried to sleep.

In her dream, she was playing a children's game of drop-
stone-and-dive. She was very good at it. She had better be
good, because the stones were eggs.

Silver spent the morning in exercise. She played the
stone game with a quick novice, faster than she was because
he was male and therefore smaller, but she did well, missing
only once during the entire morning. The Gathering knew
her special mission of the next day, so after a short noon
rest she had a fresh practice opponent for unarmed combat.

This was another woman, older and well muscled. Not as fast as her morning's opponent, but strong and full of cunning. Silver had chosen to specialize in Skytalon, a form of aerial combat, but she was familiar with several wrestling techniques to be used with a grounded combatant—or one who had grounded her. Her practice opponent, Rends-Horse-Sinew, was more versatile and clever with the cunning of middle age, but speed carried the day, and Silver triumphed. They played with thin leather gloves, of course, to avoid slashes or stab wounds. The older woman had not sharpened her talons, but Silver kept hers at razor points.

Again Silver rested. The games-sky was bright all forenoon and the floor of the sky dusty. A wind was rising. Silver threw dust on herself, then preened it off quickly. The coaches, after consulting with a Mentor, had decided her afternoon practice would be ground combat, wrestling. She reviewed quickly in her mind the style she had studied, aware that her opponent might be, like Rends-Horse-Sinew, skilled in several styles.

The opponent this time was a man, large and strong for a male. His bearing reminded her of Hunt. His name was Laugh-at-Distance, but he was from the south, and his size gave him advantage.

He was expert, it turned out, at the style she herself had studied. Both wore light gloves, but when he lashed out at her with a thumb talon, she staggered, and the pain made her wonder if she had been cut. She was allowed, by the rules, to flutter a few talons above the ground, and she did so immediately, to return his attack. She felt she must score points soon, or lose the match—bad omen on the eve of her blood match. Slightly aloft, she grappled with him. He rolled on his back, steadying himself with his wings, and returned her clasp by taking handfuls of her breast feathers. The rules forbade tearing her flesh, but he had scored a point, and they were forced to separate. Silver felt a chill.

She took the next point by hitting him with a talon hard enough to knock him down. Winded, he asked for time out. Silver was pleased. She could have disengaged from his feather-pulling, and she was too fast to allow him purchase on her breast cage. Her own blow had been timed too slowly to stun him, but she congratulated herself that he needed time out.

Then Laugh and Silver circled each other, feinting with talons. Laugh was quick, but not quick enough, she thought. Just then, he squatted and leapt into a glove-hand charge— or what looked like a glove-hand charge. As she came up and turned to block his glove hand, he corkscrewed into the air and landed on her neck. For a moment she panicked. Then her training came to her, and she rolled forward, jarring the unprepared Laugh's beak. They rolled in the dust, until judges separated them.

Silver was sure she had torn a ligament in her talon hand, and considered asking the match called off. On any other day she would have risked further injury, but she did not want to postpone the Blood Trial tomorrow. She was sweating and shivering in the chill, gusty wind. Rain began to threaten. Then Laugh went to the judges and asked that the match be declared a tie. He said he thought he might have a concussion from the force of hitting the sky floor when Silver threw him.

Though relieved, Silver was not sure a tie match was a good omen for the eve of settling blood business. At that the judges conferred and gave her the victory. Laugh refused to go on, they said, so she was the winner.

Silver dipped her head and body in a winner's curtsy, and Laugh dipped his deeper forfeit curtsy, reminding her again of Hunt. Hunt, though, never liked to fight. But the curtsy looked so like courtship. If only Hunt were here! She was sure he would be moved by her skill and daring, not to speak of her feminine grace. A worthy woman to bear his eggs! Laugh also attracted her. He fought well, and perhaps he had deliberately lost because it was the eve of her Blood Trial. That would be chivalry!

Laugh must not be married, or he would be with his wife so late in the love months. Yet she thought fondly of

Hunt. However, she mustn't think of husbands, or eggs either, until the day after tomorrow.

She lifted off the ground, leading the ceremony that vaunted her Blood Trial. A huge complicated pattern of Skybreaker Gatherers formed in the sky—a dance like courtship, but vaster, slower, more impressive. The dance reached a climax before the first drops of rain.

Laugh was a beautiful dancer, she thought as she glided down.

But she really wished Hunt were here.

Dance wished Scan would come back. She had had no answer to her letter to him; no surprise, since steering a helium ship was weather-chancy. She had not slept much. The chick woke and called from inside the egg many times during the night, and each time she had jolted awake, sure that a dark shape glided across her sky toward the nest. Yet Silver would spurn the instruments of night flight, conventions of a weakling civilization. Nor would Dance be able to see through the tentlike roof or the closed shutters.

Dance's last nightmare had sent her bating against the nest walls, and she had broken two primaries. Unpreened, bleary-eyed, she found shafts of daylight through the shutters disorienting.

Wincing with pain from where she had struck against a wall, she stirred. The chick in the egg cried "Mama," and she murmured tired reassuring sounds. She hobbled to the shutter pull and let in daylight. At least the primal horror of the night would evaporate with morning light.

Dance tugged open the east-side shutters. But the feeling of disorientation did not ease.

For one thing, the sky and the sky floor were covered with thick ice fog.

After Silver's shower and her light meal of rabbit meat (she hadn't been hungry, but rain made her want to kill something), she settled on a protected ledge for sleep.

Sprays of rain touched her, but she liked to sleep cold. Her keen muscles generated lots of heat.

The excitement of the day's combat and the Blood Trial dance dissipated slowly. The other Gatherers chattered and laughed, flitting in the storm as if it were a summer shower, or flying up to the ledges of the temple, which, though sacred, sheltered flirtations and giddy parties.

Silver didn't care. She was the center of attention, among friends and potential lovers. She knew, without looking, that Laugh had roosted where he could watch her. She chuckled softly and fell into a dreamless sleep.

Fog was a surprise to her when she awoke, but a sweet surprise. As a child, she had played stalking games by flying a few talons above a plain, so that she might pluck a snake or a mouse like a flower as she passed. It was harder to fly this way in fog, of course, because the ground was cold and offered no thermals. Dance, her enemy, could never have done it, Dance who was brood-sleepy and newly delivered of eggs. So Silver had learned from Gather spies. But Silver herself was strong enough to do it, keen from training, fasting, and virginity. She could steal right up to the high ground above the mountainside ledge that held Dance's nest.

The shutters, Dance realized, did not lock. Why should they? Scan and Dance had never anticipated such an attack. With the shutters down, and tied with odd lengths of rope, the nest seemed secure enough. This Silver might tear at the slats with her sharpened talons, but they would hold until Scan returned.

But with the shutters down, Dance could not see her enemy's approach. The fog was, after all, lifting. Dance gambled on leaving the front shutters up. Silver would have to come from the down side of the ledge, she thought.

She was wrong.

Even as Dance tied the side shutters down, Silver crouched on the high ground, clutching a dead root, only talons above the nest. She had been there since dawn, working and watching the fog lift. Now she stole forward.

The shutters would stand up to strong winds, but she had a plan for getting Dance out of the nest.

She began pelting the shutters with fair-sized stones.

The stones were awkward to throw with her long, natural talons, but her aim was not to break in. She just wanted Dance's attention.

And she wanted her out of the nest, in the air.

Dance appeared at the front of the nest, her eyes wild and unfocused.

"Golden," said Silver lightly, "come play."

Dance had expected the attack and hated not anticipating its direction. "Go away," she said bravely. "You and I have no quarrel." She cautiously drew on her flying glove and buckled it.

"We have the oldest quarrel of all!" cried Silver. "You are my twin, and we both should not live!"

Dance mustered arguments; they fell away from her. She knew Skybreaker Gatherers had answers for everything. And Silver was retreating, her expression sly wickedness.

"Go away!" Dance cried again. "My husband is returning."

"Then I will fight your husband, too. And I hope he's big, for a man."

Dance could see Silver scuttling with her hands at something above the nest. Suddenly she realized that Silver had spent the morning on the slope above the nest setting a trap. That she had laboriously piled rocks and pebbles in a huge pile, held back only by a few twigs, branches, and pebbles. The whole thing could be set off easily. Rockslide!

The nest was an old picturesque affair. It didn't have a modern foundation. It might hold if the rockslide hit it, but maybe rocks would collapse the flimsy roof and strike the babies in their eggs.

Knowing she'd fallen into a trap, Dance leapt up, half flying, half scrabbling, toward Silver. Silver held her ground, then launched delicately into the air. "Come play," she exulted.

Dance fluttered back toward the nest. Silver flapped higher, then dove toward the unsteady pile of rocks. Dance watched in horror as she pulled up short of dislodging them.

"The next time," Silver said, "I push the top rocks. Just a little bit."

"I don't want to fight!" Dance screamed.

"But I do!" Amber fury in Silver's eyes belied the pretense at gaiety.

Dance flew slightly above the rocks. She thought of rolling on her back and grabbing Silver's talons on the next pass. Silver lit slightly below the rocks, above the nest. "Or I could pull this twig." She tugged a branch.

Dance's head spun. She launched out into the air and careened past Silver, trying to rake her across the cere without touching the rock pile or allowing her to start the rockslide.

"More like it!" Silver was delighted. She launched out in chase, and the two sisters closed in hand-to-hand combat, locking talons as they tumbled in the air.

In the nest, inside the elder egg, a nameless child tried to straighten his back. The shell was so tight. It hurt. He wanted to stretch out; the egg bound him. He wanted to breathe; the egg stifled him. He wanted to reach forth his hands; the egg seemed to tighten around him.

"Mama," he called tentatively, kicking, tossing his beak against the stony shell. "Mama. Mama. Mama. *Mama*!" There was no response. He had heard his mother's heartbeat and felt her warmth; she had murmured things to him in words he tried to understand. Where was she? He was getting cold, too.

He dashed his beak against the hard shell. It scraped. He tensed his small neck and back and *pushed*. Nothing. He subsided and began to drowse. The feeling of being cramped roused him again. Something on the top of his beak felt really good when he ground it against the shell.

Outside the nest, Dance was fighting in panic. Every time she disengaged, Silver dove toward the rock pile.

Dance knew her own weakness, but worse still, she had no killer instinct. Yet there seemed no way out but to kill.

Silver had noticed Dance's concern about the roof of the nest. She lit on it and began to tear with her sharpened talons at the fabric, leaves, and wooden struts. Every time Dance flew at her, she crouched low on the roof, daring Dance to strike and dislodge parts of the roof. Already it bowed in, ready to collapse. Dance was exhausting herself and could not harry Silver away from the fragile structure.

Why, oh, why, had they not built a sturdier roof? It did little more than keep rain off. Of course nothing in its right mind ever attacked a nest. The sentients of Aeyrrhi were masters of their world. Nothing dared approach their nests.

Nothing except their own twins.

Silver crowed as she tore out talons full of fabric and leaves. Some of the struts that held these up were already broken. With a cry of macabre delight, Silver fell through the structure. She emerged a moment later.

"Mama! Mama!" screamed the chick in a steady, hysterical rhythm. Movement. Fear of falling.

Silver had the egg. Dance went cold with fear, rage, outrage. Silver flew out over the canyon, the egg clenched in her bare talons. She was crushing the egg, the live chick screaming in fear and pain in her hands. Dance beat desperately almost on top of Silver. Rage gave her power. She rolled under the other, flying belly up, and grabbed at the egg, hoping to snatch it and fly free.

And flinched a second too long, fearing her steel flying-glove blades would pierce the child's flesh. She beat up above Silver again, ready for a second pass. But at that moment, Silver howled in triumph and dropped the egg.

Even this was not the end, for without hesitation Dance went into a power dive that could surely overtake the egg, though if it did not, it would dash her to bones and feathers on the canyon floor. But Silver had anticipated her dive and followed her, fastening naked talons on her back. Dance tried to free herself, but it was too late.

What good, she thought with a stab of agony, *are these*

sharp eyes, if they can see THAT, the crushed body of my child? She had never seen the child alive, only heard it. Now, outside the egg, it was dead.

Her brain, sight, blood, and talons exploded as she tore loose of Silver and plunged to the sky floor where the child lay dead. Perhaps she meant to dash herself against the rocks. Silver had not thought beyond the murder of the child. She had thought only that it was the ultimate revenge. After all, one chick should have been killed by its twin, just as should have happened with her and Dance. She thought somehow Dance would see this, collapse with grief, give up, and allow herself to be torn apart. The egg theft had been spontaneous, not part of her original plan. Maybe, too, she thought it would goad Dance into an earnest fight. Maybe Silver, being the younger, unconsciously wanted to die.

But Dance was beyond logic, too, and pulled out of her suicidal dive only talons from the canyon floor. Fury had turned to despair. Not soft, resigned despair like that of patients she had treated, but white-hot despair that opened her throat in a scream and gave her breast muscles fiery strength to climb back up to that speck, the evil speck in her sky that was Silver, a speck she planned to pluck out and squeeze to death as she would a presumptuous starling marring her blue sky.

Silver, without plan, banked and hovered, terrified at the very battle she had sought. Too late, she made to dive left and evade Dance's rushing wings. But Dance coursed above her. Silver tried to twist still higher, but Dance, talons and glove blades fully extended, had begun her dive. Silver rolled to the left and dodged the razor-sharp weapons. She thought surely Dance would carry through her dive and be so far below that she could climb higher and thus turn to attack.

But now, Dance's despair and Dance's steel-bladed glove, symbol to Silver of decadence and over-civilization, were the very instruments of Silver's undoing.

* * *

Dance knew that she would attack again and again. To be able to check her dive just under Silver did slightly diminish the power of her dive. But she knew by now that Silver's two natural talon hands were no match for a natural talon hand and a steel-bladed glove. Dimly she was aware that Silver had made puncture wounds in her back. Hysteria had nearly closed off the blood vessels. She had an insane plan, built out of despair.

She knew she was going to kill Silver. Yes, Silver meant also to kill her. But where Silver had planned a conventional Blood Trial, with one survivor, Dance didn't really care if the fight was fair, or even if she herself survived. The child's death had released a juggernaut within her. She planned to dive at Silver, check, beat up to diving height again, and repeat the cycle until Silver killed her— or until Silver misjudged and allowed herself to be caught in flesh and steel. And Dance knew that once she had caught Silver, she would never, never let go. Until she had tightened her talons and cut, with her steel-bladed glove, through feather, flesh, and bone, severing Silver's spine.

Dance needed only one more pass. Silver yawed back and started to roll on her back, presenting talons. But she misjudged. Dance too misjudged, and her steel-bladed talons raked Silver's face. Dance barrel-rolled and, feeling purchase, tightened her glove hand, puncturing Silver's right eye and squarely slicing the other. Automatically she tightened her taloned fist; then realizing in horror the sit of her grasp, she released and fluttered away. But it was too late; Silver flapped in aimless panic. She was not dead. She was blind.

Later, after Scan returned, some Skybreaker Gatherers came to carry Silver away. She would be a virgin Mentor to them, as Praise was to Glovemaker Gatherers.

In the evening, a young tercel, just coming into adulthood, flew over Dance's and Scan's sky floor. It was Hunt. He flew close enough for them to see his flame-colored eyes. They were sad.

About Janet Kagan and "What a Wizard Does"

Janet Kagan is a lifelong reader of science fiction, so when she found out that books were actually written by people, she made up her mind then and there that she'd write some too. She's delighted to discover that people seem to have as much fun reading her work as she has writing it. So far she has accumulated as evidence of this three Asimov's Readers' Poll Awards, first place in the Cauldron vote for issue 10 of *MZB's Fantasy Magazine* in which this story first appeared, a Nebula nomination, and a Hugo.

She lives in New Jersey with her husband Rick and a pride of cats. Her novels include *Uhura's Song*, *Hellspark*, and *Mirabile*, and she's currently working on a novel about Nellie Bly. It will be interesting to see how she makes that into science fiction, but as this story shows, she has the sort of mind that looks around corners and turns ideas inside out.

What a Wizard Does

Janet Kagan

Sable rose from the comfort of her goose-down pillow to stalk to the streaked window yet again. It had been raining steadily for a week now. She had spent some of that time profitably—rousting sniggets from the rugs or (her fur dry-spelled) catching such mice and moles as the wet brought to the surface. Of itself, rain did not bother her.

What did bother her—what set her tail twitching like a black and venomous snake—was the stench of misery that coiled from the village below to seep into every corner of the house she shared with Glory Two-Eyes. This morning it would have overpowered even the best of smells Glory could conjure.

It was the stench of children trapped—kept indoors for fear of colds. Base superstition, Glory called that. Likely, it had more to do with the desire to keep the children's clothing from being muddied. In which case, Sable thought, it would be sensible to send them out without the clothing. It was certainly warm enough for most creatures (even those lacking her superb coat and her dry-spells) to go "unprotected."

The atmosphere had begun to affect the adults as well, which only added to the misery of the children.

Sable paced once more and, for something to do, made herself a moth-spell and chased it up the drapes. She was midway to the ceiling before she realized she had miscalculated the weight the drapes would hold. The drapes gave a lurch.

So disgusted was she—with the way the world smelled and with herself—that she made no magic to counter the impending disaster. Wood splintered above her, and down she and the drapes went, a tangle of black cat and blue linen.

Still too irritable to extricate herself with the ease of a spell, she clawed her way out. Ripping brought her a certain sense of satisfaction . . . until she emerged and looked up.

Glory loomed over her, hands on hips. "Well?" There was an edge to Glory's voice.

"Don't help," Sable said. "You wouldn't want me to get fat and lazy like some familiars I could name." She twitched her tail free and sniffed dramatically. There was an edge to Glory's scent as well. "The weather's not doing your personality any good either, I see. I try to get a little exercise and a little entertainment and what do I get?" Sable yawned, flashing sharp white teeth. "I get, 'Well?'" she mimicked. "Well, what good is having a wizard around the house if she won't provide a little sunshine, O great and awesome Glory Two-Eyes?"

Glory had not changed her stance. If anything, she loomed more ominously. "Meddling in the weather—"

The looming didn't impress Sable; she knew how the trick was done. "Requires enormous energy and results in terrible backlash if you're not careful," she finished for Glory. "Think of something else, then. The whole village reeks of depression and impatience and only World Entire knows what else. A few more days of this and there'll be murder done."

Glory jerked back her head, dark hair flying. "You think so?"

Irritation ran the length of Sable's spine and set her tail twitching again. "You curl up with your books and scrolls and your toms and you don't pay attention. Yes, I think so—if something or *somebody* doesn't crack the pattern."

"All right," said Glory. "Let's see what we can do."

"It's about time."

Stepping over the shredded draperies, Glory threw open the window and crooked an arm in Sable's direction. Sable preened her shoulder and said, "If you need my help to read that pattern, you're of no use to any of us." Glory sighed and set to work.

Sable knew just what she would see. The shifting currents that flowed to and from the village today eddied dark and muddy. That would have been bad enough, but there was worse. Over the village itself, the thick, dark currents slowed, then halted altogether. It was as if the village drowned in stagnant water.

Glory turned back. "You're right, Sable," she said.

Of course she was right. Offended by the implication that she might possibly have been wrong, Sable glared.

"I'd risk interfering in that to prevent a famine," Glory said, misreading Sable's glare, "but not to lift a depression." Forestalling any comment on Sable's part, Glory raised her hands and added, "I'll think of something."

"You'd better. Let something like that go on and you don't know what the populace will nightmare up. Next month they may decide that black cats are bad luck."

"What?" Glory's dark brows knitted. Sable thrust her hind leg forward and licked her heel in contempt. "You were the one who told me this business about children catching colds from playing in the rain was pure superstition."

Glory's scent changed abruptly. Sable put her heel down and looked up in time to see a smile spread slowly across Glory's face. That was what Sable had been waiting for: Glory had thought of a counterspell for the rain-soaked village.

Sable stretched her pleasure. "What would we do without magic?" she said.

The smile turned to a grin. "Come with me and I'll show you."

"You can't shift those patterns without sorcery." Sable eyed her scornfully—then thought better of it and amended the statement: "*Even* you can't."

Glory took no offense. "What a wizard does is magic," she said. "I mean to use a little neverburn, unless you have some objection." The grin was, if anything, broader.

Neverburn scarcely counted as sorcery. It was as rudimentary a spell as the *up* Sable had neglected to use when she climbed the drapes. Sable waited for a further explanation.

She received none. So Glory had taken offense after all. Glory had as fine a sense of retribution as any cat. Well, if Glory was not about to tell Sable what she had planned, Sable was not about to give her the satisfaction of asking. There was nothing for it but to follow along and see what Glory had in mind.

"Use all the neverburn you want," Sable said. "You'd overrule my objections if I had them, so I seldom do."

Glory chuckled. Sparkles of neverburn appeared between her fingertips and she set them in her hair like tiny stars. Then she stripped out of her clothes, heaping them up on the table. From the hook near the door, she took up her hooded drycloak and threw it around her.

"Are you ready?" Glory crooked an elbow.

By this time, Sable was sure her eyes were enormous, but she feigned nonchalance. She was cursed if she'd ask. "Of course," she said.

With an *up*, she sprang for Glory's elbow, then for her shoulder, and on into the voluminous hood. She *upped* a second time—the fabric of the drycloak was thin and Glory had no protection beneath it. Irritable she might be, but she had no desire to sink her claws into Glory's shoulder for purchase—that would have been admitting that Glory was getting to her.

Glory padded softly down the path that led through Silverfir Forest and into the village. The shoes she'd left behind looked so forlorn that Sable considered conjuring a family of field mice to keep them company. And fleas for Glory's abandoned gown. *Cursed* if she'd ask!

At each house along the way, Glory paused to knock. When they had been welcomed and Glory had declined offers of food and tea, Glory told each householder, "I need the children."

When asked for what purpose, she said only, "Can't you feel the oppressiveness?" The villagers could, of course, and they agreed to send the children to Glory at council hall.

Glory stopped at the post as well. Jennet Fast-Foot went for the children at the other end of town and Tomas and Cecilany rode to fetch those from the outlying farms. Glory was determined not to miss a one.

Then there was nothing to do but make for the shelter of the council hall and wait. Glory was still being stubborn, so they waited in silence. Doing her best to ignore both the stench and Glory's stubbornness, Sable dozed.

Clatter and chatter woke her. The children had begun to arrive, bringing with them a brightening of the atmosphere that Sable had not expected. Glory hadn't, after all, done anything yet.

Glory only nodded solemnly at each arrival. Awed by her manner, they tried to match her solemnity. In the end, of course, they couldn't. Little Bit and Wozzle hushed their younger sisters—toddlers both—and got giggles. Tall Rob joked, his bravado silenced by a dark frown from the much smaller Ray Golden—who then dissolved into giggles herself.

A heady scent of anticipation cleared much of the smell of misery from the council hall. *Maybe Glory has done something already,* Sable thought, surprised that she could have slept through any of Glory's magic.

Sable made a quick check of her own. No, Glory'd done no magic. Yet the atmosphere had changed. She turned her attention to the children.

They were, as Sable had expected, bundled in drycloaks

(or cloaks of a simpler sort); their heads were covered with scarves and hats. They should have smelled stifled but didn't.

Their necks were festooned with talismans—Sable couldn't remember the last time she'd seen so many in one place—and their pockets filled with charms and cookies. If they were to be involved in magic, their parents reasoned, they would need all the help they could get—and all the energy the cookies would provide.

Glory still said nothing. She sat on the council table, clasping her drawn-up knees in her bare arms, her mud-spattered toes peeking from beneath her drycloak. Sable remained hidden in the depths of the cowl, seeing but not seen.

The mayor and her council made a sudden appearance in full regalia. They bowed as one. "Glory Two-Eyes," said the mayor, "we are honored by your presence."

"Thank you, Helen of Wye, but I must ask you to leave us now. We have a great deal of work to do."

Helen of Wye glanced at the children. Annie-Tiptoe, who was the youngest, waved. Helen of Wye, somewhat embarrassed, waved back. "I must ask if what you intend bodes any danger to the children."

"There is greater danger to them if I fail to accomplish my ends."

Sable stirred within the hood and said, "Now you've worried them."

Glory answered silently, *Only the adults. The children are more excited.* A sniff of the air told Sable this was true.

"If you wish, you may send Granny Sassy, Eloise-That-Liar, and Ringgold to assist us," Glory said aloud. "In fact, I would prefer it."

Skinny Lem, at a look from Helen, dashed off into the rain to round up the three she had named. "Granny Sassy should be enough chaperone for anybody," Sable said. "Why go to the trouble to add Eloise-That-Liar and Ringgold?"

"Because what I plan will give Eloise-That-Liar a week's worth of new tales to tell," Glory said.

That made sense, until Sable realized that Glory meant to leave Ringgold unexplained. Well, Sable didn't mind Glory's quirk. Ringgold was the town's herbalist, and Sable enjoyed smelling him.

Helen of Wye did not move until the three adults named had arrived; then, with a last embarrassed wave at Annie-Tiptoe, she hurried her council away.

Granny Sassy pushed the door shut, slamming it for attention, and said, "I hope you're not messing with the weather, child. I won't have it, you know."

"I wouldn't dream of it," Glory said with a smile. Then, more solemnly, she added, "But this gloom isn't natural and must be lifted."

Granny Sassy snorted. "I'd have called it perfectly natural after a week of rain. Still . . . if you're proposing to do something about it, let's get on with it."

Glory nodded and stood. She threw back the hood of her drycloak, revealing Sable and the neverburn sparkles in her hair. There was a murmur of delight from the children. More neverburn sparkles began to appear between her fingers.

"My friends," Glory said, "you have all felt the terrible gloom in this village. With Sable's help, I've learned the cause of it."

"Oh!" said Little Bit. Her eyes were wide but Sable couldn't tell if that was in reaction to what she'd heard or what she saw. "Who's doing it to us?"

"Not who," said Glory. "*What*. Sniggets—an invasion of sniggets."

"Sniggets!" said a surprised voice from the crowd.

Little Bit turned. "Sniggets are those pesty things that cats pounce on all the time, only we can't see them," she said helpfully.

"I know what sniggets are," said the same voice, scornfully this time. "They don't bother *people*."

"This many sniggets can and do bother people," Glory said. "I admit it doesn't happen often, but it has happened and you can feel the result."

Sable said privately, "You're almost as good as Eloise-That-Liar. Sniggets, indeed."

Glory ignored her, finishing aloud, "To put an end to this problem, I'll need your help. Will you give it?"

"Oh, yes!" said Little Bit, glancing at Wozzle, her best friend. Wozzle nodded enthusiastically, first at Little Bit, then at Glory. A chorus of assent followed.

"You must do exactly as I say," Glory cautioned them, but again she received their consent.

"Good," she said. "Then let's get to it."

She moved around the room and fixed a handful of neverburn sparkles in the hair of each, kneeling to reach the little ones, standing on tiptoe to adorn Ringgold. Sable caught a distinct whiff of attraction between the two and commented, "Ah, so that's why you included Ringgold. You and your damn toms." But she breathed in the herbs and their mutual attraction with content.

"Oh, Little Bit, you look so pretty!" Wozzle said, clasping her hands together in imitation of her mother's manner.

"You look so pretty, too!" Little Bit told her, loyally. The two were constant companions and not to be outdone in their admiration for one another.

Eloise-That-Liar produced her pocket mirror. By far the prettiest young woman in the village, Eloise-That-Liar used it only to practice comic faces for her tales. Today it was passed from hand to hand, so each child could see her own spangles. Sable followed the mirror's progress through the crowd by ear, listening for the oooohs and aaaaahs.

It was Granny Sassy that Glory adorned last, and even she could not resist a peek in Eloise-That-Liar's mirror. "A good start," she told Glory in a somewhat grudging tone. "Let's see what comes next."

Glory strode to the council table. *Off, Sable,* she said voicelessly, and Sable walked down her arm to pose where she could see and be seen best.

Glory raised her arms, and there was, after some minor shushing, a silence. "Next," she said, "take off your boots and stockings."

This took a considerable length of time, with the older ones helping the younger ones—many of whom would have done much better without the help.

When they had finished the task, Glory raised her hands again. "And now, take off all the clothes that remain. You may wear your talismans and carry your charms but—this is the important part—all of your skin must be exposed to the rain."

There was a squeak of protest from one of the adolescents. Glory fixed him with a stare. "Do you wish to help the village?"

Tall Rob nodded reluctantly. His face was scarlet.

"Tall Rob," she added gently, "I would not ask anything of you I would not do myself." Without fanfare, she unbound her drycloak and doffed it, laying it beside Sable on the council table. Sable could smell Tall Rob's relief—and Ringgold's desire.

There was another scent as well, sharp and strong and as pleasing as any Sable had smelled. She could not locate the source—until Granny Sassy did an unheard-of thing: she laughed aloud.

Granny Sassy began to take off her clothes, and Sable knew the scent was her pure delight.

With much giggling and laughter, all the children peeled off their heavy, bundled clothing—cloaks, blouses, linens, trousers—everything went jumbling to the floor. The talismans went back around their necks, though several of the smallest children squealed at the coldness of some of those spells. Glory made a circuit of the room to bind charms to bare chests so they need not be carried.

Granny Sassy said, "You're a wicked wizard, Glory."

"And you're a naughty old lady, Granny—everybody knows it."

Granny Sassy laughed again. "If they didn't this morning, they will this afternoon, child."

Glory clapped her hands above her head. A shower of neverburn fountained between them, curved and cascaded to the floor around her, like the Queen's Own Fireworks. She had the attention of all. "Our work begins," she said. "The sniggets lurk in puddles on every street corner on every street in town. We are going to drive them out!"

Eloise-That-Liar cheered and was promptly joined by a dozen or more voices and a chorus of giggles.

"Here's how we do it," Glory went on. "We make loud joyful noises—sing, shout, laugh!—and jump into their puddles. It doesn't matter if five of us jump into the same one, as long as we don't miss a single puddle within the circuit of the city. Splash the sniggets out!"

She took Little Bit's hand and Little Bit took Wozzle's and Wozzle reached to her young sister's. As they all linked hands, Glory opened the door into the rain. "Sing, Ringgold!" she shouted. Ringgold started the children's chant that called the stars back from the rain, and it was immediately taken up by the children.

Over the din, Glory shouted again, "We dance to the square and part from there!"

She led them dancing, singing, shouting, and giggling into the warm summer rain.

As Granny Sassy took up the rear of the line, Sable trotted to the door to watch. Through the shielding rain, she could just barely see that the head of the line had reached the square. Glory jumped into the largest puddle with a shout of laughter and an "Out, sniggets, out!" and stood to point the children in various directions.

Two adults in cloaks froze to watch, then abruptly ran for cover. Little Bit and Wozzle were showing their younger sisters the *right* way to jump into puddles, while Eloise-That-Liar turned a cartwheel in the rain.

"You're a snob, Sable."

Sable looked up just in time to see Granny Sassy dance through the door with the end of the line.

"You can't give me fleas," Granny Sassy called, breathless but taunting. "I'd just brush 'em off. They only work on people in clothes! Snob!" she called again.

It was too much for Sable—and it was apparent that they were all going to have a great deal of fun. She darted out into the rain after them.

* * *

The next few hours were the liveliest she had ever spent, and she recalled only confused images of them. Shocked and delighted expressions on the faces of the adult villagers (sometimes both at once!), the yelps and squeals of children as they splatted into puddles over and over again, splashing each other with warm, muddy water. Eloise-That-Liar, who stood on her hands and pitched full-length and spread-eagled into the largest standing pool she could find . . . Glory dancing a circle dance with a dozen youngsters as they kicked through puddled water, neverburn still sparkling through the muddy water that dripped from her long locks of hair . . .

And above it all, the scent of joy and the bright rupture of the lines of disturbance that had entwined the village.

Sable heard the glasslike tinkle of a sequence of spells and looked up from the puddle to find herself seeing a rainbow. And it was no ordinary rainbow; it was her own private vision. Nor was it an arc—it was a complete circle, and she knew she was the very center of it.

In the back of her mind, she knew very well that each child saw the same thing: each child was the beginning and end of his or her own rainbow. . . . She could not take her eyes off it until it faded gently into the mist and was gone.

When she looked around, she saw Eloise-That-Liar stretch out her hand as if to call it back. Granny Sassy shook herself as if from a dream; the two children beside her were openmouthed in wonder.

"We've done it," said Glory with satisfaction, and the children, as if compelled, drew toward her. "Yes," she told them, "you saw. We drove all the sniggets out. You did a good job of it, too. Now you deserve a rest—go home, bathe away the mud, and tell your parents I prescribe a restorative of hot honey-lemonade and candies."

Still awed, the children quietly nodded and began to disperse. As they passed through the rain-soaked streets, they at last regained their tongues—and Sable could hear that the topic of conversation was hot honey-lemonade.

Granny Sassy looked at the handful remaining, who had been brought by rider, and said, "I'll see to hot honey-lemonade for these—I could use some myself. I'm a little hoarse from all that shouting." Very softly she added, "Thank you, Glory. I've never seen the like." She bustled the children away. Then, to restore her sharp-tongued image, she shot back over her shoulder, "Clean up, child. You look a perfect mess."

Sable considered Glory: she was streaked with mud. Her hair was matted and dripping, but the neverburn still twinkled. "She's right, you know," Sable said critically.

Glory spread her hands and looked down at herself and began to laugh. "You should talk, you didn't even dry-spell yourself."

Sable twisted to wash her shoulder and got a tongueful of mud. Disgusted, she shook violently, spattering Glory further.

"If you please, Glory Two-Eyes"—Ringgold ducked his head deferentially—"you would be welcome to bathe at my house. Sable, too, of course," he added hastily as Sable glared at him.

Aha! thought Sable at Glory, *now it comes out . . .*

Don't be such a grouch, Glory replied.

I'm wet! She shook again. This time she spelled the flying drops for emphasis: each and every one got Glory.

I'll see you dry first, Glory assured her, chuckling. Aloud, to Ringgold, she said, "We'd be delighted to accept your offer."

"And you can bet she doesn't mean just the bath," Sable commented, but Ringgold was deaf to all but Glory's magic. Glory was right, Sable reflected. *Spells or no spells, what a wizard does is magic.*

About Mercedes Lackey and "Satanic, Versus"

Misty Lackey is another one of "my" writers; I bought her first two short stories for *Sword & Sorceress* 3 and 4, and continued to buy them for both my anthologies and my magazine. And, of course, she has sold novels. Lots of them—by now, maybe more than I have. And Misty, Andre Norton, and I have just finished a collaboration, called *Tiger Burning Bright*, which should be out sometime around the time this anthology sees print.

Misty's first Diana Tregarde story, "Nightside," which was in issue 6 of my magazine and the first volume of this anthology series, is a short-story version of her novel *Children of the Night*, but this story hasn't made it into a novel—at least not yet.

Misty lives in Oklahoma with her husband, the artist Larry Dixon, somewhere between ten and twenty birds at last count, and a wide variety of other animals.

Author's Note: The character of Robert Harrison and the concept of "whoopie witches" were taken from the supernatural role-playing game "Stalking the Night Fantastic," by Richard Tucholka, and used with the creator's permission.

Satanic, Versus

A Diana Tregarde Story

Mercedes Lackey

"Mrs. Peel," intoned a suave, urbane tenor voice from the hotel doorway behind Di Tregarde, "we're needed."

The accent was faintly French rather than English, but the inflection was dead-on.

Di didn't bother to look in the mirror, although she knew there would be a reflection there. Andre LeBrel might be a two-hundred-year-old vampire, but he cast a perfectly good reflection. She was busy trying to get her false eyelashes to stick.

"In a minute, lover. The glue won't hold. I can't understand it—I bought the stuff last year for that unicorn costume and it was fine then—"

"Allow me." A thin, graceful hand appeared over her shoulder, holding a tiny tube of surgical adhesive. "I had the sinking feeling that you would forget. This glue, *chérie*, it does not age well."

"Piffle. Figure a backstage haunt would know that." She took the white plastic tube from Andre and proceeded to attach the pesky lashes properly. This time they obliged by staying put. She finished her preparations with a quick application of liner and spun around to face her partner. "Here," she said, posing, feeling more than a little smug about how well the black leather jumpsuit fit. "How do I look?"

Andre cocked his bowler to the side and leaned on his umbrella. "Ravishing. And I?" His dark eyes twinkled merrily.

Although he looked a great deal more like Timothy Dalton than Patrick McNee, anyone seeing the two of them together would have no doubt who he was supposed to be costumed as. Di was very glad they had a "pair" costume, and blessed Andre's infatuation with old TV shows.

And they are going to see us together all the time, Di told herself firmly. *Why I ever agreed to this fiasco ...*

"You look altogether too good to make me feel comfortable," she told him, snapping off the light over the mirror. "I hope you realize what you're letting yourself in for. You're going to think you're a drumstick in a pool of piranha."

Andre made a face as he followed her into the hotel room from the dressing alcove. "*Chérie,* these are only romance writers. They—"

"Are for the most part overimaginative middle-aged hausfraus, married to guys that are growing thin on top and thick on the bottom, and you're likely going to be one of a handful of males in the room. And the rest are going to be middle-aged copies of their husbands, agents, or gay." She raised an eyebrow at him. "So where do you think that leaves you?"

"Like Old Man Kangaroo, very much run after." He had the audacity to laugh at her. "Have no fear, *chérie.* I shall evade the sharp little piranha teeth."

"I just hope I can," she muttered under her breath. Under most circumstances she avoided Romance Writers of the World functions like the plague, chucked the newsletter in the garbage without reading it, and paid her dues only because Morrie pointed out that it would look really strange if she didn't belong. The RWW, she found, was a hotbed of infighting and jealousy, and "my advances are bigger than your advances, so I am writing Deathless Prose and you are writing tripe." The general attitude seemed to be that "the publishers are out to get you, the agents are out to get you, and your fellow writers are out to get you." Since Di got along perfectly well with agent and publishers, and really didn't care how well or how poorly other writers were doing, she didn't see the point.

But somehow Morrie had talked her into attending the RWW Halloween party. And for the life of her, she couldn't remember why or how.

"Why am I doing this?" she asked Andre as she snatched up her purse from the beige-draped bed, transferred everything really necessary into a black leather belt pouch, and slung the latter around her hips, making very sure the belt didn't interfere with the holster on her other hip. "You were the one who talked to Morrie on the phone."

"Because M'sieur Morrie wishes you to give his client Robert Harrison someone to talk to," the vampire reminded her. "M'sieur Harrison agreed to escort Valentine Vervain to the party in a moment of weakness equal to yours."

"Why in Hades did he agree to that?" she exclaimed, giving the sable-haired vampire a look of profound astonishment.

"Because Miss Vervain—*chérie*, that is not her real name, is it?—is one of Morrie's best clients, is newly divorced and alone, and Morrie claims most insecure, and M'sieur Harrison was kind to her," Andre replied.

Di took a quick look around the hotel room, to make sure she hadn't forgotten anything. One thing about combining her annual "make nice with the publishers" trip with Halloween, she had a chance to get together with all her old New York buddies for a real Samhain celebration, and avoid the Christmas and Thanksgiving crowds and bad weather. "I remember. That was when she did that crossover thing, and the sf people took her apart for trying to claim it was the best thing since Tolkien." She chuckled heartlessly. "The less said about that, the better. Her magic system had holes I could drive a Mack truck through. But Harrison was a gentleman and kept the bloodshed to a minimum. But Morrie doesn't know Valentine—and no, sexy, her name used to be Edith Bowman until she changed it legally—if he thinks she's as insecure as she's acting. Three quarters of what La Valentine does is an act. And everything is in Technicolor and Dolby-enhanced sound. So what's Harrison doing in town?"

She snatched up the key from the desk, and stuffed it into the pouch, as Andre held the door open for her.

"I do not know," he replied, twirling the umbrella once and waving her past. "You should ask him."

"I hope Valentine doesn't eat him alive," she said, striding down the beige hall, and frankly enjoying the appreciative look a hotel room-service clerk gave her as she sauntered by. "I wonder if she's going to wear the outfit from the cover of her last book—if she does, Harrison may decide he wants to spend the rest of the party in the men's room." She reached the end of the hall a fraction of a second before Andre, and punched the button for the elevator.

"I gather that is what we are to save him from, *chérie*," Andre pointed out wryly as the elevator arrived.

"Oh, well," she sighed, stepping into the mirror-walled cubicle. "It's only five hours, and it can't be that bad. How much trouble can a bunch of romance writers get into, anyway?"

There was enough lace, chiffon, and satin to outfit an entire Busby Berkeley musical. Di counted fifteen Harem Girls, nine Vampire Victims, three Southern Belles (the South was Out this year), a round dozen Ravished Maidens of various time periods (none of them peasants) and assorted frills and furbelows, and one "witch" in a black chiffon outfit clearly purchased from the Frederick's catalog. Aside from the "witch," she and Andre were the only ones dressed in black—and they were the only ones covered from neck to toes—though in Di's case, that was problematical; the tight black leather jumpsuit really didn't leave anything to the imagination.

The Avengers outfits had been Andre's idea, when she realized she really had agreed to go to this party. She had suggested Dracula for him and a witch for her—but he had pointed out, logically, that there was no point in coming as what they really were.

Besides, I've always wanted to get a black leather jumpsuit, and this made a good excuse to get it. And since I'm doing this as a favor to Morrie, I might be able to deduct it.

And even if I can't, the looks I'm getting are worth twice the price.

Most of the women here—and as she'd warned Andre, the suite at the Henley Palace that RWW had rented for this bash contained about eighty percent women—were in their forties at best. Most of them demonstrated amply the problems with having a sedentary job. And most of them were wearing outfits that might have been worn by their favorite heroines; though few of them went to the extent that Valentine Vervain did, of copying the exact dress from the cover of her latest book. The problem was, their heroines were all no older than twenty-two and, as described, weighed maybe ninety-five pounds. Since a great many of the ladies in question weighed at least half again that, the results were not what the wearers intended.

The sour looks Di was getting were just as flattering as the wolf whistle the bellboy had sent her way.

A quick sail through the five rooms of the suite with Andre at her side ascertained that Valentine and her escort had not yet arrived. A quick glance at Andre's face proved that he was having a very difficult time restraining his mirth. She decided then that discretion was definitely the better part of valor, and retired to the balcony with Andre and a couple of glasses of Perrier.

It was a beautiful night; one of those rare late October nights that made Di regret—briefly—moving to Connecticut. Clear, cool, and crisp, with just enough wind to sweep the effluvium of city life from the streets. Below them, hundreds of lights created a jewel-box effect. If you looked hard, you could even see a few stars beyond the light haze.

The sliding-glass door to the balcony had been opened to vent some of the heat and overwhelming perfume (Di's nose said, nothing under a hundred dollars a bottle), and Di left it that way. She parked her elbows on the balcony railing, looked down, and sighed.

Andre chuckled. "You warned me, and I did not believe. I apologize, *chérie*. It is—most remarkable."

"Hmm. Exercise that vampiric hearing of yours, and you'll get an earful," she said, watching the car lights crawl by, twenty stories below. "When they aren't slaughtering each other and playing little power-trip games, they're picking apart their agents and their editors. If you've ever wondered why I've never bothered going after the big money, it's because to get it I'd have to play by those rules."

"Then I devoutly urge you to remain with the modest ambitions, *chérie*," he said fervently. "I—"

"Excuse me?" said a masculine voice from the balcony door. It had a distinct note of desperation in it. "Are you Diana Tregarde?"

Di turned. Behind her, peering around the edge of the doorway, was a harried-looking fellow in a baggy, tweedy sweater and slacks—not a costume—with a shock of prematurely graying, sandy-brown hair, glasses, and a mustache. And a look of absolute misery.

"Robert Harrison, I presume?" she said archly. "Come, join us in the sanctuary. It's too cold out here for chiffon."

"Thank God." Harrison ducked onto the balcony with the agility of a man evading Iraqi border guards and threw himself down in an aluminum patio chair out of sight of the windows. "I think the password is, 'Morrie sent me.'"

"Recognized; pass, friend. Give the man credit; he gave you an ally and an escape route," Di chuckled. "Don't tell me; she showed up as the Sacred Priestess Askenazy."

"In a nine-foot chiffon train and see-through harem pants, yes," Harrison groaned. "And let me know I was Out of the Royal Favor for not dressing as What's-His-Name."

"Watirion," Di said helpfully. "Do you realize you can pronounce that as 'what-tire-iron'? I encourage the notion."

"But that wasn't the worst of it!" Harrison shook his head distractedly, as if somewhat in a daze. "The worst was the monologue in the cab on the way over here. Every other word was Crystal this and Vibration that, Past Life Regression, and Mystic Rituals. The woman's a whoopie witch!"

Di blinked. That was a new one on her. "A what?"

Harrison looked up, and for the first time seemed to see her. "Uh—" He hesitated. "Uh, some of what Morrie said—uh, he seemed to think you—well, you've seen things—uh, he said you know things—"

She fished the pentagram out from under the neck of her jumpsuit and flashed it briefly. "My religion is nontraditional, yes, and there are more things in heaven and earth, et cetera. Now what in Tophet is a whoopie witch?"

"It's—uh—a term some friends of mine use. It's kind of hard to explain." Harrison's brow furrowed. "Look, let me give you examples. Real witches have grimoires, sometimes handed down through their families for centuries. Whoopie witches have books they picked up at the supermarket. Usually right at the checkout counter."

"Real witches have carefully researched spells—" Di prompted.

"Whoopie witches draw a baseball diamond in chalk on the living-room floor and recite random passages from the Satanic Bible."

"When real witches make substitutions, they do so knowing the exact differences the substitute will make—"

"Whoopie witches slop taco sauce in their pentagram because it looks like blood."

"Real witches gather their ingredients by hand—" Di was beginning to enjoy this game.

"Whoopie witches have a credit card, and lots of catalogues." Harrison was grinning, and so was Andre.

"Real witches spend hours in meditation—"

"Whoopie witches sit under a pyramid they ordered from a catalogue and watch *Knott's Landing*."

"Real witches cast spells knowing that any change they make in someone's life will come back at them threefold, for good or ill—"

"Whoopie witches call up the Hideous Slime from Yosotha to eat their neighbor's poodle because the bitch got the last carton of Häagen-Dazs double-chocolate at the 7-Eleven."

"I think I've got the picture. So dear Val decided to take the so-called research she did for the Great Fantasy Novel seriously?" Di leaned back into the railing and laughed. "Oh, Robert, I pity you! Did she try to tell you that the two of you just must have been priestly lovers in a past life in Atlantis?"

"Lemuria," Harrison said gloomily. "My God, she must be supporting half the crystal miners in Arkansas."

"Don't feel too sorry for her, Robert," Di warned him. "With her advances, she can afford it. And I know some perfectly nice people in Arkansas who should only soak her for every penny they can get. Change the subject; you're safe with us—and if she decides to hit the punch bowl hard enough, you can send her back to her hotel in a cab and she'll never know the difference. What brings you to New York?"

"Morrie wants me to meet the new editors at Berkley; he thinks I've got a shot at selling them that near-space series I've been dying to do. And I had some people here in the city I really needed to see." He sighed. "And, I'll admit it, I'd been thinking about writing bodice-rippers under a pseudonym. When you know they're getting ten times what I am—"

Di shrugged. "I don't think you'd be happy doing it, unless you've written strictly to spec before. There are a lot of things you have to conform to that you might not feel comfortable doing. Listen, Harrison, you seem to know quite a bit about hot-and-cold-running esoterica—how did you—?"

Someone inside one of the other rooms screamed. Not the angry scream of a woman who had been insulted, but the soul-chilling shriek of pure terror that brands itself on the air and stops all conversation dead.

"What in—?" Harrison was on his feet, staring in the direction of the scream. Di ignored him and launched herself at the patio door, pulling the Glock-19 from the holster on her hip, and thankful she'd loaded silver-tipped bullets in the first clip.

Funny how everybody thought it couldn't be real because it was plastic . . .

"Andre—the next balcony!" she called over her shoulder, knowing the vampire could easily scramble over the concrete divider and come in through the next patio door, giving them a two-pronged angle of attack.

The scream hadn't been what alerted her—simultaneous with the scream had been the wrenching feeling in her gut that was the signal that someone had breached the fabric of the Otherworld in her presence. She didn't know who, or what—but from the stream of panicked chiffon billowing toward the door at supersonic speed, it probably wasn't nice, and it probably had a great deal to do with one of the party-goers.

Three amply endowed females (one Belle, one Ravished, one Harem) had reached the door to the next room at the same moment and jammed it, and rather than one of them pulling free, all three kept shoving harder, shrieking at the tops of their lungs in tones their agents surely recognized.

You'd think their advances failed to pay out! Di kept the Glock in her hand, but sprinted for the door. She grabbed the nearest flailing arm (Harem), planted her foot in the midsection of her neighbor (Belle), and shoved and pulled at the same time. The clot of feminine hysteria came loose with a sound of ripping cloth as a crinoline parted company with its wearer. The three women tumbled through the door, giving Di a clear launching path into the next room. She took it, diving for the shelter of a huge wooden coffee table, rolling, and aiming for the door of the last room with the Glock. And her elbow hit someone.

"What are you doing here?" asked Harrison and Di simultaneously. Harrison cowered—no, had taken cover, there was a distinct difference—behind the sofa, beside the coffee table, his own huge Magnum aimed at the same doorway.

"My job," they said—also simultaneously.

"What?" (Again in chorus.)

"This is all a very amusing study in synchronicity," said Andre, crouching just behind Harrison, bowler tipped, the sword from his umbrella out and ready. "But I suggest you both pay attention to that most boorish party-crasher over there—"

Something very large occluded the light for a moment in the next room. Then the lights went out, and Di distinctly heard the sound of the chandelier being torn from the ceiling and thrown against the wall. Di winced. *There go my dues up again.*

"I got a glimpse," Andre continued. "It was very large, perhaps ten feet tall, and—*chérie*, it looked like nothing so much as a rubber creature from a very bad movie. Except that I do not think it was rubber."

At just that moment, there was a thrashing from the other room, and Valentine Vervain, long red hair liberally beslimed, minus nine-foot train and one of her sleeves, scrambled through the door and plastered herself against the wall, where she promptly passed out.

"Valentine?" Di murmured—and snapped her head toward Harrison when he moaned, "Oh, no," in a way that made her sure he knew something.

There was a sound of things breaking in the other room, as if something was fumbling around in the dark, picking up whatever it encountered, and smashing it in frustration.

"Harrison!" she snapped. "Cough it up!"

"Valentine—she said something about getting some of her 'friends' together tonight and 'calling up her soul mate' so she could 'show that ex of hers.' I gather he appeared at the divorce hearing with a twenty-one-year-old blonde." Harrison gulped. "I figured she was just blowing it off— I never thought she had any power—"

"You'd be amazed what anger will do," Di replied grimly, keeping her eyes on the darkened doorway. "Sometimes it even transcends a total lack of talent. Put that together with the time of year—All Hallow's Eve—*Samhain*—is tomorrow. The Wall Between the Worlds is especially thin, and power flows are heavy right now. A recipe for disaster if I ever heard one."

"And here comes *M'sieur* Soul Mate," said Andre warningly.

What shambled in through the door was like nothing that Di had ever heard of. It was, indeed, about ten feet tall. It was a very dark brown. It was covered with luxuriant brown hair—all over. Otherwise, it was nude. If there were any eyes, the hair hid them completely. It was built something along the lines of a powerful body builder, taken to exaggerated proportions, and it drooled. It also stank, a combination of sulphur and musk so strong it would have brought tears to the eyes of a skunk.

"Wah-wen-ine!" it bawled, waving its arms around, as if it were blind. "Wah-wen-ine!"

"Oh, goddess," Di groaned, putting two and two together. *She called up a soul mate, and specified parameters. But she forgot to specify "human."* "Are you thinking what I'm thinking?"

The other writer nodded. "Tall, check. Dark, check. Long hair, check. Handsome—well, I suppose in some circles." Harrison stared at the thing in fascination.

"Some—*thing*—that will accept her completely as she is, and love her completely. Young, sure, he can't be more than five minutes old." Di watched the thing fumble for the door frame and cling to it. "Look at that, he can't see. So love is blind. Strong and masculine as you can get. And not too bright, which I bet she also specified. Oh, my ears and whiskers."

Valentine came to, saw the thing, and screamed.

"Wah-wen-ine!" it howled, and lunged for her. Reflexively Di and Harrison both shot. He emptied his cylinder, and one speed-loader; Di gave up after four shots, when it was obvious they were hitting the thing to no effect.

Valentine scrambled on hands and knees over the carpet, still screaming—but crawling in the wrong direction, toward the balcony, not the door.

"*Merde!*" Andre flung himself between the creature's clutching hands and its summoner, before Di could do anything.

And before Di could react to that, the thing backhanded him into a wall hard enough to put him through the plasterboard.

Valentine passed out again. Andre was already out for the count. There are some things even a vampire has a little trouble recovering from.

"Jesus!" Harrison was on his feet, fumbling for something in his pocket. Di joined him, holstering the Glock, and grabbed his arm.

"Harrison, distract it, make a noise, anything!" She pulled the athame from her boot sheath and began cutting sigils in the air with it, getting the Words of Dismissal out as fast as she could without slurring the syllables.

Harrison didn't even hesitate; he grabbed a couple of tin serving trays from the coffee table, shook off their contents, and banged them together.

The thing turned its head toward him, its hands just inches away from its goal. "Wah-wen-ine?" it said.

Harrison banged the trays again. It lunged toward the sound. It was a lot faster than Di had thought.

Evidently Harrison made the same error in judgment. It missed him by inches, and he scrambled out of the way by the width of a hair, just as Di concluded the Ritual of Dismissal.

To no effect.

"Hurry up, will you?" Harrison yelped as the thing threw the couch into the wall and lunged again.

"I'm trying!" she replied through clenched teeth—though not loud enough to distract the thing, which had concluded that either (a) Harrison was Valentine or (b) Harrison was keeping it from Valentine. Whichever, it had gone from wailing Valentine's name to simply wailing, and lunging after Harrison, who was dodging with commendable agility for a man of middle age.

Of course, he had a lot of incentive.

She tried three more dismissals, still with no effect. The room was trashed, and Harrison was getting winded, and running out of heavy, expensive things to throw. . . .

And the only thing she could think of was the "incantation" she used—as a joke—to make the stoplights change in her favor.

Oh, well. A cockamamie incantation pulled it up—"By the Seven Rings of Zsa Zsa Gabor and the Rock of Elizabeth Taylor I command thee!" she shouted, stepping between the thing and Harrison (who was beginning to stumble). "By the Six Wives of Eddie Fisher and the Words of Karnak the Great I compel thee! Freeze, buddy!"

Power rose through her, crested over her—and hit the thing. And the thing—stopped. It whimpered, and struggled a little against invisible bonds, but seemed unable to move.

Harrison dropped to the carpet, right on top of a spill of guacamole and ground-in tortilla chips, whimpering a little himself.

I have to get rid of this thing, quick, before it breaks the compulsion— She closed her eyes, trusted to instinct, and shouted the first thing that came into her mind. The Parking Ritual, with one change . . .

"Great Squat, send him to a spot, and I'll send you three nuns—"

Mage-energies raged through the room, whirling about her, invisible, intangible to eyes and ears, but she felt them. She was the heart of the whirlwind, she and the other—

There was a pop of displaced air. She opened her eyes

to see that the creature was gone—but the mage-energies continued to whirl—faster—

"Je-sus," said Harrison. "How did you—?"

She waved frantically to silence him as the energies sensed his presence and began to circle in on him.

"Great Squat, thanks for the spot!" she yelled desperately, trying to complete the incantation before Harrison could be pulled in. "Your nuns are in the mail!"

The energies swirled up and away, satisfied. Andre groaned, stirred, and began extracting himself from the powdered sheet-rock wall. Harrison stumbled over to give him a hand.

Just as someone pounded on the outer door of the suite.

"Police!" came a muffled voice. "Open the door!"

"It's open!" Di yelled back, unzipping her belt pouch and pulling out her wallet.

Three people—two uniformed NYPD, and one fellow in a suit with an impressive .357 Magnum in his hand—peered cautiously into the room.

"Jee-zus Christ," one said in awe.

"Who?" the dazed Valentine murmured, hand hanging limply over her forehead. "What hap . . .?"

Andre appeared beside Di, bowler in hand, umbrella spotless, innocent-looking again.

Di fished her Hartford PD Special OP's ID out of her wallet and handed it to the man in the suit. "This lady," she said angrily, pointing to Valentine, "played a little Halloween joke that got out of hand. Her accomplices went out the back door, then down the fire escape. If you hurry you might be able to catch them."

The two NYPD officers looked around at the destruction, and didn't seem any too inclined to chase after whoever was responsible. Di checked out of the corner of her eye; Harrison's own .44 had vanished as mysteriously as it had appeared.

"Are you certain this woman is responsible?" asked the hard-faced, suited individual with a frown as he holstered his .357. He wasn't paying much attention to the plastic handgrip in the holster at Di's hip, for which she was grateful.

House detective, I bet. With any luck, he's never seen a Glock.

Di nodded. "These two gentlemen will back me up as witnesses," she said. "I suspect some of the ladies from the party will be able to do so as well, once you explain that Ms. Vervain was playing a not-very-nice joke on them. Personally, I think she ought to be held accountable for the damages."

And keep my RWW dues from going through the roof.

"Well, I think so too, miss." The detective hauled Valentine ungently to her feet. The writer was still confused, and it wasn't an act this time. "Ma'am," he said sternly to the dazed redhead, "I think you'd better come with me. I think we have a few questions to ask you."

Di projected outraged innocence and harmlessness at them as hard as she could. The camouflage trick worked, which after this evening was more than she had expected. The two uniformed officers didn't even look at her weapon; they just followed the detective out, without a single backward glance.

Harrison cleared his throat, audibly. She turned and raised an eyebrow at him.

"You—I thought you were just a writer—"

"And I thought you were just a writer," she countered. "So we're even."

"But—" He took a good look at her face, and evidently thought better of prying. "What did you do with that—thing? That was the strangest incantation I've ever heard!"

She shrugged and began picking her way through the mess of smashed furniture, spilled drinks, and crushed and ground-in refreshments. "I have no idea. Valentine brought it in with something screwy, I got rid of it the same way. And that critter has no idea how lucky he was."

"Why?" asked Harrison as she and Andre reached the door.

"Why?" She turned and smiled sweetly. "Do you have any idea how hard it is to get a parking place in Manhattan at this time of night?"

About George Barr and "Brontharn"

When I first started *Marion Zimmer Bradley's Fantasy Magazine*, I turned to my old friend, the well-known sf/fantasy artist George Barr, for the cover painting for my first issue. The title story was called "Skycastle" and George painted a beautiful flying castle, a line drawing of which now appears on the front of the T-shirts we made up for the magazine. George continued to do covers for us, and by issue 4, I had discovered that he could write as well. He wrote the cover story and painted the cover for both issues 4 and 11. This is the story from issue 11; I hope that you enjoy it as much as I did.

George lives in San Jose, California.

Brontharn

George Barr

"**H**is Highness, Prince Derro Silverlance, of the Kingdom of Fairland!"

The herald's staff rapped the requisite three times on the black slate floor, sending echoes about the great hall despite heavy draperies overhanging the cold stone walls, and the buzzing throng of courtiers assembled for the—by now—familiar occasion.

Amberly sat straight in her throne, her face carefully expressionless, as the latest suitor descended the stairs.

Prince Derro, unlike so many who had presented themselves in the two years Amberly had been of marriageable age, was not bedecked in regal splendor. His bearing was regal enough; he didn't need brocades and jewels to convince anyone he was of royal birth. He wore a simple black tunic over grey hose, girded with a broad, silver-studded belt, and had a deep red woolen cloak thrown back over one shoulder.

He didn't swagger, nor did he appear conscious at all of the court about him. His manner seemed less a performance than simply natural behavior.

Princess Amberly's first impression was that he was striking. But as he approached, she amended that to strikingly *handsome*. Prince Derro Silverlance was the hero of every maiden's dream made flesh.

If she accepted his suit her father would be pleased. Fairland was wealthy; it would be a good marriage and a profitable alliance. She would be envied by all the girls of the court . . . and, truth to tell, many of the married ladies as well.

She might even—in time—learn to care for him. If good looks could only guarantee happiness, she should be in heaven, for he was certainly the most dashingly beautiful of all the men who'd come seeking her hand.

She wished it were that easy . . . that she could simply nod, smile, and let it all be over.

If only she could . . .

If only she'd not asked for her father's promise.

She'd been fourteen and it was her birthday. Before the entire court her doting father had asked if she had some special birthday wish he might grant.

"Yes," she replied boldly, "but you *wouldn't* grant it."

"Why?" he laughed. "Would it cost me the crown jewels?"

"No," she said. "It would require you to break custom, and you wouldn't do it."

Her father seemed hurt that she'd think him so hardhearted. "My darling," he said, drawing her close, "I give you my word. I cannot relinquish my crown, nor set May Day into June on your whim, but what I can do to make you happy I will do most willingly."

Amberly looked about at the smiling court. They were imagining she wanted some childish fantasy like a formal ball she—at fourteen—would be allowed to attend, an out-of-season hunt, or a harvest fair in the middle of summer. They all saw her as her father did: a girl who'd been pampered and indulged, with little imagination and no reason for ambition. And they were right . . . partly. She *had* been pampered, and she really *didn't* aspire to much beyond her already royal position.

But Amberly remembered her sister who, three years before, had come closer than anyone else realized to taking poison when she'd been married off against her will to a man she neither knew nor loved. Amberly had seen her despair, and lived in horrified anticipation of sharing her sister's fate.

"Father," she said, "I want only your promise that when it comes time for me to be wed, you will allow *me* to choose my husband. I will try to make a good marriage, but I'd rather live a spinster all my life than marry a man I do not love. Will you do that for me, as you have promised . . . or is it too much for a daughter to ask of her father?"

He might have reneged on his vow had it not been made in front of the entire court. Even so, there were many who'd have understood . . . perhaps all. But King Ferris Oakenshield was a proud and honorable man; he stood by his word lest anyone accuse him of being untrue, even to a child.

There'd have been no problem. There were plenty of suitors . . . many who set hearts fluttering throughout the castle. And Amberly would surely have been smitten by one or another of the fine handsome men who presented themselves before her.

Except for that promise, Amberly's fate would have been out of her hands. Her father would long since have given her to a worthy prince of a rich kingdom. She'd have hated it—just as much as her sister had—but she'd have lived with it. Generations of women since time began had endured such arranged marriages and managed somehow to find a measure of fulfillment in their lives. Her own mother had not been entirely unhappy.

But Amberly had been given the right to choose for herself, and she could make no choice.

Not ever . . .

. . . because she was in love, and it was an impossible love. Not that law forbade it; such laws had not even been *imagined*, let alone enacted. She might as well request permission to wed a pine tree or a mountain peak. She'd have as much chance for acceptance, a family, and happiness.

Two years before Prince Derro Silverlance of Fairland entered the audience hall of King Ferris Oakenshield to seek the hand of a young princess, that princess—bored with her samplers, her dolls, and her ladies-in-waiting—had indulged in a secret pleasure she'd shared with no one; she'd gone exploring.

She left the castle by way of a tunnel hidden behind her great-great-grandfather's crypt, deep within the mountain. It was a way known only to the members of the royal family, dug generations ago as an ultimate means of escape in case of a siege.

She spoke to almost no one for fear her education might betray itself in her speech and give her away. It made such explorations more secretive and exciting to imagine herself a spy or a sorceress bent on some secret and dangerous mission.

In rough dress of homespun and a shawl to hide her bright hair, Amberly had become acquainted with most of the lanes and byways within half a day's walking distance. She knew the shops, the inns, the mill, the smithy, even the brothels.

There'd been no war for near a century. Amberly herself was the only member of the family—so far as she knew—who'd ever actually made use of the passage. It wasn't the most pleasant place in the world . . . dank, dark, filled with rustlings and eerie echoings.

Twenty paces beyond the crypt, the man-made tunnel connected with a natural limestone cave that honeycombed the mountain. There were numerous dark, unexplored branches leading away from the main passage, and many small openings in the steep mountainside that let in faint daylight occasionally to give glimpses of chambers she was certain were full of bats and thick with spiderwebs.

Amberly had always kept to the well-defined trail that led down to a small waterfall. There she was required to crouch low, squeeze through a small crevice, and push aside thorny brush that grew thickly about the stream.

But once past this there was a mountain trail to the village. It was an outing that took most of the day, so the princess didn't take it unless she was fairly certain she would not be missed.

On this fateful occasion she had known her father would be involved with envoys from a neighboring kingdom, and she was bored enough that she didn't much care if her ladies-in-waiting were distressed at not finding her. She dressed carefully, stole a torch from a sconce in the crypt, and moved slowly into the hand-hewn tunnel.

Though she carried tinder, she always waited to light the torch until she emerged from the tight passage. In such cramped quarters, she disliked its smoke and stench. Feeling her way along the rough stone, she had no fear of being lost, as there were no branches until she reached the cave. She could easily determine when she'd arrived there by the change in the texture of the wall.

The tunnel, upon merging with the cavern, joined first a natural passageway between the solid mountain and a fretted screen of limestone that had formed over the countless ages. Slim columns had descended in a straight line from a crack in the stone overhead, meeting with others arising from the floor. Close together, they'd branched, spread, filled in, and created a delicate network of lacy stone. Water still dripped over it, gradually filling in the openings with minute deposits of dissolved minerals.

Upon entering this narrow hallway, Amberly became aware of two things. First: the morning sun through the porous face of the cliff made the torch unnecessary. The light was dim, but sufficient. Second: there was a sound she'd not heard before . . . something more than the dripping water and the rustling of bats. It was like heavy breathing . . . almost snoring.

Cautiously she crept forward. Sound was deceptive in

the cavern. Echoes made it difficult to discern the direction of a noise. What she heard might be a bear, or simply an amplified reflection of her own breath.

With the sunlight behind it, the stone screen had become a translucent veil pierced with tiny bright holes. It was beautiful and seemed somehow magical. Delicate traceries of subtly glowing color wound through it.

Never having come through this early before, Amberly had not been aware of the beauty of the cave. She'd seen it only lit by the light of a smoking torch, looking dangerous and forbidding, filled with deep holes and ominous pillars that looked like shrouded statues.

Carefully she leaned forward and with one eye peered through a small hole in the stone. The scene that met her gaze was unreal . . . dreamlike . . . enchanted.

Water, dripping from the ceiling, caught the light and sparkled like jewels. Light, like that in a cathedral, filled the air, reflecting softly from wet stone. A few larger openings, straight enough to admit pure sunlight, formed slanting beams of radiance filled with dancing notes and falling gems.

The sound of water, so eerie in darkness, seemed suddenly like music . . . fairy music to match the enchantment of the moment.

But it didn't mask the soft sound that had urged her to extra caution.

Then she saw, in a recess across the cavern, a slight movement. A young man lay there, apparently asleep. Though muscular of build, his face seemed that of a boy . . . not handsome, exactly, but open and appealing. He was nearly naked, wearing only a brief garment that looked to be made of the skins of many small animals sewn crudely together.

Leaning against the wall beside him was a club: a gnarled, thorny, quite dangerous-looking length of tapered wood at least half his height. That—and the skins he wore—gave an appearance of savagery and barbarism very much at odds with the untouched innocence of his face.

His hand moved. Evidently not soundly asleep, he caressed a small grey-furred animal curled up at his side.

A mouse, she thought, enchanted at the sweetness of it. *He has a pet mouse.*

Then the little animal raised its head to sniff the air. To her utter astonishment it was not a mouse at all ... nor anything remotely related to a mouse. The boy's pet was the tiniest dog she'd ever seen. It was not a puppy; its proportions were those of a full-grown dog. In fact, it looked very like a wolf, yet was small enough that he could have carried it curled in the palm of his hand.

It sniffed again and its head turned to stare directly toward her. Though it couldn't possibly see her, its nose wrinkled as it bared its white teeth in a snarl.

Not wishing to alarm the young man, Amberly moved quickly along the trail until she'd emerged from behind the limestone screen.

Suddenly disoriented, the girl stared in amazement.

Having peered through the hole in the stone with only one eye, she'd had no immediate way to guess the distance across the cave. Now in the open, she saw that the cavern was larger than she'd remembered. It was *immense*. Between her and the skin-clad stranger stretched a floor as vast as the great audience hall of the castle, though not so neatly paved. There were formations like great tree trunks rising out of deep pools of crystal-clear water ... hills, hollows, and ravines.

She screamed involuntarily as her foot slipped into a narrow crevice and wedged tightly.

The little wolf stood up, growling, and launched itself toward her as the young man blinked and peered after it.

For what seemed an incredibly long time the snarling, grey-furred creature bounded across the cavern. And her mind balked at accepting what she saw.

It was *distance* ... the distance across that huge chamber ... that had made the wolf seem so small. It was anything *but* small as it approached. It was a full-sized beast of the forest, as large as any the castle huntsman had ever brought in.

And that meant—no, it was beyond belief! But it was true! The young man she'd assumed was a lost child of the woods was in reality a creature out of myth. He scrambled to his feet to follow the wolf, and with each long stride loomed ever larger to her horrified gaze.

He stood fully *six times* the height of a normal man.

In this cave beneath her home lived a *giant*! In all the nursery tales, never had she heard of one so huge. He could devour a human being as quickly and easily as a man might eat a rabbit ... take off a head in a single bite.

"Galbor!" the giant shouted, his voice filling the chamber, reverberating from the stone walls, terrifying the princess with its immensity. Such a voice could never have emerged from a human throat. The great heraldic trumpets in the gate towers did not sound with such depth and resonance.

The wolf stopped ... evidently well trained to its master's commands. Mere feet away from her, its yellow eyes seemed to burn into Amberly's. Its pink tongue, dripping, licked its black lips. But it did not attack.

In moments the giant had covered the distance to arrive beside his pet. He knelt and bent toward the princess, who felt her bones turn to water.

So close, and so huge, the great being's face still managed to retain that look of boyishness that had so charmed her. "Who are you?" the giant asked, his voice soft ... like whispering thunder. "And what are you doing here in Carrowyn?"

"Carrowyn?" she said, astonished that the huge man would speak a language she could comprehend ... and suddenly hopeful that she might survive this day. If he spoke, she reasoned, he had a mind. Intelligence. He'd spent time in converse with others ... others who were akin to her, at least in that they spoke the same tongue.

"Carrowyn," he repeated, then gestured sweepingly to

encompass the entire cavern. "This is Carrowyn ... the ancestral home of my people."

"*My* home is atop this mountain," she replied. "My father rules this land."

"Aaah," he said, nodding. Sitting back on his heels, he seemed lost in thought.

Taking advantage of his diverted attention, Amberly cautiously extricated her foot from the crevice and prepared to dart back behind the limestone curtain and into the tunnel. The wolf, perhaps, might follow, but the giant surely could not.

"If your father rules," he said, leaning forward again, "then he is a *king*, is he not? I've heard of kings. You are then a ... *princess*?"

"Yes," she admitted, wondering if she would be held for ransom, "the youngest of three. I am Amberly, daughter of King Ferris Oakenshield, and Princess of Carin. This is the land of *Carin*, not Carrowyn."

Again the giant nodded. "It has been many ages since my people lived here. Long before you little ones came, this mountain was ours, and this cavern our home. We called it Carrowyn then. That was before I was born. Carin is not so different ... *smaller* ... like you.

"I came back to see it, to see if the legends were true."

Despite his immense size, and the presence of the slavering grey wolf that obeyed his command, Amberly no longer felt afraid ... and was surprised at the realization.

"How many of you are there?" she asked. "There's been no rumor of giants in these mountains. None at all."

The huge being looked for a moment like a forlorn child. "I came alone. If there are others of my people still living, I don't know where they'd be. My father died beneath an avalanche before I was born. And my mother ..." His face hardened. "My mother was slain by a brave knight when I was but a toddler. I've been told your people still tell tales of heroism in conquering the Ogress of Kerrywood Fen. I am her son: Brontharn ... perhaps the last of all my kind."

Amberly gasped. "It is an old tale. No one really believes it. It was supposed to have happened over *a hundred years ago*. How can you be her son?"

Brontharn spread his hands—each big enough to grasp her like a puppet—and shrugged. "I don't know how many years ago it was. We are a long-lived people. I have barely reached my full growth, and have not yet grown a beard. My father had a beard almost to his waist, I was told, and he was over two hundred years old when he died . . . and not yet grey. I really don't know how long we're supposed to live. There's no one left to ask."

He sounded so lonely that had he been nearer her size, the princess would have put an arm around him to comfort him. But she could hardly have encircled his ankle with *both* her arms.

Such gestures were to imply that the one embraced was more protected and secure. The thought should have been funny in this situation, but Amberly did not feel like laughing. She felt deeply the giant's isolation.

In the visits that followed, the princess heard how Brontharn had been led as a child to the great forests in the south by an old dwarf named Gutwort. He had raised the colossal boy—as well as possible—as his own.

Old Gutwort, being about half human height, had been able to move among men without too much trouble, and had learned much of their doings, their history, and their legends. All this he'd taught to his young charge, as well as what he knew of the giants themselves.

Isolated from both their kind, visited only occasionally by forest gnomes, and encountering on rare instances a fairy or an elf, their life was lonely and hard. They'd lived on wild boar and elk. There was little else big enough to feed Brontharn, and gathering sufficient food for the growing giant had not been easy. But it had not been a totally unpleasant experience.

He'd learned from Gutwort how his mother had stained her fair face with pitch, strung moss in her long hair, then gibbered and wailed to frighten men out of Kerrywood Fen. But the ruse had worked against her when she became legendary, and the object of knightly quest by men hoping to build a reputation for bravery.

Her presence had been put to use by several who'd seized the opportunity to escape blame for deeds they might otherwise not have dared commit. Rivals in business . . . and in love . . . disappeared. Their bodies were discovered in the marshes and the "Ogress" assumed a more deadly reputation. Thefts of sheep, goats, and cattle were attributed to her, and more than one impatient heir came to his inheritance sooner than he ought to have when wealthy fathers or uncles reportedly fell prey to the monster of the fen.

The brave knight who'd slain her did so by having an entire troop of armed lackeys surround and distract her so he could creep through the undergrowth and use an ax on the back of her ankle. With the tendon cut, she'd fallen, and his lance was waiting for her throat.

No one had ever bothered to see the quiet beauty beneath the simple disguise.

Amberly wept at the tale.

Many times Brontharn would take the princess out through a huge exit from the cavern, about which she had not known. The sprawling maze of caves had many chambers and corridors that had very probably never been explored by man . . . almost certainly so, or some provision would have been made to defend the castle against attack from below.

The giant's own portal was a high, narrow cleft behind a stand of ancient pines. It looked as though the trees, which were probably over a century old, had been planted deliberately to conceal what must once have been the door to the caverns of Carrowyn. Brontharn wondered if his own father might have set them there. Gutwort, who could only have heard of it from the giant's parents, had described to him in detail the location of the cleft, and the trees that concealed it.

Amberly and Brontharn, with Galbor the wolf, would sit together in the forest, basking in the sun, exchanging accounts of their lives. Often she'd wear her loveliest gowns, her jewels and tiaras, because he had a great delight in beautiful things.

Through the trees they could see the castle atop the mountain, and it seemed a distant, foreign place to her. In all of that great fortress, she had not one true friend, and—save for her father—no one she truly loved.

"*I* love you, Amberly," Brontharn said one afternoon.

He needn't have said it; she'd known it for months. But hearing it was pleasant, and it allowed her to speak her own love in return.

"Destiny has played a cruel joke on us," she said. "All we can ever be is friends, and even that is doomed. You cannot stay here much longer, for the herdsmen are complaining at the loss of their sheep and cattle. They suspect each other right now, but how long can it be before you are discovered? I don't want you to meet your mother's fate."

"I know," he nodded. "It was a vain pilgrimage on which I came. I wanted just to *see* the caverns of Carrowyn . . . to know that Gutwort's tales were true. I had no expectation of meeting anyone at all . . . least of all someone like you."

He reached one huge hand toward her and Amberly nestled into his palm. His skin was like soft leather, but warm and alive. She rested her arm upon his thumb, as though it were the arm of a couch, and stroked the broad nail with her fingertips. It was agony to be limited to such an ineffectual touch when everything in her ached to embrace.

Her pain was echoed in his boyish face.

Though he'd lived a hundred years—longer than any man she'd ever known—her heart accepted the evidence she could see, and to her he was but a youth. The tears forming in his eyes were a young man's tears.

"What will you do?" she asked. "Where will you go?"

"Back to the forest, I suppose," Brontharn replied after a long moment. "Old Gutwort is long dead, of course. But there are a few humans in the deep woods. I should not be bothered by brave knights. There is a mountain upon which I may build myself a castle. It will take many years ... but I will *have* many years, and little else to occupy my time.

"I think I may throw a scare into a few villages on my way home. If rumor spreads that there is a giant in the land, perhaps some other of my people may hear of it and come seeking me." He sighed, his eyes showing little hope. "But in all the years I lived there with Gutwort, none of the gnomes, fairies, or elves we encountered had heard of another giant since the death of my mother."

Amberly could not control her tears. "I cannot bear to think of you so alone. Could I not come with you? Would it not be better to have a *friend*, even if that's all I can ever be?"

The sweet face of the huge creature smiled gently. "No," he said sadly. "You would grow old and die long before my house was completed. You would live your life in a forest grotto, without family, friends, or companions. *I* would have the joy of your company, but not at the cost of your life and fulfillment.

"Here ... in a while ... you'll find someone of your own kind you can love. With him you will have children ... a family ... and know that your life has had some meaning. I cannot take you from what fate surely meant for you to have."

They said sad good-byes one early morning when the cavern was most beautiful. Amberly doubted she would ever go there again. It had stopped being simply a means of exit from the castle. It was a magical world called Carrowyn ... a name that no one else would ever know.

Amberly went on with the business of being a princess. Her duty was to marry well, to benefit the kingdom, and to bring honor to her family name . . . then to raise strong sons for her *husband's* kingdom.

But the arrangements she herself had made specified that she would marry for *love* . . . a man of her own choosing. A man she agreed to marry would have every right and reason to believe he'd found favor in her eyes. And she did not know if any man ever could.

Torn between a genuine sense of who and what she was, and her responsibilities to that position . . . and the love that would forever lie between her and whatever man she accepted in marriage . . . Amberly tried desperately to think of a way she could give back to her father the authority to make the choice for her.

It would have been easy except for her pride, which would not allow her to appear to have been unable—because of being a female—to accept the responsibility she'd demanded.

She watched Prince Derro Silverlance of the Kingdom of Fairland approach the throne. *Shall it be he?* she thought. *He's handsome enough. And it would be a good alliance.*

"My lady," he said . . . loud enough to be heard, but not so loud as to give the impression that he was performing for the benefit of the court. He bowed low . . . gracefully, but not delicately. He was a man familiar with the courtly graces, but he was a man.

"Prince Derro," she responded, extending her hand for his kiss. "We are honored at your presence."

"Oh, no, my lady," he said politely, "the honor is entirely mine. We in Fairland had heard rumor of your beauty, but I'd not expected a goddess out of legend."

It was a pretty speech, but others before him had used it . . . or variations of it. Amberly was aware of the fact that she wasn't *ugly,* but she hardly considered herself in the *goddess* category. She smiled the expected smile and bowed her head demurely. It wasn't proper, even for a princess, to accept such praise as though it were expected.

"After all the knights and heroes who have presented

themselves to you," Prince Derro continued, "and not stirred your heart, it is bold and presumptuous of me to consider that *I* might be the one to win your favor. But I'd not be worthy of my title if I did not make the attempt."

"Am I a *prize*, then, to be sought as proof of knightly valor?" she asked, not totally in jest.

"A prize, yes," he responded, his eyes sincere. "Worthy of the greatest deeds. I come because I do not wish to spend the rest of my life wondering if you might have been mine if only I'd had the courage to try."

"And what brave deeds have you performed," she asked, "other than risking my refusal?"

The prince smiled acknowledgment of her barb, seemingly pleased that she was not so gullible as to be won by flowery declarations.

"It is customary to bring an offering," he replied. "But I would beggar the Kingdom of Fairland and not be able to tempt you with treasures more than have already been offered by the brave men before me.

"You've not been swayed by silks from the East, the ivory tusks of elephants, nor even—it has been said—by jewels stolen from a dragon's hoard. A throne carved of a single block of jasper has been offered to you, as well as a cloak of golden gryphon feathers. I have no such treasures. And it would hardly be complimentary of me to assume that if you did not love me, you could be *purchased* with a gift of sufficient value."

Behind him, four lackeys eased down the stairway what appeared to be a carriage swathed in velvet. No one had yet offered a royal coach . . . but he had just finished saying he wasn't intending to try buying her favor.

As they drew it forward over the slate paving of the great hall, Amberly could see that the wheels were ordinary in appearance, neither carved nor gilded. She awaited his explanation.

"I will someday be king of Fairland," Prince Derro said. "But until then I cannot offer you its wealth. What I offer is myself, my love, my devotion, and proof that I would brave *anything* in your service and defense.

"I found no dragon, no gryphon to conquer in your name. But I bring you evidence of my valor."

The velvet draperies were whipped from the cart, and Amberly stared into the glazed eyes of Brontharn of Carrowyn.

He could not see her. His head, alone, was all the cart contained. Brontharn would build no castle . . . nor would he live out his long life in loneliness. If he were in truth the last of his kind, then giants walked the earth no more.

"Father?" the princess said, her voice barely a whisper.

"Yes, my dear?" the king replied from his throne beside her. He clasped her outstretched hand, marveling at how cold her fingers were.

"I will wed," Amberly said to him and to the hushed assembly. "Anyone. Anyone you choose." She looked into Prince Derro's uncomprehending eyes. "Anyone at all . . . but *him*."

No one in the kingdom ever guessed the reason for her tears.

About Phyllis Ann Karr and "The Robber Girl, the Sea Witch, and the Little Mermaid's Voice"

Phyllis Ann Karr was born in 1944 "to wonderful parents." Among the stories her mother read to her were Anderson's fairy tales, and "The Snow Queen" was one of her favorites, largely because of the Little Robber Girl.

She lives in Wisconsin with her husband, and is getting back into one of her earliest enthusiasms, amateur theater, playing one of the poker buddies in a community theater production of *The Odd Couple*.

The Robber Girl, the Sea Witch, and the Little Mermaid's Voice

Phyllis Ann Karr

There was the time I made a friend out of a little opera singer.

Say "opera singer," and people think of a large body standing in the middle of the stage singing arias and duets with other large bodies. But my friend was only in the chorus, with a body not much bigger than a child's and a voice not much bigger than her body, although it was a good, sweet little voice, and earned her just about enough money to put a little roof over her head and a little porridge in her bowl.

The way I befriended her was by putting my pistol to the head of a rich young rogue who tried mistaking her for another kind of woman one night on her way home from the Opera House. I helped myself to his purse for my pains, and gave him a kick into the bargain, which may have helped teach him his lesson. Or maybe not—some people never learn a thing. I went away and spent his money somewhere else, but not before taking the time to see my new little friend home safe and promising to look her up if I ever came back to her city.

I found myself back in her country after about a year. During that year I had had adventures, and I was carrying three new prize possessions in my pockets, along with a comfortable supply of money.

I had robbed a rascally magician and in his wallet, along with his coins, I found some lotion in a vial just big enough for the label that read, in tiny handwriting: "To See Spirits, One Drop On Either Eyelid. To Hear Spirits, One Drop In Either Ear. To Talk With Spirits, One Drop On The Tongue." There was so little of the lotion that I hadn't tried it yet.

Then I'd been on a ship that was attacked by pirates. When they boarded, I kept them off with my pistols until a fellow passenger and I got clear, and he was so grateful he gave me one of the necklaces he had that a great wizard had made for him out of seahorses' eyes and fish's gills. Whoever wore one of those necklaces could breathe under any amount of water, so we were both able to swim ashore, stopping on the bottom whenever we needed a rest.

The last of my prizes was a pack of cards. Not just any cards. Oh, no! Every court card had the face of some famous personage, and all the faces could sing and talk. Those cards could always win for anybody they happened to like, and the only reason the gypsy, whose mother's they had been, let me trade him two horses—I had three at the time—for them was because they had taken a dislike to him, and the king of clubs was missing, besides.

Well, when I got back to her city, I found my friend the little opera singer flat in her bed, with a doctor bending over her.

"She has been very, very sick, this little one," he said, "but I think that at last she is on the mend. Only providing, however, that she has good food, warm blankets, and the will to get better."

"Why shouldn't she?" said I, thinking that everyone always has plenty of that kind of will.

"You see," said the old leech, "her voice is gone. She can whisper, yes, and with time and good nursing she may someday be able to murmur a little, but I fear she will never sing again."

With that, he left some medicine and went off on his rounds of other patients.

As I said, my purse was pleasantly heavy just then, so I went out and bought food for her bare cupboard, a couple of bottles of good wine, two goose-down feather beds, and a supply of wax candles. When I got back, lit the candles, propped my friend up for dinner, and wrapped her in one of the feather beds, I saw she was crying.

Her tears rolled down all the time I fed her and got wine and medicine into her, and at last she whispered to me, "You might as well have let him have his way with me last year. Without my voice, it is the only way left for me to earn my living."

"Stuff and nonsense!" I told her.

"No, it isn't," she whispered back, shaking her head weakly. "I don't have the legs for ballet, or the fingers for sewing, and I'm not like you, to live by my wits and hardiness. I have only one thing left to sell, and . . . I think I would as soon be dead."

That sent a chill through me, but I told her things would look better in the morning, and she wasn't to be a little fool in the meantime. Then I got a sleeping draught into her, laid her down and tucked her in snug as a caterpillar in its cocoon, and hoped she'd have good dreams. And then I wrapped myself up in the other goose-down feather bed and settled in to keep watch.

I got out my talking cards to play a little patience, but they grumbled so loudly at the splinters in the table and the dumb "plebeian" king of clubs I'd put in from another pack, that I was afraid they'd wake the little sleeper up. So I put them away again and let the bottle of wine keep me company all alone.

Back when I was just a robber brat I had learned that getting drunk can be dangerous, and that taught me how to make a good friend of wine by sipping it just a little at a time. No, it wasn't the wine that made the air in the garret room shimmer around us toward midnight. It wasn't the wine that made the candle flames curtsy like tiny dancers in flowing silk skirts, or that seemed to brush the cracked windowpane from the *inside*.

I've hobnobbed with Death in person—I can tell when the air is full of something not quite canny. Deciding it was time to try my lotion, I put a drop on each of my eyelids, one in each of my ears, and one on my tongue.

No, it wasn't canny, what was in that little room with us; but it wasn't frightening, either. Over my singer's bed a fair young woman was hovering, so beautiful I might have thought she was an angel, except that she had no wings. In fact, I can't say for sure whether she had a real body, or just a long gauzy robe that flowed like the candle flames. It seemed to be flowing around limbs and a trunk, as fine as anybody could ever imagine, but it was as transparent as her face and hands and long lovely hair, and I couldn't see anything through the gauze but the shadowy garret walls. What she was, was a glowing outline against the beams and shadows and flaking whitewash.

She was stroking the sleeping girl's forehead, and smoothing the pillow in its worn, patched pillowcase.

"Hello," I said softly, standing up but feeling quiet. "You haven't come to take her, have you? I'll give you a fight if you have."

The spirit looked at me and shook her head. "No—to give her all the help that lies within my power to give. How is it that you can see me?"

I showed her the lotion. "But who are you?" I asked.

"I am one of the children of the air," she replied, still stroking my friend's forehead. "We go wherever we can, bringing fresh breezes, soothing dreams, and every other healing thing we can. In this way, we earn souls as immortal as those of human beings."

"It isn't a bad plan," I remarked. "I know plenty of people born with souls who don't know what to do with them."

"I fear not. Whenever the children of the earth cause

us to shed tears of sorrow at their naughtiness and mischief, it lengthens our time of trial. But by giving this poor child all the help that lay within your power," she added more happily, "you are helping me, also, to earn my soul and fly to Heaven all the faster."

"Oh, so we're 'the children of the earth,' are we?" I observed. When the spirit nodded, I went on, "Well, it's some comfort to know we're doing all this double good in the world, but it'll be a lot better if we can help her to some purpose. Did you happen to be here when the old leech told me about"—I glanced down to be sure my friend was still sleeping—"her voice?"

The air-child nodded again. "I used to have a very sweet voice," she mused, "or so they said. If only there were some way . . ."

"You've got a pretty nice voice now."

"All of the children of the air have sweet voices, but only other children of the air—and folk who use magic lotion—can hear us. That would be no use to a mortal singer, but if only there were some way I could give her the voice I had when I was a mermaid, I'm sure she could go on earning her living in the opera."

"So you used to be a 'child of the sea'?" I asked.

"Yes. I fell in love with a human prince, and sold my old voice to the sea witch for a draught that divided my tail into a pair of the props that humans call legs." She sighed. "He was very kind and very handsome, and if he had married me, he would have given me a soul at once."

"I think I've heard about you," I told her. "But they say he *did* marry you."

"What? Who says that?"

"Oh, people. The people who tell these tales and make plays out of them."

"But what do they say happened to the princess he really married?"

"Who? Oh, you must mean the one he almost married— the way they tell it—but you found out just in time that she was the old sea witch in disguise, out to cheat everybody."

I saw tears, transparent as the rest of her, form in the air-child's eyes and roll down her clear cheeks, like dewdrops if dewdrops could roll down a soap bubble without breaking it. "But the princess was so good and kind! It was not her fault that she had not actually been the one who rescued him from drowning, and she made him so loving a wife! They were happy together all their lives, and they always remembered me—even before they knew my whole story. And now that they are both in Heaven, they look forward to the day I join them again. How can people make up such a wicked tale about her?"

"Be careful," said I. "Lengthening your time of trial, aren't you?"

"Yes, because of the people who make up such tales! And the sea witch was surely very unpleasant, but she was fair and kept her word, and never broke it at all until my sisters begged her and sold her their long hair for a way that I could turn back into a mermaid, after all. It was a very wicked way, and I'm grateful I did not take it, but it was the only way she had it in her power to offer me. How can people twist it all around?"

"*Snip snap snurre, basse lurre!*" said I, seeing another tear ready to roll, and hoping to head it off. "It's simply the way of the world, and no good crying about it. Just tell me how to get there, and I'll go visit the old witch and see what I can do about getting your voice back for my friend here."

"But the sea witch took my voice by cutting off my tongue," the air-child said doubtfully. "I was only dreaming—I don't see how we *could* give it to this little singer, at least while she still has her own tongue."

I answered, "You can be sure that the witch wouldn't have been content to take your voice away from you if that was the end of it completely. Anyway, we can try. I think I've already had a few glimpses of your people, the time I had to swim back from a pirate attack, and I've been wanting another look at the bottom of the sea ever since, so it might as well be now, and we'll see if we can't do a good turn while we're about it."

"Oh, are you one of the people with a necklace of enchanted fish's gills and seahorses' eyes? I heard about it from some of my sisters of the air, the ones who stayed around you when you wore the necklaces, so that you could breathe. But the sea witch is very unpleasant. Her garden-forest is full of polyps that can catch a grown merman and hold him fast, and her house is made from the bones of drowned humans. Are you sure you want to face her?"

"I've seen worse," said I. "Besides, she'll have a hard time of it if she wants to outdo my own wicked old robber woman of a mother, and I could always handle *her*, from the time she used to carry me on her shoulders. But don't worry—I'll find some honest way to get your voice back, so as not to lengthen your time of trial."

So the next day I put more drops of lotion on my eyes, ears, and tongue, and off we set. First we looked some nurses over, and when the air-child pointed a kind one out to me, I hired her to take care of the opera singer while we were gone. Then we went down to the harbor and the air-child showed me which ship to take.

We set sail late that afternoon, and that night in my cabin I tried to explain the situation to my cards. They still didn't much like me, even after I'd taken the "common" king of clubs out of their midst. But they seemed to be very much impressed with the child of the air, and shared my own feelings about the little opera singer, so I hoped for the best from them.

Next morning I used the lotion again, and the air-child pointed out some whirlpools in the water. I could hardly make them out, the ship was giving them such a careful margin, but it wouldn't have been any good trying to make the captain sail closer.

I took my necklace out and asked how it worked. "Does it trap the nearest one of you air-children somehow?"

For the first time since I'd met her, I heard her laugh, a cheerful, musical laugh that floated up like the lovely ghosts of notes from pure silver bells. "Trap us?" she cried. "Oh, no! It ... enables us, invites us ... there's no human word that is quite right for it, but, you see, if we could stay around humans under the water by our own efforts, no one would ever drown. Sometimes we can keep humans alive for a while by ourselves, but if they are too far out or too deeply under, the water forces us up away from them again, unless they have some such magic as your necklace to which we can cling."

I put it on, and she gathered herself into it. She was so close around me that I couldn't see her any longer, only sense her feelings, but overboard we went. Some of the sailors saw me dive, but I ignored their shouts, swam to the nearest whirlpool, and rode it down to the bottom.

That was a fine, exciting ride, but I would never try it again without the right kind of magic. Even with my necklace and the air-child in it, I had a hard time catching my breath around some of the turns.

At the bottom I found nothing around the whirlpools but bare gray sand. Beyond the sand was a seething black mire. On the other side of the mire, I saw the witch's forest-garden of polyps reaching out for anything they could catch in their hundreds of squirming tentacles. And in the middle of the forest, I could just make out the house of drowned people's bones, squatting in a muddy clearing.

The sand was easy to cross, so long as I watched out for the whirlpools. The mire wasn't too much of a problem: all we had to do was swim up high enough to stay out of danger from the heat. The polyps were trickier, but if the air-child had been able to dart between them safely when she was the little mermaid, I could surely do it now, especially with her riding around me to nudge me whenever one reached at me from behind, and to keep reminding me with her emotion that I shouldn't stop to tease any of them.

The sea witch was a wizened, wrinkled old thing with breasts as floppy as wet sponges, what I could see of them through the water snakes she wore in place of a robe, crawling all over her and her long, thin, finny fishtail. She was letting a little toad pick tidbits out of her mouth, for all the world like a fine lady feeding sugar to a pet canary. Her teeth looked like pearls rotted half away, gaping and uneven. I noticed that one of her upper dogteeth was missing and the other one was broken off a little shorter than the teeth around it. The room she sat in had no roof, I suppose the better to catch bodies and things when they came drifting down through the water.

"If you were a child of the sea," the witch said, with a glance at me, "I would know exactly why you have come. Since you are a child of the land, I don't, but it must be a very foolish reason for you to put yourself in so much danger."

"You don't frighten me, old witch," I told her. "If it got around that you killed people who came to you, nobody would ever come again, and then where would you be?"

"Where I am now," she answered. "In the middle of my forest of dangerous polyps that keep me safe from most intruders. It is they that you have to fear more than me. But do you think I care whether anyone ever comes to me or not?"

"Yes," said I, "I think you do. If they didn't come to buy help from you, where would you get your little treasures? Like that pretty rug woven from mermaids' hair on the wall behind you?" I guessed it was the hair the little mermaid's sisters had sold her. "Or somebody's sweet voice?" I went on.

"Ah! So you've heard about that, have you?" She gave her hand a languid flip, and the toad somersaulted a little distance away through the water. Then she shook off some of her snakes, reached out, and took a scallop shell down from a niche that was made out of somebody's old shoulder blade. She opened the shell like a box, and it sent out a soft ruby glow. A jewel lay inside it like a pearl—a great red jewel shaped something like a long little heart—and when she picked it up, it began singing in a voice so sweet that the toad swam to my knee and nuzzled it like a trusting puppy, and I didn't even feel like tweaking the web between its toes.

The air around my head thrummed as I felt the air-child remember the voice that had been hers when she was the little mermaid.

"This is the prize of all my collection," the sea witch said. "Once it was the voice of the sea king's youngest daughter—her little tongue—and if you or anyone else were to put it in your mouth and suck it like a piece of candy until it dissolved, it would become your voice."

"Really?" I asked, thinking how simply that solved one of our problems. "Why haven't you ever done it yourself, then?"

She laughed. "Because I like my own voice the way it is, harsh and scratchy."

"The better to frighten your customers with."

She cackled and nodded. "I see that we understand each other, you and I. Yes, and besides that, one can never hear one's own voice quite as it sounds to other ears. Keeping this as my little music box, I can always enjoy it exactly as it really is, whenever I tire of the sound of my own wheeze in my ears."

"Yes, I've heard the story," said I. "They say that what you really wanted was the sea king's throne, and that you tempted his daughter and cheated her pitifully to get it."

"Who says that?" the witch asked curiously.

"Oh, the people who tell these tales and make plays out of them."

"What would I want with the old king's throne?" The sea witch cackled again. "Let him keep it, with all the headaches of ruling the seven seas! I do very well for myself here, thank you! letting people alone and letting them let me alone, except when they come seeking me out for themselves. I tempted the poor little mermaid, they say? Far from it, I said all that I could to talk her out of it, but she would insist on loving her prince, little as he or his fine soul were worth it. I warned her of everything that would happen to her, all the pain she would have to endure when every step she took with her human legs would feel as if she danced on knives sharp enough to make the blood flow. And I set my price so high I thought that must discourage her when nothing else did. But it did not, so why shouldn't I have reaped some benefit, where no one else did?" She touched the jewel-voice and laughed again. "So now she is sea foam on the waves, centuries before her time, and nothing left of her except her voice."

It seemed that the sea witch knew nothing about the little mermaid's having been turned into a child of the air, and I didn't see fit to enlighten her.

She closed the scallop shell, put it back on the shelf, and chuckled. "Of course they may tell whatever lies they like, up there in the human lands, for that's the way of the world."

"Exactly what I always say," I agreed.

"Do you, now? Yes, I might expect it of someone like you. But you still don't say what you came to me for."

I whistled a few notes before I replied, "Why, for somebody's sweet voice, of course. The little mermaid's will do."

The sea witch cackled with delight and rubbed her bony hands together. "What, my prize, the prettiest treasure in all my collection? So you want that, do you? And what do you expect to pay for it, you saucy young human?"

"Nothing," I told her coolly. "I expect to win it from you with a game of cards."

"Cards? Yes, I know what they are. And how, my chick-abiddy, do you hope to play with pasteboard things here beneath the sea?"

"If you're as skillful an old witch as you pretend," said I, "you'll think of something."

She chuckled and hissed a few words to her snakes. They swam up and wove themselves into a ceiling and latticework above and around us. Then the witch puffed her cheeks out and blew. The water flowed away from us and stopped just short of the snakes, leaving us in a big bubble of air.

"I can breathe air as easily as water," the sea witch said, her laugh sounding not too much different from the way it had before, but echoing more. "Well, what will you stake against my little mermaid's voice? Your heart, perhaps?" Oh, no, she was not going to get me that easily! "The cards themselves," I answered, pulling them out of my pocket, where the air-child around me had kept them dry along with my clothes.

"My dear, packs of cards have fallen to me in plenty from shipwrecks and such."

"Yes, but cards like these?" I spread them out on a flat rock that lay between us.

"Ho-hum!" said the king of spades, who was Alexander the Great.

"Where are we this time?" asked the queen of hearts, who was Helen of Troy, pretending that I hadn't explained things to them the night before.

Looking interested, the sea witch picked them up and held them spread in her knobby fingers. "Do you sing, too, my pretty faces?" she wanted to know.

The knave of diamonds, who was Roland, blew his horn, and they all pitched into a chorus of "The Tree in the Forest."

The sea witch nodded and said, "Yes, these are very fine. In fact, if you'd rather, I might be talked into trading the little mermaid's voice for all these cards, with one or two other little trinkets thrown in. Say, two or three of your toes. Toes from living people are rare enough at this depth."

"I can guess they are," I answered, shaking my head, "and I don't like to think what kind of witchcraft you could work with them. No, I'll just keep all my toes, thank you, and it's a game or no deal at all." If she had asked for a few coins, or even the jeweled rings and things I'd gathered over the years, I might have agreed ... or then again, maybe not, because by playing, I had a chance to keep the cards and all for myself, and I thought it ought to be a better chance now that they'd heard me refuse to trade them outright. After all, what card would want to risk living at the bottom of the sea?

I misjudged those cards. More self-willed and mischievous even than an ordinary pack, they were. Maybe a little spiteful, too.

I had to explain all the rules to the sea witch, of course, and its being her first game ought to have given me one advantage, anyway. And then, I shuffled long enough and carelessly enough to let my cards fall into whatever order they liked. But when I dealt them out, I got a hand that needed just one card to make it perfect ... and that one card was the king of clubs!

So the sea witch won, with diamonds, and I felt a sort of sigh around my neck. It was the air-child trembling with disappointment, there in the necklace I had never taken off, even though I no longer needed it as long as the sea witch kept her room filled with air.

I gave the cards a reproachful glance. The knave of clubs winked up at me and said, "She'll keep us safer than we ever were with you, galloping around the world the way you do."

"We want to settle down," the queen of clubs added.

And the ace, which I hadn't even known could talk, put in, "But you wouldn't so much as consider selling us to her."

The sea witch chuckled again and gathered up the cards, because they were hers now. Fairly, I suppose, since I had played fairly, and so had she: I know how to watch for cheating and sleight of hand. But never, never trust any pack of cards!

They had continued singing the whole time we played, and they sounded as fine as any chorus I ever heard in the Opera House, I'll say that for them. "I might still sell you the little mermaid's voice," the sea witch said, "now that I have all these others. . . ." and she ran her fingers lovingly over the cards, who purred like contented old cats.

"Not for my toes," said I.

"Well, well, what else then?" Looking me over as if she found it hard to make up her mind—and I'm sure she had it already made up by the time we'd started our game, the old sea biddy!—she said at last, "Your necklace then."

"What, this old thing?" said I.

"Old things are sometimes best," said she. "And, looking at it, I think we should agree that it belongs down here. Only I warn you: First you must put the necklace into my hand, before I put the little mermaid's voice into yours."

I hesitated a long time, pretending to finger the necklace that had let me find my way to her alive. Even if she knew that, did she know how it worked?

"You want my necklace, do you," said I at last, "to make a dry space for the cards, where they'll never be in any danger of the water breaking in on them?" Of course she knew I must have *some* kind of magic in order to be here alive, and I wanted to pay the cards back by making them nervous. The sea witch's leathery old skin was drying out and cracking in the dry air, so I knew she would have to let the seawater flow back in around her soon. "But I won't let go my end of the necklace," I went on, "until I can put my fingers around the shell with the little mermaid's voice in it."

"I agree to that." The witch cackled again. "But when once our bargain is completed, if you should drown on your way up, my snakes will bring you back to me, and I will keep your body and the little mermaid's voice, too."

"In that case," said I, "you can make a box out of my skull and keep the scallop shell between my jaws. But once we start, it's only fair to finish the trade as fast as we can."

I'll say this for the old sea witch, that she never made the least attempt to cheat me. She made her own rules, and they might be loaded in her favor to begin with; but once she stated them, she stuck to them fair as Justice— and it's not very often you can find *that* in the world!

The moment I had the scallop shell tucked in my pocket, and she had the necklace wrapped around the cards, she snapped her knuckly fingers, the snakes whisked themselves out of their latticework, and the water clumped back in on us like an avalanche rushing from all sides at once— from east and west and north and south and up from beneath as well as down from above—and the force of all the other directions shot me up and out of her house in spite of the force from above.

Well, I wouldn't have been able to get out of there through dry air, anyway. But I was sorry to miss seeing whatever happened to those cards. Because, you see, the air-child stayed around *me*. As she had explained to me in the ship, the necklace didn't bind her, but only enabled her to stay with its wearer if she chose. I never knew if there was another air-child in the sea near the witch's house, or if any of them would have considered it a good deed worth doing to keep that pack dry; but I doubt it. Maybe the sea witch used more of her own magic in time. Meanwhile, I had problems of my own.

Instead of going back the way we had come, I was trying to bob straight up for the surface. We couldn't avoid the polyps that way, however; the hungry forest arched high over the house made out of dead folks' bones, its black branches rising up around us on every side, flowing back and forth every way in every current, and snapping their thousands of pods at us. They couldn't have held the air-child—she seemed to be having a hard time staying with me anyway—but one of them just touched my hand and grabbed it tight enough to leave an ugly red patch when I yanked free. If enough of them had gotten a real hold, they could have kept me there until the snakes came to collect my bones for the next room the sea witch wanted to add to her house. That is, if the snakes themselves dared swim up between those sticky dark branches. If everything the polyps caught didn't just stay wrapped in their coils until they let it go of their own accord.

I'm sure they would have gotten me half a dozen times from behind, if the air-child hadn't watched my back and nudged me like a tiny puff of breeze hinting me away from the long strands whenever they reached out for a shoulder or piece of neck. Between that and filling my nostrils, she must have had harder work of it than I did, and I wasn't exactly lazing my way up to the surface. If every now and then she slipped and floated a short way away from me, like a huge, ghostly bubble, before she could catch her balance and get back around me again, who could blame her, poor child? Not I! Not when I stopped gasping, anyway.

Why make a longer story of it? Once out of range of the witch's forest-garden, all we had to dodge was a shark or two, and eventually a big sea turtle slipped up beneath me, took me onto its back, and brought me the rest of the way to the surface.

By now the lotion was pretty well worn off or washed away, but I had just enough left in the bottle for a drop on my right eyelid, one in my left ear, and one on my tongue. There was my air-child, gasping a bit herself after her exertions, and whispering in the turtle's ear.

Then she turned to me, her face all radiant, and sang, "Oh, thank you, thank you! Such a deed as this is worth three years to me! But how could I have done it if I had not grown up a child of the sea? And how would I ever have become a child of the air, if it had not been for the sea witch—even though she did not mean it. But you have meant a good deed all around, and bless you for it forever!"

The blessing might prove useful someday or other, but for now a dry ship and a good meal would be handier. I remarked as much to her, and, sure enough, in a few hours, with the air-child scouting ahead and the turtle swimming diligently after her, we found a ship heading back to the city we'd come from the day before. The air-child gave me one parting kiss on the forehead, but naturally none of the sailors noticed it as they hauled me aboard; and that was the last I've ever seen or heard of her, until and unless I can find more of that lotion. But by then she may be in Heaven.

I got back to the city and gave my singer the little mermaid's voice, telling her it was a throat lozenge from a physician who was too rich and famous to come calling in person. She sucked it down, and afterward said he must be the most wonderful physician anyone ever heard of, for giving her a remedy that brought her voice back better than it ever was before.

She doesn't sing in the chorus any longer. Now she is a famous principal with the opera, standing up in the middle of the stage singing arias and duets, and her body has even started plumping out with all the good food. The last time I went to see her sing, I got so boisterous with my applause that the management threw me out of the Opera House. They said I had no knowledge of how to appreciate fine music. *Snip, snap, snurre*! It's the way of the world.

About Selina Rosen and "They Never Approve"

Selina lives in rural Arkansas with her son, her roommates, and various assorted animals. She is active in the local synagogue and the local Society for Creative Anachronism group, although she's cutting back a bit on the latter to allow herself more time to write. (Writing takes a lot more time and energy than one would think—the old line about "Sit down at the typewriter and open a vein" isn't quite a joke.)

And speaking of opening veins, here is a story with a definitely unusual slant on vampirism.

They Never Approve

Selina Rosen

They had decided they didn't like her before I ever brought her home.

Hell, they didn't even give her a chance.

Ten minutes into dinner I saw Mom and Dad exchange that look. I know *that* look. It's the one that says they agree about something. It doesn't happen very often, but when it does, it invariably means that I'm in trouble.

But she hadn't *done* a damn thing. In fact, she couldn't have been behaving more properly if she had been trying, and she wasn't trying.

Virginia was always every bit the lady. That's why I liked her so much more than the girls I went to school with.

But *they* didn't like her.

She had impeccable manners. She was polite. She was courteous. She was intelligent.

None of *that* mattered.

She was wearing normal clothes, and she was beautiful. *That* didn't matter either.

Only one thing mattered to them, and she wasn't out of

the house five minutes when they started in on me. "Of all the girls you know . . . You have to bring one of *those* home."

I didn't stick around. I went to my room.

I slammed my door, but the door didn't stop me hearing them, and their words still sting my brain with the intensity of their disapproval.

It was always the same with them. No matter what I did. All I had to do was tell them that I had a girlfriend and they promptly made up a list of what was acceptable and what was not.

Talking soon turned into screaming—sometimes my parents were louder when they were agreeing than when they were disagreeing. I didn't even try not to listen. Maybe I should have.

"I think I could have accepted anything but that!" my mother screamed.

"He's only sixteen. Let's just hope to God that it's only a schoolboy crush and that he'll grow out of it."

"If he lives through it," Mom screamed.

"I don't think anyone has died yet," my father reassured her.

"Lily Simmons's daughter Janet came damn close. She wound up in intensive care. My God, Bill, they had to give the girl three blood transfusions, or had you forgotten that? What do we do?"

"Tell him he can't see her anymore." I guess that sounded logical to my dad.

"Oh, come on, Bill. You know Steve. If you tell him he can't see her, that's just going to make him want to see her more."

My dad gave a grunt of agreement. "Maybe we're over-reacting. Remember your parents' reaction to me. . . ."

"Bill, you wore a leather jacket and rode a motorbike. When you were feeling really rebellious, maybe you smoked a little reefer. This girl is a *vampire*. She sucks out people's blood."

My mother was obviously outraged that my father would

even think to link the two together. "There's a big difference."

"Okay, okay, Ellen. Calm down. What I was trying to say was that it's just a fad. A disgusting and perverted one, but really no different than any of the others, and like all the others, this one will die out. Besides, I don't think Steve wants to be a vampire. He just likes the girl."

"Bill, think about what you just said. I went with you all of five days when I put on a leather jacket and climbed on the back of your motorbike. A week later I was smoking grass with you. Steve is totally infatuated with this girl. How long can it be before he's wearing solid black, slicking his hair back with grease, and sleeping in inversion boots? After that, it won't be long till he's drinking blood."

"You're right. All we can do is tell him he can't see her anymore. I know it's weak, but what else can we do? If we have to lock him in his room, I don't want him seeing this girl anymore." My father's words were firm and final, and meant not a damn thing.

"Short of locking him in his room I don't see how we can stop him seeing her, and as I told you, forbidding him to see her is just going to make him want to see her more."

"What else can we do?" Dad's voice raised a pitch. "If you've got any better ideas, why don't we hear *them*?"

Mom made a bunch of gurgling sounds that meant that she was out of ideas.

I couldn't take any more.

They didn't understand love.

They didn't understand anything.

I stormed out of my room. I guess I just wanted to say my piece.

"You're just like everyone else!" I said accusingly. "You don't even try to understand. We live in a world where nothing is sure. At any minute some bureaucrat somewhere could punch a button and we could all go up in a puff of nuclear smoke. Vampires are just trying to improve their chances of survival. How can you put them down for that? They don't fly through the night and suck out the blood of unsuspecting victims. They don't take anyone's blood. All their donors give willingly. It's done very cleanly, just like in the hospital. No huge fangs digging into flesh. What happened to Janet Simmons was her own fault. Some people get off on having their blood drunk. Janet gave to three separate groups that day. None of them knew she had given already."

Mother looked at Father, and gave him the famous "Where have we gone wrong?" look.

Dad shook his head in disbelief and shame, and almost looked at me for a second, something that he had avoided doing for years.

Then Mother broke into tears. "My God, Steve," she sobbed, "have you listened to what you're saying? Drinking blood!" She shrieked, "Human blood, for Christ's sake!"

She had always done that. Probably because it had always worked. She'd tried reasoning with me, now she'd cry, and if that didn't work, later she could always try her secret weapon—*threats*.

I stood my ground and didn't bat an eye. I knew what I was talking about. I was talking about vampirism, and it was a sure bet that I knew a lot more about that than they did. There are more kinds of vampires in this world than those that feed on blood.

My parents were vampires. Instead of blood, they fed on people's spirits, their souls. They used and manipulated people. My father as a lawyer, my mother as a real estate agent, had both ruined their share of people, and they had never given it a second thought.

But let someone drink a little blood, and they were mortified.

They were being hypocrites, and I told them so.

They both started talking, or rather screaming, at once. There wasn't too much that was actually coherent. But it was obvious that, among other things, they thought I was warped, ungrateful, and being led around by my nose, that Virginia was pulling the string.

Finally, Mother out-screamed Father. "You're not like this, Steve. Listen to yourself. You're defending these people. It's that girl. She's filling your head with a bunch of nonsense...."

"It's not nonsense," I said. My anger slapped at the back of my teeth, trying to find the words with which to escape. I finally had to be happy at just blurting out, "I have my own brain. Virginia doesn't tell me what to do or what to think."

They both started screaming at once again, and I went back to my room. I don't even think they knew that I had gone. They had never dealt with me as their offspring. They always dealt with me as a problem. One they could never quite solve.

I lay on my bed and listened to them trying to blame something or someone for my behavior.

Thirty minutes of "It's that girl's fault." Followed by thirty minutes each of "It's your fault. It's your mother's fault. It's the school's fault," and finally back to "It's that girl's fault!"

As usual, someone was at fault, and it wasn't either of them.

I sneaked out of the house. It wasn't that hard. They were so preoccupied with trying to figure out how they could keep me locked in my room that I walked right out of it and out the front door without either of them seeing me.

I walked the street, hands in pockets, head down. This was all my fault. I should have known better than to bring Virginia to meet them. They were selfish jerks.

Because I had really thought they would like her. Because for once I thought that they might actually approve of my choice.

I am a damned fool. I always have been, and I probably always will be.

My misery folded in on itself, and at that time, I had no idea where I was or where I was going. I was just walking. Trying to put some distance between myself and the screaming back at the house. Trying to find some peace of mind.

I never did.

Looking back now, I can only conclude that it was fate that guided my unsure footsteps.

My tangled thoughts were interrupted by sound. Sirens! They were close. Too close. The cop car whisked past me.

It took me a few seconds to realize what that lump in the road ahead was. It wasn't till I saw all the cop cars that it really shot home.

It was a body. I froze in place for a second. That sweater. The red sweater with the white stars on it. I'd only seen one like it. The one that belonged to Janet Simmons.

I started moving again, toward the body. Why I don't really know. Morbid curiosity, I guess. I wanted to see what Janet looked like. Maybe I wanted to see if she were really dead. Or maybe fate was still guiding me, and I had no choice over where I went.

I was almost upon the scene when someone hollered out, "There's one of them!"

There were sirens and cop cars and ambulances and confusion. It was several moments before I realized the man was pointing at me.

I ran. I didn't want to face the fury or the outrage in the crowd. Didn't want to try to explain that this was the worst thing that could have happened for Virginia and her kind. Because now there was a confirmed death and that would mean witch hunts and persecution tenfold what it had been.

I had no doubt that if the mob caught me, they would pound a stake through my heart and ask questions later. I ran through yards and jumped fences, but I was never a fast runner, and they were closing in on me. Then, suddenly, someone grabbed me and pulled me back into the bushes. I struggled. I started to scream, and a hand was wrapped firmly across my mouth. I bit it, and my attacker let out a muffled cry as my mouth filled with blood. The blood was warm and sweet and I swallowed. I almost instantly felt different, and I knew that whoever had grabbed me was not human. I looked up into Virginia's pained eyes. All struggling ceased. Virginia removed her hand and held it.

I started to apologize, and she put a finger over my lips. I could hear my pursuers all around us. They were so close I held my breath.

Then they gave up and moved on.

"I'm sorry," I told Virginia when I was sure it was safe. "I didn't know it was you."

"You have no idea how sorry you will be." Her voice was sad and distant; I felt instantly chilled. "Steve, it's too late to go back now. We better get out of here before they come back."

She took my hand, and I followed. Nothing mattered. I was with Virginia, and no matter the reason, I was happy just to be with her, to feel her hand in mine.

Her hand in mine! Wasn't this the hand I had just bitten? It felt warm and smooth and undamaged. I stopped suddenly and jerked the hand into my field of vision. It was clear. I checked the other. No sign of the bite. I began to wonder if perhaps I had imagined the whole thing, but the taste of blood still hung sweet in my mouth.

I looked at Virginia, and displayed a set of very healthy fangs. "It's not just a game we're playing, Steve." She kissed me ever so gently on the lips. "Join me, Steve."

I would have followed her to the ends of the earth and back. She was the first girl I had ever loved. Correction, she was the only *woman* I *ever* loved.

I went with her. Their den was in a back alley in the basement of an abandoned warehouse. She shared the dwelling with three male vampires. I was a little upset about that.

So were they.

"Damn it, Virginia," one said, "not another one."

I found out later the reason for such an outburst. The boy (or Billy, as I later came to know him) had been her first. They called him Count.

Billy had never understood Virginia's needs. The rest of them did, and I soon learned.

"Chill, Count. This is not time for one of your tantrums. Janet Simmons is dead," Virginia said. There were a few moments of absolute silence.

"You do it?"

I recognized the boy; it was Larry. Now, I knew Larry real well. We had grown up on the same block. We had played in Little League together. We had been caught trying to drill a hole in the wall so we could watch the girls shower. But what I never would have guessed was that he was a vampire. Larry just wasn't the type. He was shy, quiet, the absolute last person you would expect to be drinking blood.

Before I go any further, let me dispel some myths about vampires.

The sun does not kill vampires. Grant you, it does hurt their eyes a little, but a good pair of Polarizers will take care of that.

Crosses and garlic have no effect on them. Or holy water, or any of that stuff.

They do have a reflection.

They don't turn into bats.

A wooden stake through the heart will kill them. But so will a bullet in the same place. Their heart is their weak spot.

Maybe this is going to sound like I am really stupid. But until Larry asked, it had never entered my mind that Virginia might have killed Janet. Or maybe I just knew Virginia enough to know that she couldn't do such a thing.

"No, I didn't," Virginia said hotly.

"Don't act so holier-than-thou, Virgi." Someone else I knew! Stewart! I had always liked Stewart. But right then, I could have slapped him. "We all drink blood. You more than us. And she was one of your favorite donors." It was the way he said it that made the hair stand up on the back of my neck. He didn't care whether she had killed Janet or not. He just didn't want her to lie about it.

"I haven't been to Janet for blood since I found out she was giving to other groups," Virginia defended herself.

"Get real, Stewart. You know Virginia doesn't like to share." Count drew his words out, and his lip curled into a snarl as he started at me with utter contempt.

"I really don't have time for this stuff." Virginia's voice was filled with rage and an authority I had never heard her use before. To my amazement, even Count looked frightened.

"What is it? What happened?" The arrogance had completely left Stewart's voice.

"The cops were there. In force. They chased Steve. If they had caught him, they would have lynched him."

"Can they link him to you?" Count asked, the anger daring to enter his voice again.

"I should think so," Stewart said, looking at his nails. "She's been sporting him for weeks."

Larry asked the obvious question. "Was it a vampire kill?"

"Yes."

"Will the cops know that?" Larry asked nervously.

"They already do." Virginia's brow knotted up with worry.

"You do it?" Count asked me.

I was more than a little taken aback. Till then, they had talked about me as if I were a nonentity. I think I was more shocked at being acknowledged than by the accusation. "I didn't kill her," I screamed at him, then added in a purely childish manner, "Maybe I did!"

They laughed at me then. They all did. Except Virginia.

"Can the laugh track, jerks. We've got a real problem on our hands, here. Thanks to Janet's carelessness, every vampire in this city is going to be under suspicion. Us more than the others. We're going to have to hide out till this all blows over."

"What about feeding?" Steve asked hungrily.

Virginia looked tired, rubbed her eyes. "Dawn approaches. Let's get some sleep."

Virginia took me to a secluded part of the warehouse. That was a private time. A time for her and me, and no one else.

It never came to mind to think about what my parents might be thinking or doing. It never occurred to me that at the happiest moment in my life they were making moves to destroy me.

"Look at this." I woke up to Stewart screaming and something thrown in my face. It took a few moments for me to come fully aware of my surroundings. By the time I sat up, Virginia was already reading the paper. She sighed deeply. "What now, Virgi?" Stewart asked in a panic. "What do we do now?"

"For starters we all calm down." It wasn't a suggestion when Virginia said it; it was a command. "The worst thing we can do right now is panic."

Count entered the room. "I think the solution is simple. Let Steve go back to his parents."

"What if I don't want to go back to my parents?" I screamed. "What does this have to do with me anyway?"

Virginia handed me the paper then. "High School Girl Killed by Local Vampire Gang" was the headline. I read on. Basically it was pretty much what we had expected.

Till you got to the third paragraph.

Steven Johnson, a 16-year-old friend of the deceased, walked up to the murder scene and was taken hostage by the gang. The authorities suspect ... My parents were offering a reward for any information leading to my safe return.

I didn't read on. Obviously, my father had used his clout to turn my running away into a kidnapping. There was only one thing to do and I knew it, but I didn't do it.

"He's got to go back," Stewart said. "You can see that, can't you, Virgi?"

"It'll be bad enough over Janet's death, but add kidnapping to that and they won't be happy till they hunt us down and kill us all." Surprisingly, Count's voice was calm.

Virginia's voice was even cooler. "He's one of us now. He belongs to us."

"To you, you mean!" Count's calm shattered. "You don't give a damn what happens to him. Or any of us, for that matter. If he goes back . . ."

"He needs blood. . . ."

"It's not too late for him, *yet*. He could break free. He could remain normal. . . ."

"I'm sure he doesn't want to, Count. Who in their right mind would choose to be normal when they could be immortal?" Virginia held up her hand as he started to continue. "Count, you're just hungry. We'll feel better after we eat."

"And just how are we going to feed?" It was Larry who came to Count's defense. "Count's right. With Janet dead, the heat is on anyway. How are we going to feed with him around? They think we kidnapped him for God's sake!"

"They're right." What they said made perfect sense, and I managed to keep my hormones at bay long enough to figure it out. "I should go back, just to take the heat off."

"No!" Virginia was adamant. "We all stay together."

"You're being unreasonable, Virgi," Count said, regaining some of his calm now that the tide seemed to have turned his way.

Virginia turned to him and smiled smugly. "Oh, am I, bright boy? Then how about this? Let's say Steve goes back. Do you really think that's going to take the heat off? No. The main issue there is Janet's death. They'll question Steve." I watched as Count's face sank. He knew the words she spoke were true.

"I won't tell." I was a little hurt by the accusation, but I didn't want to go, and I secretly hoped they would find a reason why I *couldn't*.

"You wouldn't want to," it was Stewart who spoke, "but you would. They would word a question cleverly, and . . ." He threw up his hands in exasperation. "So, what now, Virgi? I don't know about everyone else, but I'm hungry." Larry and Count nodded in agreement.

"It will be dark soon. We are creatures of the night. It will conceal and protect us. We will hunt and we will feed."

At night, we dressed all in black and took to the streets: the dark ones on the old side of town, where only hoods, hookers, derelicts, and politicians—around election time—go. We found a willing donor right away. We all went into a dark alley and then the tube and bags came out. Now, I was the kid that passed out the one time in my life I had a blood test, so I was a little shocked at my reaction to the blood-taking ritual. I watched the blood flow into the bag from the tube in the man's arm and felt no nausea. Instead, there was a strange feeling of satisfaction. When the bag was full, we paid the man and went on hunting.

"Just a little now, Virgi," Stewart begged. "I'm starving."

"Don't be a fool, man," Count said hotly. "Last thing we need is to have someone catch us feeding."

Thirty minutes later we found another willing donor. With both bags full, we went "home."

I'll never forget that first time. I had to force myself to drink the first few drops. The next thing I remember, Stewart was cussing me and taking the bag away. It was the total fulfillment of all I had ever dared to dream. I felt like I could do anything, go anywhere. I realized that to be a vampire, blood isn't just a food—it's a drug. It becomes your way of life, and then you can never go home.

For about a week, we had to be extra careful, and then everything seemed to cool down. Like any news story, after it's told fifty times, it loses its impact.

We were able to move a little more freely around town, which is to say that there wasn't a cop around every corner we turned.

Then the powers-that-be decided that Janet's death was not a form of murder at all, but a form of suicide.

Vampires were once again free to walk the streets.

Except me. I was still officially missing. Although now they were saying that I had probably run away.

Most nights I got left at the warehouse alone. I felt left out but had to agree that it was an added risk that we shouldn't take too often.

Except for that, I couldn't complain about my life. I had my friends, I had Virginia, and I had plenty of blood.

Then some stupid jerk went berserk. He used his teeth for more than show, and chewed some poor hooker up. Then he killed a wino.

Then a cop.

After that, no vampire was safe on the streets, and the blood supply dried up. No one was willing to give blood if they thought they might be chewed up. Even the derelicts wanted a stiffer price, and we were running out of money. Some of the other groups were resorting to violence. They would abduct their donors, tie them up, and take the blood.

For all practical purposes, they were mugging people for their blood.

Virginia refused to do this, so we went hungry a lot.

I watched the sunrise through the tears in my eyes. My path was clear. I turned on the radio, and the morning news confirmed my fears. My life had been shattered. I dug around till I found my old clothes. The clothes that weren't black. The ones I had been wearing the night my life had begun. It was appropriate that I should wear them on the day that that life was destroyed.

"The young woman was shot seventeen times before she fell dead. . . ."

I slung the radio into the wall. I found a pair of sunglasses. I dried my tears and put the glasses on. It had been a long time since I had been outside in the daylight. I didn't like it.

I now see the light for what it is: the enemy of man. For nothing can hide in it. All that is ugly in man can be seen clearly only in the light. The dark hides man's ugliness and, for that matter, his beauty. In darkness, all men are equal. No one can judge you if they can't see you. That is why so many fear the dark.

They fear what they cannot judge.

When I got to the house, no one was home. I showered and changed into the black garments I had brought with me. I sat down in the living room and turned on the TV. I watched soaps. The news came on at 12:00, and I damn near turned it off.

I should have.

They were saying that Virginia, Larry, Stewart, and Count were the "Killer Vampires." I suppose that cleaned things up for them for a while, till the killing started again. I wanted them all dead. The cops, the newsmen, and the killer vampire who had ruined everything.

But all that would have to wait. First, I had to get some money. If my parents had taught me one thing, it was that you can't get anywhere without that. Then I had to make everyone believe that I was a normal, mundane person. My parents had always been great at that. No one would have ever guessed that they harbored all those hidden neuroses. Once I had money and had proved I was "normal," then I could take everyone down. One at a time.

I smiled and waited. It was all so simple. If only I had thought of it before. It was too late for the others. For Virginia.

I couldn't think about them. If I did, I would be dragged down into despair and become unable to avenge their deaths. I thought this all out in the hours that I sat waiting for my parents to return.

When I heard the key turn in the lock, all I could feel was a sense of anticlimax. I heard someone enter, and a sack of groceries hit the floor.

"My God . . . Steve, is that you?"

"It's me, Mom." I stood up and turned to face her.

"My God, you're one of *them*." I heard the disgust and disapproval in her voice. They never had approved. Not once. Of anything.

I smiled, showing my fangs. "Tell me, do you and Dad still have that giant life insurance policy naming me as beneficiary?" Her eyes grew large as I approached. "Did you ever think of how ironic it is that they call it *life* insurance?"

About Jennifer Roberson and "Never Look at a Gift Sword in the Horse's Mouth"

Jennifer is another of the writers whose first story I published, in the first of the *Sword & Sorceress* anthologies. She went on to a very successful—and busy—career, but still managed to find time to write the occasional story for me, including one for the first issue of *Marion Zimmer Bradley's Fantasy Magazine* and this, the cover story for issue 16.

She is the author of two fantasy series: "Chronicles of the Cheysuli" and the "Sword Dancer" cycle, as well as a historical reinterpretation of the Robin Hood legend, called *Lady of the Forest*, which emphasizes Marian's point of view. Her newest historical fiction, *Glen of Sorrows*, is due out about the same time as this anthology, and she has done a fantasy collaboration with Melanie Rawn and Kate Elliot, *The Golden Key*, due out sometime in 1996.

In addition to writing, she trains and exhibits Labrador retrievers and Cardigan Welsh corgis. She lives near Phoenix with four dogs and two cats.

Never Look at a Gift Sword in the Horse's Mouth

Or: The Horse Who Would Be King

Jennifer Roberson

My master had a problem. He knew it. I knew it. But nobody else knew it. And we needed to keep it that way.

"You're a magician," I told him comfortingly. "Use some smoke and mirrors, a little sleight of hand, a pinch of razzle-dazzle—no one will even notice."

The morning, for Britain, was bright: the halfhearted sun was a tarnished, brass-colored splotch in the haze of reluctant day. Birds chirped. Bees buzzed. Mice rustled. Down the hill, a camp dog barked.

My master slumped disconsolately against the broken tree stump in the hollow of the hill, rump planted precariously near an anthill. The ants, as yet, were oblivious; unfortunately, so was he.

"Magician," he muttered disgustedly, "I'm bloody Merlin, you fool!" I considered polite ways of pointing out the anthill and the potential consequences of taking up residence, however temporary, in its immediate environs, but decided the topic at hand was more immediate. My master was touchily proud of his position as the most exalted, learned, and powerful magician Britain had ever known, and protected that reputation with a fervor verging on obsession . . . any challenges to his authority, intended or no, required delicate attention.

"I know that," I reminded him, implying mild reproof; a long and peculiar acquaintanceship allowed me great latitude in familiarity. "You've taken great pains for some years now to establish exactly who you are, with commensurate reputation. No one in all of Britain doesn't know who you are."

He cast me a baleful glance from dark, brooding eyes overshadowed with thick, untidy dark hair only infrequently combed or cut. "And there's the rub," he complained. "I'm a victim of my own success. I'm left no room for failure."

I snorted. "There's no reason you shouldn't be successful this time."

"No reason!" The baleful glare reasserted itself as affronted outrage. "I'm supposed to supply Britain with the greatest hero-king she's ever known, and you say, ever so blithely"—with the soft-spoken, icy precision that cuts the legs out from lesser souls—"there's no reason I shouldn't be successful?"

I ignored the ice and derision. "No reason at all. Trust me."

Merlin glared, surrendering verbal acrobatics; none of them worked, with me. "Trust you."

"Yes."

With elegant precision, my master said distinctly, "You are a horse."

A moot point, and unworthy of discussion. I tossed my head, flopping my dark gray forelock eloquently between upstanding ears. "I'm confident you'll find someone for the job."

Merlin ground his teeth, spitting out his commentary with a repressed passion that underscored his frustration. "It can't be just anyone, don't you see? It must be someone very special. Someone unique in all respects.

Someone perfectly suited to unite all the warring tribes so Britain can fend off foreign invaders."

I looked down my nose, a posture better suited to me than to him, as my nose was considerably longer. "You just need someone who can kiss a lot of ass," I told him, "although why anyone would want an ass when there's a perfectly presentable horse available, I don't know."

"Don't be so arrogant," Merlin sniffed. "After all, I made you."

"And I'll be the making of you." I gazed back at the encampment some distance away. Smoke clogged the trees, drifting hither and yon. I heard the sounds of laughter, raillery, arguments, mock fighting, weapons practice. The air stank of smoke, burned meat, and unwashed human bodies. "We haven't failed yet. We'll come up with a plan."

Merlin heaved a sigh, picking idly at a snag in his second-best enchanter's robe. "Not just any plan. It has to be very delicate. Very selective, so there's no question as to the outcome. I can't just point at a fellow and say: 'That's the man there, don't you know, rightwise born king of all England.'"

I cocked a hoof, standing hipshot. "Why not?"

"It smacks of dictatorship. They won't like it, from me. These people like signs, and portents, and omens ... they're a superstitious lot, bound up by ritualistic gobbledy-gook—never mind such things are as easy to arrange as buying a girl for the night." He glowered at me. "Not that I can buy one, mind you ... whose idea was it that Merlin had to be chaste?"

"You had to be something," I reminded him. "You needed a gimmick. Nobody cares if you sing, or tell stories, or swill wine with the best of them—what sets a man apart in these immoral times is his chastity."

He flapped a hand at a bee. "You might have picked something easier on me. Or at least let me geld you, so we suffer equally."

I pointedly ignored the suggestion. "As to signs and

portents and ritualistic gobbledygook, you've been the one arranging those very things for years now."

He snapped a loose thread free of his robe, inspecting it morosely. If he kept at it, part of the robe would unravel and hence become third-best. "I have to make them think they've something to do with it ... or else make it so obvious there's only one conclusion."

"Tests are good for that. They weed out the inappropriate."

The line of his mouth crimped. "I hate to make the kingship of all Britain contingent upon a test."

"Why? Makes as much sense as drawing names out of a pot."

I pawed at damp turf, digging an idle hole. We all have our bad habits. "After all, it's you who'll be running the realm."

Merlin thought about it. "I need the right sort of man. A very particular type of man. Stupid enough to be malleable, but wise enough to know his limits. Young enough to be suitably idealistic, big enough to be impressive."

I plucked a succulent clot of turf from the damp ground, shook it free of mud, ground it to bits between my teeth.

"There's always Artie."

Truly taken aback, Merlin gazed at me in horror. "You can't be serious!"

"He's pretty good at carrying your baggage around, and he always feeds me on time."

"Artie's thick in the head."

"All the better for you." I smiled, displaying teeth. "He's young enough, big enough, certainly stupid enough—and he listens to you."

"Because he knows if he doesn't I'll turn him into a frog."

"No, you wouldn't. Artie's an innocent. You'd never hurt him like that."

Merlin just scowled; he hates it whenever I remind him he's not the tyrant he pretends to be.

I switched my tail. "It's a good idea, and you know it. He's been quiet since we arrived, so no one knows much about him. He looks enough like Uther to qualify as his bastard; and anyway, Uther's dead. He won't care."

Merlin grunted. "Who's his mother, then?"

I ruminated a moment. "What about that woman living out on the edge of nowhere in Cornwall? At Tintagel? She's supposed to be a trifle touched in the head, too."

"Gorlois's widow?" Dark brows lanced down. "That's Ygraine. No one's seen her for years. She lives out there with a couple of servants and a castle full of cats."

"That's what I mean. She won't put up much of a fuss. And if she does, just keep sending her merchants with wagons full of wares. Shopping will keep her mind off things."

"Uther's bastard, got on Ygraine." Merlin chewed a lip. "It could work."

"Of course it could."

"I'll have to concoct some bizarre tale full of supposed magic and superstitious nonsense to account for the bedding."

"Uther bedded half the women in Britain."

"But he's allergic to cats. He'd never have bedded Ygraine, or he'd have sneezed for a month."

I waggled dark-tipped ears. "You'll think of something. You've done it before." With my help, of course, but we don't always mention that.

"And something to prove Artie's worthy." Merlin chewed a ragged fingernail. Very bad habit. "That will be the hard part."

I disagreed. "Just figure out a straightforward test with all the right sort of bells and whistles, then contrive the thing so Artie passes when no one else can."

"Ants!" Merlin cried, leaping to his feet. In a frenzy of activity unbecoming to the most exalted enchanter Britain had ever known, he beat off the ants with both hands. "Begone!" he thundered.

I winced, wondering if England would keep her ants. The last time Merlin had been so irritated, we'd been in Ireland, with snakes.

Though someone else got the credit for that.

Artie came up to see me at midday. All the other horses were picketed at tents or elsewhere in the trees, but everyone had learned very quickly that the big gray horse with the sword-shaped blaze on his face was not to be bothered.

I nickered a greeting as he made his way up the hill, using horse language in case anyone else was around. Only Artie and Merlin knew I could talk, and we'd decided it was better left that way. Actually, I think it was because Merlin didn't like sharing his notoriety; a talking horse would siphon some of the attention from him.

Artie wore that distant, slack-jawed expression that others took for stupidity, including my master. In truth, Artie wasn't that stupid. He just daydreamed a lot.

I'd asked him once what he thought about when he turned himself sideways to the day and wandered the dreaming lands that separated waking life from sleep. He'd just hunched his big shoulders and answered "Things," in that infuriatingly unspecific way that said everything he needed to say, and nothing at all of what I wanted to hear.

But that's Artie, God love him.

For a man as big as Artie, he knew how to walk quietly. I heard nary a crackle of underbrush and deadfall as he climbed the hill to me. I smelled the oatcake before he dug it out of his tunic, expanding nostrils to breathe heavily at him.

"All right, all right . . ." Smiling widely, Artie unknotted the corner of his tunic and caught most of the crumbs before they fell. His hands were huge and gentle, cupping my muzzle tenderly as I lipped up the oatcake.

Once finished, I put one large nostril up against his face. We traded breaths a moment, reasserting our bond, and then Artie patted me firmly on one shoulder, smacking palm audibly.

"More swordplay today," he told me. "Kay will have his turn."

"What about you?" I asked.

Artie shook his head, hitching one shoulder. "Not for me."

"Why not? Ector'd let you."

"Kay would complain."

"Let him. Merlin paid enough coin for your fosterage—let it buy you a chance, too."

But Artie just shrugged again. "Doesn't matter."

I eyed him thoughtfully. "They've been at you again, haven't they?"

Another shrug as he stroked the underside of my jaw.

"You're big enough to beat them all at their own game, Artie."

"That's what they want me to do."

"So, you'll let them call you names without trying to make them stop."

"They'll say whatever they want, anyway."

"If you learned some of the skills—"

"No." Wrinkles marred his forehead beneath the lank light brown hair. "I'm good at what I do. I don't need to be like them."

"You could be better than them."

Artie just shook his head.

I rested my chin on his shoulder and leaned. "There's more to life than fetching and carrying for Merlin."

He laughed. "I could say the same to you."

"But I'm a horse, Artie. That's what horses do."

"And I'm just Artie. It's good enough for me."

I snorted damply at him. He just wiped his face clean and cast me a reproachful glance.

The trouble with people like Artie is you can never reason with them. Especially when they're right.

Merlin, hunched over his grimoire, looked up crossly as I stuck my head inside the flaps of his tent. His expression cleared as he saw me. "What is it?"

"Have you made any progress on your plans for Artie's test?"

He scowled. He had changed from his second-best robe to his third-best, which meant he'd probably unraveled enough of his second-best to make it the new third-best, thereby elevating the former third to second.

"No," he said shortly.

"I think I may have the answer."

"Oh?" He shut the grimoire and placed it back on its tripod, rising to stand before me. "Pray tell me, horse, what Britain's greatest magician can do to deliver a king?"

"I told you. There's Artie—"

Merlin made a rude sound. "It's a stupid idea."

"Why? Would you rather have someone like Kay make a play for the realm?"

Merlin snorted. "Kay's a hotheaded, braying fool."

"While Artie's a kind man who wants the best for everyone."

"Kind men don't make good kings."

"With your attitude, you could make up the difference."

We glared at one another. Merlin broke it off. "All right, enough already. What do you suggest?"

"This," I said, and told him.

The night was cool, crisp, very dark, save for the spill of argent moonlight glinting through leaves and branches. Merlin slid off my back, muttering under his breath of foolish ideas and superstitious nonsense. The grimoire, wrapped in pure black silk, was tucked under an arm; he hitched it more securely between elbow and hip, and stalked ahead of me through the darkness.

"Over there," I told him. "On the other side of that tree."

He went around the designated tree and stopped at the huddled rock formation. Not large, not small; kind of medium, worn smooth by time and dampness. "This?"

"That." I plodded onward and stopped beside him. "Appropriately unique, wouldn't you say?"

"It's a rock."

"Not just a rock. The rock. Have you no imagination?"

Merlin grunted. "I suppose it will do."

"It had better, if you're to maintain your reputation." I ignored the sideways scowl. "You said there was a spell for what we need."

"Oh, I can melt the rock with no real difficulty, and even fuse it back. I just don't understand why I should."

"Leave that to me."

Merlin stared at me fixedly. "Look here," he said finally, "you've given me a lot of good ideas over the years, but you can't deny the fact you're a horse. How do I know this trick of yours will work?"

"It won't cost either of us anything to find out."

Merlin heaved a sigh. "You're being obtuse, as always."

I reached out a forehoof and banged it off the rock. "If it's to be done by dawn, we'd better get busy."

"All this just for Artie."

"All this just for England—and your reputation."

Merlin sat down, opened the grimoire, and began to page through it.

"Here," he rasped at last. "This one should do it."

It was nearly dawn. I blinked myself awake, peered blurrily at the rock, then blew out a blade of grass that had lodged itself in one nostril as I'd grazed earlier. "Now for the sword," I murmured.

Merlin was alarmed. "Sword? What sword? You said nothing about a sword. I didn't bring one with me."

"That's my part," I told him. "All right. Close your eyes. Sit very still. Don't move until I say so."

"Are you sure this is going to work?"

"I'm sure it won't work if you don't do as I tell you."

Merlin gritted his teeth. Closed his eyes. Sat very still.

"No peeking," I warned. "This is very delicate magic."

"I'm the magician," he muttered. "I know a little about such things."

"Shhhh."

Merlin held his tongue.

It wasn't so bad, after all: just a small piece of myself, made over into something else. My head ached a little, and my knees were a bit wobbly, but in the end the task was accomplished with little fanfare. I bent, put my head down close to his lap, and let the sword fall.

"Now," I told Merlin.

He caught it, clasped it, gazed in awe upon it. "A sword," he whispered. Hands caressed the weapon, wary of the blade. "A sword," he said again.

I saw the acquisitive glint in dark eyes. "Artie's sword," I told him.

"Artie's . . ." He looked up at me. From his posture on the ground, I loomed over him.

"Artie's," I said pointedly. "Now it's your turn."

"My turn?"

I thrust my nose toward the rock. "Melt it. Put the blade in it, with the hilt left standing upright. Fuse the stone back."

Merlin was aghast. "You want me to seal it up?"

"For now."

"What good is it, then? How will it ever be used?"

"It will be used to determine a king."

Merlin made an inelegant sound in the back of his throat. "That'll be the day."

"Tomorrow," I said. Then, reconsidering, "Sometime today, that is."

"This is the most ridiculous thing I ever heard—"

"Just do it," I told him. "There's a lot riding on this."

Merlin sighed and set the grimoire aside, heaving himself up with the sword clasped in both hands. He strode to the stone, shut his eyes, held the sword above his head. And hissed the incantation.

The air crackled and turned blue. All the hair rose on

my body. Stone parted, then flowed aside. It swallowed the naked blade as Merlin thrust it downward. Then it flowed back, cradling the blade, and remained completely liquefied until Merlin spoke once more. A single sibilant word that made it stone again. The blue light went away. The crackle died out.

"There," he rasped hoarsely. "Stuck in the rock, forever."

Splay-legged, I shook my entire body as violently as I could to rid myself of the itch left by all the magic. "Give it a few hours."

He scooped up the grimoire, wrapped it in silk again, gazed wearily at me out of bloodshot eyes. "This will determine a king?"

"Signs and portents," I told him. "Ritualistic gobbledygook. But I think it will do the trick."

"What do we do next?"

"You wake everybody up at dawn and parade them up here. Tell them it's been revealed to you that Whosoever Pulleth This Sword From the Stone Shall Be Rightwise Born King of All England."

"What?" Merlin croaked.

"Trust me," I told him.

Merlin, being Merlin, enticed everyone to the rock by dawn, promising them who knows what in the elegant, eloquent pomposity of language that impresses those mere mortals who can't decipher it.

Artie, being Artie, meandered up through morning mist and stopped next to me, rooting through his tunic for an oatcake.

"Go down with the others," I murmured from the side of my mouth, pitching my voice so no one else could hear.

"What for?" Artie untied knots.

"Just do what I say. Listen to Merlin."

Artie squinted through the dawn haze and listened briefly as Merlin harangued the gathering. "He's just going on again," Artie said finally. "He does that sometimes."

"You're supposed to be down there with the others."

"Here." He held out a crumbled oatcake.

I shoved his hand aside, knocking the cake to the ground in a shower of crumbs. "I don't want the bloody thing! Just go down with the others and take your turn!"

"My turn?" Artie, squatting to gather up the largest of the crumbs, peered up at me. "What am I supposed to do?"

"Have a shot at the sword," I told him.

"What sword—? Oh, that sword." He straightened, frowning. "How did that get there?"

"Magic," I hissed. "Go get in line, will you?"

Artie stared at the sword thrusting boldly upright in the stone. "Seems to me if someone went to all the trouble to put that sword in the rock, we ought to leave it there."

I tucked my nose into the small of his back and shoved him down the hill. He staggered a few steps, caught his balance, looked aggrievedly back at me. I glared at him ominously.

Merlin, seeing this, cut off his exhortation. He motioned curtly at Artie. "Get in line. Get in line. Everyone has his chance."

Kay's voice rose above the murmurs. "Come on, Artie! Afraid to fail in front of everybody?"

I scowled down at him. Artie just shrugged his shoulders, scratching at lank brown hair.

It took a while, as expected. Each man had his pull, then stepped aside, muttering, and waited with the others to watch the next attempt. So far, all had failed. I nodded across at Merlin, who orchestrated the trial. But it wasn't until I saw the wild glint in his eyes that I realized Artie was missing.

I trotted over to Merlin. "Where is he?" I hissed.

"I thought you were with him!" Merlin waved his hands in an approximation of a spell, just to keep the crowd distracted.

"I sent him down to stand in line."

"This is the end of the line. Artie isn't in it."

Trust Artie—never mind. "I'll find him," I said grimly. "Just send everyone back to bashing at one another to find out who's the best swordsman."

"I just went through this whole rigmarole about finding the Rightwise Born King of All England," Merlin growled. "What do I tell them now?"

I swung away from him. "You'll think of something. I've got to look for Artie."

Eventually, Artie found me. In a black mood I grazed the hilltop near the sword in the stone, tearing up clumps of turf. I wasn't really hungry, but it was something to do.

"I need a sword," he said.

I lifted my head and glared at him. "Where have you been?"

He hitched slabbed shoulders. "I went for a walk."

"You were supposed to try to pull the sword from the stone, like everybody else."

He toed a stone out of its bed. "I didn't feel like it."

"But now you need a sword."

"Not that one. One for Kay. He broke his."

I reached out and grabbed a hunk of tunic with my teeth, then dragged him ungently over to the rock. "Try this one, Artie."

"It's in a rock. I can't."

"Trust me," I suggested. "Kay won't mind."

Artie heaved a sigh and wrapped one big hand around the grip. He tugged.

Nothing happened.

"Try both hands," I said.

Artie did. Nothing happened. "See?" he said. "It's supposed to stay in the rock."

Alarums sounded. "No, no. Try again. Harder, this time."

He did. Then gave it up as a bad job. "I'll go see if I can borrow a sword for Kay."

"Wait—" I grabbed the back of his tunic. "Humor me,

will you? Look . . . you just grab it and pull—" I locked my teeth around the hilt and dragged the thing from the stone.

Artie just blinked at me.

"Take it." My words were warped by the grip in my mouth. "Take the thing, will you?"

Obligingly Artie took the sword.

"Quick like a bunny," I told him, "run down the hill to Merlin and show him what you've got."

"But—Kay needs it."

"Don't give it to Kay. Take it to Merlin."

"Why?"

I leaned my chin on his shoulder. "Have I ever steered you wrong?"

Artie, being Artie, didn't argue with the obvious.

Smugly, I waited on the hilltop for Merlin's Voice of Pronouncement to roll throughout the forest, setting leaves and saplings to shaking. But I didn't hear anything at all out of Merlin until he came racing up the hill, stumbling over rocks. Mostly, he just panted.

"What did you do?" he demanded. "By God, I ought to sell you off to Welsh archers. They shoot horses, don't they?"

"Now, now," I said mildly, "things can't be that bad. Did Artie bring you the sword?"

"He wandered by with a sword, said something about Kay, then wandered off again. By the time I figured out just exactly what sword he had—I never did see it—he'd given the thing to Kay!"

"Oh, God. And now Kay's—?"

"—spouting off to everyone with ears that he's Rightwise Born King of All England," Merlin finished, panting a little. "Couldn't you have come up with a shorter title?"

My mind raced. "But you didn't announce it, did you? As Merlin?"

"Not officially, no. I haven't said anything."

Relief bubbled. "Then we're safe."

Merlin's expression was crazed. "How can we be safe,

blast you? Kay's got the bloody thing, and Artie's out looking for baby rabbits."

"Out looking—? Never mind." I thought a moment. "Go get it back."

"Get what back—the sword? On what pretext?"

"Tell Kay he's got to draw the sword from the stone again. That it doesn't count unless everyone witnesses it. That's fair, isn't it?"

"Oh, God," he muttered. "Why do I ever let you get me into these things?"

"Just go round up Kay and everyone else and take them to the stone. I'll see if I can flush Artie."

"You didn't have much luck last time."

"Kay," I said firmly.

Gnashing his teeth, Merlin dragged up the trailing hem of his third-best—no, his second-best—robe and went back down the hill.

"Rabbits," I murmured thoughtfully, and went off in the other direction.

I found Artie sprawled facedown in front of a burrow. His expression was rapt. "You gave him the sword," I said.

Artie jumped, rolling to his side, then clapped a hand to his heart. "You scared me to death!"

"I'll do more than that if you don't get your rump up from the ground and come with me back to the stone."

Artie got up slowly, picking grass and leaves from hair and clothing. "Kay needed it."

"I told you to take it to Merlin."

"I did."

"You took it near Merlin. There's a difference."

"He would have used his Voice of Pronouncement. It hurts my head when he does that."

"It's supposed to. It's so you'll realize what he's saying is something important."

On cue, Merlin's bellow worked its way through the trees. Artie winced. "See?"

I nudged his shoulder. "You'll have time for rabbits later. Right now there's work to be done."

By the time I got Artie back to the stone, Merlin was looking a little frazzled. He saw us coming, stopped waving his arms, and glared balefully at Artie. Kay, I saw, stood in a belligerent posture at the front of the crowd. The sword hung from one hand.

I dropped my head down to Artie's shoulder, leaning weight into it. "Promise me one thing," I said. "Try the sword, this time."

"I tried before. It didn't work."

"Artie—please. If you love me, give it a try."

Artie stopped short, swung on his heels, slung both arms around my neck. "But of course I love you!"

The watching crowd snickered. Kay said something snide, but I couldn't quite catch it.

"All right," I hissed, "that's enough. Don't make a scene—yet."

Artie disentangled his arms from neck and mane. His eyes were suspiciously bright, and his cheeks were damp.

A soft-hearted fool, our Artie.

"Go stand with the others," I murmured.

Obligingly Artie went off to stand at the edge of the throng. As usual, people made comments.

Merlin turned back and thrust his arms into the air. The Voice of Pronouncement bellowed forth once more. "So there can be no doubt as to who shall rule Britain, I pledge to you that Whosoever Pulleth This Sword From the Stone Shall Rightwise Be Born King of All England!"

A voice from the back of the crowd: "We did this once, already."

Merlin glared at them all. "Do it *again*!"

Kay didn't move.

Merlin scowled at him. "Put the sword back."

He didn't so much as twitch.

"Put the sword back."

Kay's eyes narrowed. "Make me."

A single massive in-drawn breath nearly sucked the leaves from the trees. Expectancy abounded.

Merlin took two steps to Kay. He leaned forward slightly. No one dared to breathe.

Very softly, Merlin said: "Put. The sword. *Back*."

Everyone on the hillside clapped hands over ears as the final word crashed through the forest. Trees fell. Lightning flashed. Camp dogs barked, while picketed horses squealed.

I, of course, didn't, though I had to unpin my ears with effort.

Somewhat hurriedly, Kay went over and stuffed the blade back into the rock. But his intransigence remained firm. "I get first crack."

"Fine," Merlin gritted. "First Kay, then everyone else." He stabbed a look at Artie. "You too, this time!"

Artie nodded glumly.

England's greatest magician waved impatient hands. "All right. Let's get going. We don't have all day."

Kay tried, and failed. Three times, in all, grunting and straining, sweat running from his red face. Then two of his friends caught him by either elbow and pulled him bodily away.

"Next!" Merlin called.

Everyone had a try. Lastly came Artie.

"It won't work," he muttered to us. "I tried this already."

Merlin stuck his face into Artie's. "Just *do* it!"

Sighing, Artie wrapped both hands around the grip and yanked.

Nothing happened.

"Oh, God," Merlin breathed. "I'm ruined. I'm finished. It's over. It's done with. Finis—"

"Shut up," I hissed. "He's not done yet."

But he was. Artie tried twice more. The sword didn't budge.

"Keep your hands on the grip," I said quickly. Then, to Merlin: "Your Voice of Pronouncement! Now!"

"What am I supposed to Pronounce?"

"And make some fog. Hurry!"

"Hell, fog's easy."

It was. Almost instantly the forest was choking in fog.

"Hey!" someone called. "What's all this, then?"

I shut my teeth on the grip and dragged the sword yet again out of the stone. "Here," I mumbled to Artie. "Hold the blasted thing."

"Again?" he asked wonderingly.

"The Voice!" I hissed at Merlin. "Britain has a king!"

Merlin began Pronouncing.

"For God's sake," I said desperately, "make the fog disappear! No one can see anything!"

In mid-syllable the fog winked out, leaving Merlin Pronouncing enthusiastically, me blinking owl-eyed, and Artie—dear, sweet Artie—clutching the sword.

"Whosoever Pulleth This Sword From the Stone—"

"Here," someone said, "I didn't see anything!"

"—Is Rightwise Born King—"

"Not Artie!" Kay shouted. "My God, not *Artie!*"

"—of All England!" Merlin finished. "The End."

"Not yet," I said aggrievedly.

"For me, it is," he rasped. "I need a drink."

"Artie didn't do it!" Kay shouted. "It wasn't Artie at all! I was standing right here—I saw—" He dragged in a wheezing breath. "Merlin's *horse* did it!"

Heavy silence ensued. And Kay, who is not entirely a fool, realized what he'd said, what it sounded like, and what it might do for his future.

I selected that moment to bestow upon the earth my undeniably horsey essence in a noisy, lengthy stream.

Glumly Kay looked at Artie. "Long live the king."

Very quietly.

As I knew he would, Artie came up to see me later. I stood hipshot in the moonlight, whuffling a greeting. I smelled oatcakes.

Artie untied a knot and held it out. I lipped it up gingerly. "Where's the sword?" I asked, once I'd finished the cake.

"Merlin's got it. He says he doesn't trust me with it yet. He says I'd probably give it to Kay, or somebody equally unsuitable."

"Well, you did once."

"But don't you see? I'm not suitable, either!"

"The sword says you are."

"That sword says nothing at all! You pulled it out!"

I didn't answer at once.

Artie nodded firmly. "Twice, you pulled it out."

"Yes, well . . . you can't very well expect a horse to be King of All England."

"You can't expect me to be, either!"

"Too late, Artie. Merlin's done his Pronouncing."

"But I can't be Whosoever Pulleth," he insisted. "It wouldn't be right."

"Rightwise," I murmured. "And, Artie—it doesn't really matter that much. This is how things are done."

"What things?"

"Important things. They happen the way people make them happen, and then other people sing songs and tell stories and write about them the way they wished they'd happened." I twitched a shoulder. "It's just the way life is."

"I never wanted to be king."

"Maybe that's why you'll be a good one."

"Will I?" He brightened. "Are you sure?"

"Leave it to Merlin. He'll see it comes out all right."

Artie hooked an arm over my withers. "You're the finest horse I've ever known."

"Thank you."

"I'd like to do something for you. Something grand and wise and kingly, so no one will ever forget you."

"They'll forget me, Artie. I'm only a horse, after all."

Artie looked worried. "But you're sort of the glue that holds us all together!"

I winced. "Let's not mention glue, shall we?"

"All right." He brightened. "I'll name my firstborn son after you!"

I snorted. "After a horse? That's not very kingly—and the son might object, once he's old enough."

"But I have to do something."

It wasn't worth arguing over. Besides, it would hurt nothing. Part of me was already on permanent loan. "Do as you will, then," I said. "It's Excalibur."

"Your name?"

"Yes."

Artie grinned. "I'll see you're never forgotten! I'll see to it the name lives on forever and ever!"

"Artie . . ." But I let it go. "Thanks, Artie. I appreciate it."

He hugged my neck tightly. "Excalibur," he whispered. "A good name for a horse."

"Go to bed," I suggested. "You've got a full day ahead tomorrow."

"I suppose." He slapped me in farewell. "I'll bring you an oatcake in the morning."

He meant it, I knew. I also knew he'd already fed me the last of the oatcakes. "Go on," I said, and nudged him very gently.

Waving good night, Artie went back to the camp.

"All right," I said. "You can come out now."

He came, drifting out of the darkness like a nightwraith. "So," he said. "Excalibur, is it?"

"Yes."

Faint accusation: "You never told me."

"True Names contain magic. You know better than that."

"But Artie intends to let everyone know it. It won't be you, anymore."

I twitched an ear. "It doesn't matter, now. I have no part in the story. Let him use it as he will."

Merlin stroked my nose. "We've made England a king, old friend."

"Artie will do fine."

Fingers drifted up beneath the forelock, then brushed it aside. The dark eyes so full of magic were bright in the moonlight as he studied my forehead. "So that's where it came from."

I twitched a shoulder dismissively.

"Powerful magic, that. More than I'd risk."

I shook the forelock back into place. "Doesn't matter, does it? It's over and done with."

"I suppose so." He patted me on the shoulder. "A good plan, old friend. Most assuredly, my reputation will survive."

"And your name." I swished my tail. "Artie—and England—will need you."

"And Excalibur." Which was no longer me.

Another pat, and then Merlin, who knew, was gone. I shook my head again, aware of a vague tingle in the place beneath my forelock where the sword-shaped blaze had been.

I gazed up at the waning moon. "A kingdom for a horse?"

No. I rephrased it.

A horse for a kingdom.

About Mara Grey and "The White Snake"

Mara Grey is a landscape designer, writer, and Celtic harper. She lives on Whidbey Island, Washington, in a house surrounded by herbs, flowers, cedar trees, chickadees, jays, and wrens.

And she writes unusual stories, like this one.

The White Snake

Mara Grey

"**H**ey, kid, where'd you get that stick?"

The gruff, tight voice came from an old man sitting hunched on the porch of a shabby house. Paint peeled off the siding and the steps sagged; dead bushes lined the sidewalk.

"My dad's place, under an old tree. Why?"

The boy looked about fourteen, skinny, a bit too big for his clothes. He stood at the edge of the dusty summer road, a dog at his heels, swinging the stick.

Heat pressed down on the house, on the road; the air smelled of dry grass and pungent weeds. Crows swooped and cawed over the nearby fields. The only shade lay under the porch roof, where the old man leaned forward eagerly, like a hound scenting its quarry.

"Can I hold it a minute?"

He tried to smile, but his face, like his body, seemed crooked, as if inhabited by something twisted, wrong.

The boy scratched one ear for a few seconds and looked down at the ground, then walked through the overgrown yard and up the steps.

"Here. I can't see what you'd want with it, but hold it as long as you like."

The old man didn't seem to hear. He fingered the stick slowly, caressingly, crouching over it like a miser over a bag of gold.

"Years I've looked," he whispered, "years and years. But it was here all the time. The tree was here. Here! Who would have thought it?"

Suddenly he straightened up.

"Could you find the tree again?"

"The one the stick came from? Sure. I told you it's on my dad's farm. Biggest tree in the county, maybe even the state."

Again the old man's mouth contorted into a kind of smile.

"I'd like you to do something for me. I'll pay you for it, fifty dollars. All you have to do is catch something for me, something that lives in a hole at the bottom of that tree."

The boy's eyes widened and his mouth opened in amazement.

"How'd you know there was a hole there? I never saw anything come out of it, though. You want to pay fifty dollars? That's crazy."

The old man pulled a battered wallet out of his back pocket and counted out five ten-dollar bills. He held them up in his right hand.

"Here's the money. I'll give you a sack and all you have to do is wait at the base of that tree."

He paused to put the money back in the wallet.

"There's seven snakes in that hole. Let the first six go, but put the last one in this sack and bring it back to me."

The boy tapped one shoe on the floor for a minute and stared off into the distance.

"How'd you find out about all this? What makes you so sure they'll be there? What do you want with a snake?"

"It's a secret," the old man whispered. "My father told me the secret when I was about your age, the way his father told him. I've traveled for sixty years, gone just about anywhere you could name just to find the secret."

The boy looked at him warily, as if he expected him to jump up and foam at the mouth, like the madman he seemed to be.

"Well, okay. I guess there's no harm in looking. Where's the sack?"

The old man, his hands trembling slightly and his eyes gleaming with excitement, opened the screen door and went inside. A few minutes later he returned with a burlap bag and a piece of twine.

"Tie it tight, now. Don't want him getting away at the last moment."

"Don't worry. I'm good at tying knots. It's almost suppertime, so I might not be able to do it till tomorrow. Is that soon enough?"

"Sure. But bring him here as soon as you can. I'll be waiting."

The boy took the sack, called his dog away from the back of the yard, and strolled off up the street, still swinging the stick.

The old man ran a hand over his face and said softly, chuckling to himself, "He'll get it. Just wait. He'll get it."

The old man spent most of the next day on the porch, watching clouds build up over the hot, flat land, looking up the road. He sat, stood up, and sat again.

Then, late in the afternoon, he went down the rickety steps and stood out by the road. The boy was coming, whistling, alone. Across the road, the crows startled into the stormy sky, loud, complaining.

The old man reached hastily for the sack as soon as the boy came close and looked inside.

"A white one, yes, I should have known."

"I waited a long time before the first one came out, then they came so quickly I could hardly count them. But the last was this one, as white as one of my dad's Sunday shirts."

The old man pulled out his wallet and handed the boy the five ten-dollar bills. Then he thought a moment.

"I've got an appointment in town in a few minutes, but I don't want to wait any longer. I'll give you another five dollars if you stay and help me cook it."

"You're going to eat a snake?" Amazement and a bit of disgust colored the boy's voice. "Well, so long as it's not me, I don't care. Why not?"

Overhead, the clouds piled up higher; there was a roll of thunder.

In the kitchen, a small room with yellow paint on the dirty walls, the old man took the snake out of the bag.

It was white as frost, white as foam on sea waves, white as the petals of plum blossoms, but its eyes were black, rimmed with gold. They seemed ancient, old, wise as though they'd seen worlds die, only to be born again. A red tongue flickered in and out of the small mouth as it tried to pour away from the old man's hands.

He put it in a pot on the stove, filled the pot with water, and lit the burner. Then he picked up a small metal bowl.

"Now, listen. The instructions said to seal up the pot, not to let the steam get out. I haven't got time, but here's a paste I made up. Put a lid on the pot and stick the paste around the edges. And don't you or anyone else eat a bite of that snake!"

"No way. I wouldn't do that for anything!"

The old man took a last look into the pot and whispered something to himself. Then he shuffled out of the room.

Rain spattered the windows and lightning pierced the dull afternoon light as the storm broke. Inside, the boy carefully pressed the paste into the crack between the lid and the pot.

"He's crazy. He must be. Oh, well, it can't hurt to help him a bit. I'll leave as soon as he gets back."

Before he finished, the water in the pot boiled. As the boy tried to push a bit of paste over the last bit of crack left to seal, his thumb came down across a gush of scalding steam.

"Oh, hell, that hurts."

He backed away from the stove, then stuck his burned finger in his mouth.

And the world changed.

First, all colors brightened. The yellow paint on the kitchen walls became a blend of many shades of gold, orange, silver; the shabby house almost seemed to glow. The cracked linoleum on the floor shone with a light that seemed to come from beneath it.

Then the sounds began, soft musical twitterings and chirpings, as if flocks of birds were perched just outside the door. In one direction, he could hear waves on a beach; if he turned another way, he heard wind blowing across an immense forest or a fire rustling on someone's hearth.

He stood in the center of the old man's kitchen, turning around and around, staring at the walls, the stove, the sink as if, somehow, they could help him make sense of what was happening.

He knew, he knew . . . what?

Feeling as if new eyes had been given him, the boy strained to use them, to stretch sight farther and farther, out through the walls, past the town, farther than he had ever traveled.

He thought of the sea and it was there, the waves pushing up a sandy beach, almost touching his toes, then sliding down, back into the surf.

He raised a hand slowly to touch the folded rock of a mountain, stooped to marvel at a pale, delicate flower growing out of a crevice, a crack at the edge of a cliff.

Suddenly he had wings, and he leaned forward onto the wind. Soaring over a landscape a hundred miles wide, he looked down and saw rabbits, weasels, wrens, thrushes, quail. Each one spoke its own language, but each one's mind was open to him, understood.

Finally, he pulled himself back into his own body, still standing on the worn linoleum of the old house, still watching rain drip down the windows. He shook his head and leaned against the table, trying to understand what had happened.

The door opened. Chuckling with excitement, the old man strode into the room, then stopped as if struck by knowledge himself.

"You got it. All of it." His voice was flat, final.

The boy turned and met his eyes, unable to speak, to explain.

But he saw more than an old man; he saw the man there had been at twenty, at thirty, full of hope and driven by a dream of power. He felt an intolerable loneliness, a hopeless yearning focused into one desire.

Disappointment after disappointment came into his mind; the weight of years of longing for knowledge and finding nothing bowed his shoulders. His gift became burden as well as joy.

Pity burned through him.

"I'm sorry. The steam hurt my finger. All I did was put it in my mouth. It was only the steam. I'm sorry."

The old man looked at him a few seconds, then grabbed the pot and slammed it against the wall. Hot broth and what remained of the snake spilled across the floor, almost touching the boy's shoes.

"Get out, get out!" His hoarse voice cracked at the edge of a scream. "Get out before I kill you!"

The boy just looked at him with eyes already older than the old man's own and stooped down to put the meat and bones of the snake into the burlap bag.

Then he said, "This is mine. I'll bury it under the tree. I can't give you anything but this: If you go to the next town, you'll find a job, something small to help you start over again."

"Damn you, get out. I don't want your help. Just get out."

The boy closed the door, turned toward the rainbow gently touching the fields, and started walking. Inside, the old man picked up the pot and threw it at the wall again. Then he started sobbing.

About eluki bes shahar and "Queeneyes"

This story, which took second place in the Cauldron vote for issue 11, is about heroism, which can sometimes take most unexpected forms.

eluki bes shahar lives in upstate New York with six cats and "almost enough books." She writes both science fiction/fantasy as well as Regency romances, under both her own name and the pen name Rosemary Edghill.

Queeneyes

eluki bes shahar

Everyone knew you had to be virgin for the Sight. Avarach knew it better than most; for her it wasn't just a singer's tale but a real true way out of the Choirdip barrio.

Avarach was twelve. And the Choosers were coming this year.

She would go with them. She knew it. She had to. The Sight was a part of her earliest memories, a bright-winged numen that warmed her when there was no fire and fed her on futures when food was scant.

Queeneyes, the gift was called in the barrio, though it came to boys as often as girls. But the boys must be gelded to keep it past youth, and many lost it then in spite of the surgeon's knife.

Far better to be a girl, Avarach thought, and hoarded each sample of her specialness like hot autumnal gold.

Sometimes the visions were jumbled, other times they were just plain wrong. Avarach had taught herself by slow trial and error to understand their grammarie, but true knowledge would only come when the Choosers took her,

placed their imprimatur upon her gift, and taught her the
ways of it. Now it strained, bewilderingly, at the limits of
her understanding, demanding as some new-caught wild
thing, avid and importunate.

Meanwhile she had to survive. In the Choirdip barrio
survival meant work, no matter what your age.

Avarach found work—and learning of a sort—in a tum-
bledown shop at the edge of Choirdip's barrio where she
cleaned and fetched and counted and was paid in food and
castoffs too poor to sell. Avarach had come to this service
through a small dispute as to the ownership of a loaf of
bread. Her hand still bore the scar of the knife, but instead
of slow murder or slavery at the hands of the thieftakers,
Avarach had been taken in and taught. Quick enough for
a Harkady scribe, her mistress said—and laughed, though
Avarach never knew why.

Her mistress's name was Cheyne, and Cheyne wore two
pieces of green turquoise in her left ear and a dangly gold
moon in her right. Her little shop was filled with books,
and perhaps she was right in what she said about Avarach,
but only the Chapterhouse in Harkady possessed the arca-
num of reading and writing, and Avarach had no wish to
give up mother and family and home for the dubious bene-
fits of literacy. So she laughed with Mistress Cheyne and
took her pay.

This day Avarach stood counting—matching pairs of
dice in one of the windowless rooms that made up Mistress
Cheyne's establishment. Each set must match in size and
weight and color, and young eyes were sharpest. Outside
the sky was the phoenix-blue of early spring, but Avarach's
mind and stomach and perhaps her heart were fixed on the
two loaves of brown bread Mistress Cheyne had promised
her when the day was over. Nimbly she sorted the dice:
the shaved with the shaved, the weighted with the weighted,
and the true and honest matched by size. In a fortnight the
Choosers would come and then all of this would be over:
only a dream, a bitter prelude to her real life.

"When you're done there, sweep the front room all the

way to the street," said Mistress Cheyne, grading loose gemstones in the strong light of candles and mirrors. Nearly as good as direct sun, and a deal safer to use in the Choirdip barrio.

"Soon I won't be coming back here."

The news was too good to keep, and something almost-Sighted in her heart urged Avarach to tell. Mistress Cheyne raised her eyes from her work, regarding Avarach with a bland disbelief that made words come hot and easy.

"The Choosers are coming in two weeks. There'll be a fair, and the magistrate swears holiday. Anyone who wants can go to the Crownpriests—it's a fine if they stop you— they test for the Sight—they'll choose me—"

"Have you Seen it?" Mistress Cheyne asked. Avarach stopped. In all her gaudy scraps of vision it was the one thing she had never seen: the moment when she became a legend.

"I know they'll choose me. And then we'll all go away, Mama and Granddam and baby Egland and even the twins, and—"

The still look on Cheyne's face stopped her. That look meant danger, and Avarach froze in response. They stared at each other for a long moment, and then Cheyne spoke.

"The Choosers will take only you."

Only her? But that couldn't be. She was young yet, a child, surely they would know that and see, and take her mother with them—mother and grandmother and of course they could not leave the children behind. . . .

"The College will be your mother and father," Cheyne said as if she too had the Sight, could look and see each frantic turning, each evasion of Avarach's willingness to know. "The Crownpriests test any who come to them claiming the Sight, for only so can the Starharp be reclaimed by the world. Those who have it they will take. That is the law. But queen's eyes have their price. From that moment all ties of blood and family are—"

"No!" Avarach started up and away, thudding into a

table as she retreated. It rocked to the floor with a breaking
sound and spilled a tray of spices.

Cheyne didn't move.

"—severed," she finished inexorably.

Avarach ran.

Liar, liar, liar, the words she wanted to say rose stran-
glingly in Avarach's throat. She ran through the twisting
alleyways, trying to outrun her humiliation. Stupid, she'd
been so stupid, prattling on about how special she was,
and now Cheyne would laugh, and tell. . . .

But Cheyne would neither laugh nor tell, and Cheyne
knew everything, and always told the truth. Avarach slowed
down, pulled to a walk by the burning stitch in her side
and the bleak pain in her chest.

The Crownpriests would not care for her mother, her
brothers, or her family. And the gift she had counted on
to save all of them could only save her.

She tried to summon her gift, to grab its bright wings
and force it to show her happy futures. But her Sight was
erratic, untrained. Surety in the Sight was the gift the
Crownpriests gave, the heritage Avarach had always been
certain would be hers. Above the canted rooftops she could
see the gleaming gold of the palace towers, beautiful and
far in a clean bright world that only the brightness in
Avarach would let her reach. She yearned for that greatness,
the world of certainty and honor a universe away from her
own. The world she could reach.

She could still have it. They would still take her. They
would.

But only her.

Her footsteps took Avarach in the direction of the Bazaar.
She passed the fine house, near the Trade Gate and the
caravans, where Mother Dace's wares lounged and lingered
and fanned themselves in the sun. Pomegranate lips and
beetle-wing eyelids, glittering with glass and false gold

and scented ripe as a festival garden. Their skin had the sheen of bathing and oiling, the ripeness of plentiful food and often. Dace took care of her wares and took care to keep them fresh—just last year when Avarach had begun to bleed, Dace had come and offered Avarach's mother a whole gold coin for a year of Avarach's time. A year could lead to another year, to more, to a villa in the cool hills north of Choirdip and a protector who would weight her wrists and ankles with gauds that were not glass and gilded tin.

But there were other ways. The ways of heroes to bend and stretch the world to their design. Of warrior-priestesses, cloaked in white and sheathed in glittering mail, riding at the right hand of judges and priests, dispensing truth and justice and law in the bright sun.

Virgin for the Sight.

It was late when Avarach reached home—lateness caused in part by remembering she had not taken—or earned—the bread that Cheyne had promised her. The early spring day had turned to bone-cold winter when the sun set, and the little lane was blue with dusk. Oil that could be eaten was too precious to burn.

Avarach came to her front door and lifted the latch. The room beyond was as blue and cold as the street behind. No fire in the grate. Not even a stoup of hot water to warm her.

The baby lay swaddled near the ashes of the fire. The twins were nowhere to be seen.

"Mother?" said Avarach.

Her grandmother entered at the sound, letting the drape that concealed the doorway to the interior room fall behind her. Ignoring Avarach, she shuffled past her to the door and barred it for night.

"Granddam?"

Avarach's grandmother looked at her. Her eyes were hard and bright, her hair—if any—concealed beneath a threadbare scarf.

"Your mother's sick."

Avarach shrugged, one-shouldered. Her mother had been sick as long as she could remember—since the twins were born, and they were nearly eight. Five children born only to die had not helped. The baby—not yet a year old—was the last fruit of her parents' marriage, and Avarach's father had not lived to see him.

"Very sick this time," Granddam said. "She's going to die."

Now Avarach registered the too-stillness of the house. The twins must be with a neighbor. She listened hard, and imagination painted her mother's labored breathing. Winterkill, the barrio called it. An affliction of the weak, the cold, and the hungry.

"We have to get her a doctor, Granddam."

Her grandmother laughed and spat into the cold hearth.

"And do you think a doctor is going to come here, my fine lady? Doctors want coin." Slowly she began laying a new fire in the grate. Sticks and scavengings. Hoarded chips of coal.

The baby began to cry. He was hungry—Avarach's mother was still suckling him.

"There's some—there is!"

"And did I spend it on her and not the taxman, my Marram wouldn't forgive me—not and see the lot of you taken to pay the rate."

Avarach picked up her small brother, wet and cold and furious with neglect.

"What there was to spare went to the apothecary. There's nothing more."

The old woman took a carefully curled spill and lit it from the firepot on the mantel. The yellow light cast the room into sharp relief: the walls, whitewashed and painted with flowers before Avarach was born, now grey except for the pale silhouettes of furniture sold; grey with the dirt there was not strength or resource to remove.

Poverty.

There had never been money, even while her soldier-father had been alive. Avarach had grown up doing without, living for the day she would ride out on a fine horse wearing silk and vair and armor of silver and gold. Crownpriestess. Hero.

But while she had dreamed, the elegancies of cleanliness, warmth, and comfort had been surrendered, battles lost, until all that was left was the naked struggle to live.

And they were going to lose it.

Avarach lay on her hard bed, twelve years old and filled with glory. A few feet away her mother tossed and coughed and muttered. The poppy-head tea that Granddam had bought helped only a little, and had to be saved for the worst.

The Sight stretched Avarach like an old wineskin, creaking and dangerous and filled with prophecy, but this time it turned her vision outward, not in.

Without Marram there would be no family. The baby would die, the twins would disappear into one of the roving bands of child-thieves that plagued Choirdip—if they were lucky. And Granddam . . . Who would care for a quarrelsome old woman, or offer her a seat by their fire?

But Avarach would be safe. Feted by the Crownpriests, cherished for her Sight, fed on wine and white bread, and dressed in clean new wool.

Climbing to heroism over the bodies of her family.

But there's nothing I can do! Avarach pleaded with the darkness. It's the future—I can't change it! There's nothing I can do—nothing!

Just out of reach, the power and the promise. She would be chosen by the Crownpriests and rise high in the councils of the Crown of Alarra. Her voice would shape the law. Pensions would be paid and almshouses founded. The widows of heroes would not starve in the street.

Someday.

In the morning Marram was worse. Avarach spent a fruitless hour trying to feed the baby warm gruel from a wooden spoon. She wasted more than he ate and wept for the loss.

Granddam went to beg and borrow from the neighbors. The twins came home and left again as quickly, frightened in the presence of disaster, going to the marketplace to scavenge and steal and hasten the day when ill luck caught them and fastened iron collars about their necks until their bond was paid.

And what Avarach must do waited, standing so heavy and dark in the road to her future that if she looked up she must surely see it.

Granddam came home with a basket over which the cloth lay flaccid. Egland had cried himself to sleep again. He lay by the fire in a basket too poor to sell.

Avarach met her grandmother's eyes.

"It's good you're back. I'm going out." Avarach pushed the door wide and stepped into the street.

She knew where she was going but pretended she did not. She went instead to Mistress Cheyne's house, hoping for some upstart miracle that would let her bargain with the future.

But the shutters and door were barred, even at this late hour, and no one came for all Avarach's knocking. At last she gave up and went where she must.

The fine house near the Trade Gate had a servant's entrance. Avarach knew enough to go there instead of to the front door with its ornaments of gryphons and phoenixes.

"Go away, beggar brat!" said the cook who opened it.

"I want to see Mother Dace!" said Avarach desperately. "She wants to see me. She said so."

The room where Avarach was brought to wait was grand beyond imagining. There were carpets on the colored tile floors and painted walls of wood and stone. A silver bowl so big that the profits from its sale would feed everyone who lived on her street for a year sat on a table with a top that was a picture made of colored glass.

Avarach's new future reached for her, black and suffocating. An end to all magic. She fought an urge to run, and the knowledge of failure.

I do this myself! Avarach said in fierce silence. By myself and for myself, and for no one's will but mine!

Mother Dace would pay. A gold coin for a year of her time—enough to buy life and honesty for her mother and grandmother and brothers. There might be more—at least silver. Her family needed it to live. There was no one but her to earn it.

Avarach had always wanted to save the world. Now she knew where she had to start.

A week later a girl called Queeneyes stood in that room and waited for Mother Dace to come. She had left her home and given up her name to come here. Mother Dace had chosen the new one, not knowing how it hurt.

Avarach would never tell her. In a handful of days she had learned to answer to it, had learned the taste of fat capon and the feel of scented oils on her skin. The Sight that still burned within her cast shattered sparks of might-be futures across her vision; all doomed now.

She could still run. There was still time. The man was not here yet. She was not watched. But if she broke her word Dace would want her gold back, and the gold had been spent already, on bread and oil and brandy and medicine from the doctor—strong poppy sirup that let her mother sleep and heal.

The only repayment there could be was in kind—if not Avarach, then her brothers; gelded and sold (if they survived it), they would earn back the money Dace had spent on Avarach's virginity.

Queeneyes smoothed sweaty palms down her thin white linen robe and thought she understood how it would be. But she was wrong.

He was perfumed and elegant and knew what he was about; an elemental contract, loveless as a pawnshop. But he was not angry with her, and gave her instructions it was impossible to mistake. And in the ludicrous heave and clutch of embrangled bodies, she felt the Sight forsake her in an uprush of flight—all bright possibility battered to earth and remade in clay; the might-have-beens savaged from her waking mind, leaving behind them only the knowledge of what she had lost.

And what she had gained.

The Choosers came to the city of Choirdip on a bright spring day when the sun shone white and rain had washed the air to gleaming purity. They came in pomp and panoply, a feast for all the senses, and established themselves in the Market Square where any child who dared might come to them, to gaze into their bowl of cloudy crystal and be Chosen.

Many came, to dare and risk and hope, but the child Avarach was not among them. The hero Queeneyes was in a back room at Mother Dace's, saving the world.

About Jo Clayton and "Arakney's Web"

Jo Clayton lives among the gentle hills of Portland, doing her writing as she listens to Oregon's rain pattering on the geraniums and the blue rose in red clay pots on her balcony, while her cats chase each other over, around, and through a dozen bookcases. Perhaps they're chasing Arakney, Jo's wandering sorceress. . . .

Arakney's Web

Jo Clayton

"**W**hoa, Dapple, easy now."

The van slowed to a stop in the shadow of a cluster of trees with slender white trunks and sticky, saw-edged leaves, bright green and newly unfolded from the bud. The horse sagged into his harness, shaking his big head, foam spattering the clumps of grass growing around his knees.

Arakney Ko'eem dropped the reins over the curving mudshield, shifted on the lumpy cushion. "I think we've lost them." She started to comb her fingers through the tangled mass of coarse grey hair that fell about her shoulders, but the windknots blocked her. "F'lich!" She turned her head, addressed the canvas curtains that shut off the front of the van. "Piri, find my brush, will you? That's the last time I try a new do in a place I don't know. Hairpins are expensive and I've lost every c'fillacher one."

The Osuni pushed his head through the curtains. " 'Kney, you shock me." He grinned at her. "My ears, my poor little ears." He wiggled them and had a lot to wiggle; they were large for his size, with no lobes and pointed tips. "What'd you expect, that last story you told? Lady Fox and the Pig, t' t'. Headman saw he better have a care for his cracklin' before his wives got the idea."

"Pah! He annoyed me." She took the brush from him and attacked the knots.

Piri crawled through and sat beside her. He looked a lot like the peachpit monkeys fathers carve for their children— a peachpit monkey with a strip of tightly curled maroon fleece that went from ear to ear.

He scratched at the inside of his elbow as he watched her divide her hair and begin braiding it. "Marewole Moor. Hunh. Headman's youngest, Michi, what a pest, eh? He and his pack of wigglets, they cornered me night b'fore last and pitched tales at me about the moor. Yankin' my leg, some of it, but some of it, they scared themselves, see it in the gooseflesh, hear it in the whispers."

"So?" Her fingers wove briskly through the thick grey hair. "Can you reach back, get me something to tie this off?"

"Here. I come prepared." He held out his hand, two thin leather thongs dangling over the fingers. "What I think, the Yasroub didn't so much lose us, they turned round and went home, telling each other they'd let the moor take care of us."

Arakney took the thongs, secured her braids, and flipped them over her shoulders. "You pick up anything about people living in here? I don't like the look of that storm."

Clouds were piling up in the west and sweeping toward them; the wind was heavy with rain and the strong acrid smell of the heather.

"Witches and werefolk according to the wigglets."

"Whatever they are, they need a roof like anyone else on a rainy day. Get your flute, Piri, see what you can call to us." She stood. "While you're doing that, I'll tend poor Dap, he's had a hard run and earned his grain."

Piri sat cross-legged on the roof of the van, eyes closed, breath coming slow and steady as he prepared himself, then he lifted the heavy silver flute to his lips and began

to play, an eerie, scarcely audible melody that flowed out
to fill the skybowl and tickle the ears of everything under
that bowl.

The girl came trotting around the trees, fought her body
to a stop when she saw Arakney standing with her hand
on Dapple's neck. Her eyes were the same color as her
short rough hair, the brownish red of a fox's coat; her skin
was olive, her body supple with youth and something else.

Dapple snorted and shifted uneasily, his head jerking up
and down. Arakney soothed him with one hand while she
watched the girl. "We mean no harm to you," she said.
"We're lost and need shelter from that." She nodded at
the clouds boiling toward them. "Tell us where we can
find it, then we'll let you go."

Curiosity sparked in the foxy eyes, but the girl shook
her head. "This is Marewole Moor, you'll find no shelter
here."

"Now, m'dear, it's not nice to lie to your elders."

"I don't lie." Her eyes darting about, her bare feet
shifting on the hard earth, the girl was testing out the flute's
spell, hunting weak spots and pushing against them.

"By implication, you do. And most cleverly, too. Use
that cleverness, child, think on what brought you here. Piri
has other tunes he can play."

The girl sniffed, wiggled her nose; she'd managed to gain
some play in the mesh that held her and was unobtrusively
working herself into the shadow under the trees. "If that's
what your word's worth, why should I lead you anywhere?"

Arakney scratched Dapple gently between the eyes; he
snorted and nuzzled at her. "I'm a story spinner," she said
impatiently, "not a brigand. Look at me, what could I do
to harm anyone?"

The girl went still, red-brown eyes opening wide. "Cha-
la, you a Spinner, where's your Gourd?" She folded her
arms across her narrow chest. "And would you know *The
Witch of Hesley Dell*? I've never heard the whole of it and
I'd like to."

Arakney laughed. "I've heard a dozen versions, you'll have to sing me yours sometime." She stepped away from Dapple, took her Gourd from its pouch, and chanted as she shook it, the soft shsss-shsss almost lost in the bluster of the wind. "Red was her hair and green her eyes and her soul was black as a grandmama's pot. She loved with a love as true as fire, as strong and as steady as a summer wind." She dropped the Gourd back into its pouch. "And that's all you get without a taste from the pot or the clink of silver."

The girl stopped fighting the spellbond, fears eased by the Gourd's soft shsss and the Spinner's Chantvoice. "How'd you get all the way to here? And why?"

"A slight miscalculation on my part."

"Wrong story?" A nimble brow arching high, a tilt of her head—she was fire and flash now that her wariness had dropped away.

Arakney blinked. "Something like that."

The girl scratched behind an ear. "Him up there, he can rest his lip."

A chatter of her bare feet on the grass, then she darted to the van, flowing up onto the seat with the sure fluidity of youth at its peak, her words streaming back over her shoulder as she moved. "Take too long to try telling you, I'll ride with you, show you the way. Cha-la, shift it, Spinner, the dark's coming fast." Before the last word was out, she was sitting on the worn cushions frowning impatiently at Arakney.

Dapple ambled through heather shadows and the slanting sun rays that escaped the thickening clouds, the van rattling behind him, lurching across the uneven earth as he followed the elk trace their guide pointed out.

Arakney clucked encouragement to Dapple, then turned to the girl. "Arakney Ko'eem. You?"

"Yohn. The chook where I live is called Raevlis." She spoke in quick broken phrases, fitting them between the jolts. "It's where I'm taking you. Turn now, this way."

She pointed, then shifted the direction of her finger. "You see that nice flat green spot up there? Pretty, isn't it? Drive on that and you won't stop sinking till you bounce off Fadda Ameeser's head. Go straight till the siltong grove, there, that dark green lump, you can just see it in the light that's left. You'll go north from there till you reach a tor, it's a short fat one, doesn't show from here, that's where Raevlis is, tucked into a bend of the Tal-pikang."

"A river? Ah, that's good, it'll give us a way to go when it's time to go. You're young to be out alone."

Yohn flounced indignantly on the lumpy cushion. "I made marriageable my last birthday."

"So?"

She giggled, an infectious gurgling sound that tickled Arakney's ears. "Visitations. The Holy Places."

"Oh?"

"Don't girls do that where you come from? Where are you from anyway, Arakney Ko'eem? If it's not rude to ask."

"Not rude, but it's a question that's a bit difficult to answer. Tell me about this Visitation thing. This is a new piece of the world to me, I'll need new stories to fit it."

Yohn grinned. "Make one of me, eh? Cha-la, I run the heather, dance in the moonlight, sleep a while and travel on, tokens in my pouch, one two three. See this?" She brought out a small glass vial with a wax stopper; it waved with the lurching of the van and glittered in the distant lightning.

"Ah."

"It's for water from Kinayom's Well." She tucked the vial away again, missing the pouch the first time as a wheel dropped into a hole and wobbled out again. "That's the spring atop Gratcher Tor where Kinayom flew the first time. They say when you sleep there, if you get the charm right, you'll dream your lover's face. Or at least a sign that'll show you who he is when he comes."

Arakney nodded. "Adrina's Dream is a tale like that. Have you heard that one?"

"Nay. You'll sing it for us, huh?"

"We'll see, we'll see."

Yohn squeezed her mobile face into a comic grimace, then sat with her hands dangling between her knees, her body swaying with the shift of the seat. "The second place is the Granddaddy Ayyanga on Poryo Tor, you ever seen an ayyanga tree?"

"Nay. Not by that name, at least."

"Cha-la, you'd know it if you had. It's bigger than some chooks, with trunks all round like sentinels, each year a new ring of them. There's this bug that lives in its top branches and galls grow round it that have the most wonderful smell. You're supposed to cut one of them loose and wrap it tight so the scent stays in. That's for putting in with clothes and keeping your homefast strong."

The wind was getting louder and stronger; Arakney raised her voice so she could be heard above it. "That one I must admit is new. There's a story for each of these places?"

"Yah sure."

"I'd like to hear them before I move on, unless it's something you don't tell outsiders."

"Oh, nay. The last's the Bower. On Journister Tor. Sarang the Bearman planted alda vines there and tended them seven years to 'tice his love to him and teach her the heart of life. You chew one of the leaves and sit in vigil and sometime during the night, a thing comes to you and it's your secret thing. You don't ever tell that, not even to your dearest love. But Sarang's story's no secret, everyone knows it."

"I see."

"When a girl can show water, gall, and leaf, then the old ones know she's fit for wiving. 'S what I meant to do, but I can start again another day. . . ." She grinned. "When I can sleep dry not soggy nor snuffling."

Half an hour later darkness plunged down on them as if the blustery storm winds had blown out the sun. Yohn

ran ahead of Dapple, foxfire glimmering about her head
and shoulders as she led them through the dangers of the
night.

Piri clung to the back of the driver's seat and watched
the girl's long easy stride as she loped into the whirling
darkness. "Were," he yelled in Arakney's ear. "You sure
you want to do this?"

"If that youngster's a sample," she yelled back, wind
whipping the words from her mouth almost before they
formed, "her folk like stories. I can work with that."

Two small dark forms came swooping from the darkness;
they slowed, blurred into small boys who trotted beside
Yohn, talking to her in low rapid voices.

A moment later she ran back to the van, swung up, and
plopped onto the cushion beside Arakney. "You better
stop," she said.

"Trouble? Whoa, Dapple, whoa boy."

"Oggeri in the chook." A jag of lightning showed Yohn
with her fingers laced together, squeezed them until the
bones showed white; her ears were laid back and her hair
stood out in a stiff halo. "Swal said it was a whole swarm
of 'em. Him and Hersty they're cousins of mine so when
they saw me, they came out the heather to give me word."
Her eyes darted about, whites gleaming. "I don't know
what to do. . . ."

Arakney took Yohn's straining hands, eased them apart,
held them between her own. "Quiet now, you're a clever
one, so use it." She smiled as more lightning showed the
rigidity melting from the girl. "First, who or what are
Oggeri?"

Yohn blinked. "They mostly live in the desert on t'other
side the moor, but every now and then a bunch take a
notion and swarm the moor, eating their way 'cross."

"Eating?" She moved her head close to Yohn's so she
could hear and see a little of the girl's face.

"Uh-huh." Yohn's face was pinched, her eyes ringed
with white. "Swal says they sneaked up when it started

getting dark and . . ." She broke off, eyes squinting; mouth twisted as she fought back tears.

"Swarm. How many would that be?"

Yohn took a deep breath, pulled her hands loose. "Swal says more of them than us, he din't stay to count."

"So?"

"I dunno. Maybe five hands of them."

"How did they manage to sneak up on a were-settlement?"

"I don't understand. . . ."

"Don't be silly, child. You needn't try to deny the obvious." She brushed at wisps of hair that escaped the braids and blew about her face, irritating her. "If I'm going to help you . . ."

Yohn's tongue flicked across her lips. "Are you?"

"Yes."

"Why?"

"Because I can." *Because, silly child, I'd rather have friends at my back than foes or indifference.* "So, how did they manage to surprise your folk?"

Yohn turned her head. "Swal, come here a minute. 'S all right. Come on."

The clot of darkness that was Swal muttered to his cousin, then came sidling closer, hugging the clumps of heather until he was beside the van, looking up at Yohn. The flickering lightning showed Arakney a dark boy with huge brown eyes and rough brown hair clipped close to his head, curly brown fur on the backs of his hands. "What?"

"Wasn't it Chrang's watch? How'd they get past without him blowing the horn?"

Swal shrugged. "Dunno, 'twas no different than always getting on for supper, you know, then there was Oggeri everywhere, two three of 'em for each chup, they jump up so fast seems like no one could turn, you know, 'cept Komchin, he shook 'em off an' went bear an' bust the Suryo loose long enough to reach horn, like I said, and then tads and we was running off so fast I din't see what else happened." He started as the other boy sidled up and brushed against him. "Hersty?"

Hersty was wee and sleek as a silver cat with eyes that glittered like polished pewter in the unsteady flashes. He pointed at Arakney. "Who she?"

Arakney leaned around Yohn. "I spin a tale or two and sing a song if folk sit still to listen. What do they look like, these Oggeri?"

"Din't see them up close," Swal said.

Hersty shook his head, his long white hair flying out above his limber, pointed ears.

"Flappy things," Swal said. "Taller'n Komchin by more'n a head."

"And they stink. Oooo phah!" Hersty pinched his nose.

"It was like they was lying on the ground and come flying up in your face," Swal said. "You know, like leaves."

"An' their hands're bones," Hersty said. "An' they rattle when they walk."

Arakney felt Piri's hand tighten on her shoulder; she didn't look at him. Ancient enemies, from another place, another time. *I thought we'd seen the last of them.* Her stomach knotted as she remembered her arrogant words. *Because I can. Cha-la, as the child said, that's true enough. Because I will, that's truer yet. None of their business, though. Let's get on with it.* "Yohn, that tor you were talking about, can you climb up the back side of it, I mean without being seen from your chook?"

"Cha-la, a baby could do it." Yohn twisted round. "Swal, you and Hersty go in front and lead us, huh?" As the boys went trotting away, she leaned back, sighed. "Tads like them run the heather a lot, practicing their turns, you know. They'll remember it better than me."

"Whoa, Dap, whoa boy." Arakney wiped the spatter of raindrops from her face and scowled up at the huge rustling blotch atop the tor. "Can we get through that?"

Yohn's full lips twitched into a brief smile but there was none in her eyes. "It's only a baby ayyanga. It'll be easy enough to get to the other side, nothing grows under an ayyanga."

"Only a baby, hm?" Arakney shook her head. She swung down from the seat and began unclipping the harness from the van. While she worked, she talked. "Yohn, tell your cousins to take Dapple into the heather and stay with him till this is over. There's a possibility that things will go wrong for us and I don't want him hurt. I'm fond of him. He's a good horse, old Dap." She patted his flank as she moved along him, stripping the harness off him. More raindrops slanted into her, intermittent and separate still, the outriders on the storm.

Arakney eased through the last rank of secondary trunks, the newest ones, limber and pale with a tender bark that bled at a touch. Overhead the ayyanga's long, blade-shaped leaves rattled in the wind, and bits of papery bark broke loose. She settled cross-legged on the lip of a cliff that fell straight down to the chook that was a scattering of long, narrow stone houses intermittently visible in the shifting light from the roughly circular common outlined by the bonfires that burned around a pit where something was being roasted over a bed of coals. She heard a hissing intake of breath behind her as Yohn saw that. "Quiet," she murmured. She'd thought about telling the girl to stay behind with her cousins, but didn't waste her breath trying it. "Sit down and be patient. If we rush at this, we'll just get everyone killed."

Flat black forms hurried in and out of the firelight, tearing thatch from roofs and building a shelter over the pit. The wind teased at the fires, whipping bits of burning wood at the houses. The stone wouldn't burn, but here and there thatching started to smoke; the Oggeri ignored it and continued with preparations for the feast.

Arakney took the Gourd from its pouch, held it in her lap.

Piri was close beside her, sitting in the next gap between the secondary trunks, his night sight turning his eyes to yellow fire. "Do you see any of the Were?"

"Nay, 'Kney, but there's . . . mmm . . . I can see about five of the Oggeri hanging about the biggest house. Guards, you think?"

"Could be. Yohn?"

"That's the Suryo's Chup." The girl's voice was wire taut. "It's meant to be a safe place, so I s'pose it's easiest to guard."

Arakney ran her thumb over the waxy, pimpled surface of the Gourd. "Yohn," she said. "Listen, this is important. Don't distract us. You hear? You must be quiet and sit still."

"Yes. I understand."

"If you can't do that, best you go join your cousins."

"I said I understand." Quiet as drifting thistledown the girl moved round behind Piri and settled herself beside him, cross-legged, hands on thighs.

Arakney looked at Piri, nodded, lifted the Gourd, and began shaking it gently, shsssh shsssh sh shsssh. When she sang, it was in the Old Tongue, words that belonged to days before Yohn's first ancestor saw light, and her voice was a whisper sliding on the wind.

Patches of thready mist formed on the black water of the slow-flowing river, formed and drifted toward the fires. Piri's long breaths were heavy in her ears, then the sound from the flute lifted her chant.

The fog merged with the rain, pulling the silver lines of falling water into itself, weaving a web as delicate as smoke and stronger than steel, anchored by the flutesong's cable.

It passed through the scattered houses, catching Oggeri as it tightened, driving them closer and closer together until they were a clump of black leaves fluttering in the chup's common mead, rustling about the fire. . . .

She sang a double note into the chant and the fire exploded.

The Oggeri burned.

Three days later when Arakney clucked to Dapple and started him from Raevlis on the River, Swal and Hersty led a pack of youngers dancing around her, giving her a send-off with the charm she'd crafted for them to help them fight off the next wave of Oggeri that were bound to come this way. She looked around, but didn't see Yohn among them. *Gone back to her own affairs, no doubt.* She sighed, a little hurt; she'd grown fond of the girl. ''That's the way the world whimpers,'' she murmured to herself and listened to the children singing their charm.

''Shillilly shallilly,'' they chanted.

> Shillilly shallilly
> sing we of Oggeri
> Kaniem o kickanem
> how do we break them
> hammer their toes
> pull on their nose
> chew on their fingerbones
> laugh at their moans
> shillilly shallilly
> sing we of Oggeri
> Sik tay surral tay tay u curral
> Hajina waven sassina paven
> Efta ta KOKE! Mista ka YOKE!
> Shillilly Shallilly
> Sing we of Oggeri
> Poor little beasties gone up in smoke.

The sound of the children's voices followed them until they rounded a low tor smothered in ayyanga trunks.

A red fox came scrambling down the slope to trot beside Dapple, yellow eyes laughing as she looked over her shoulder—as if to say, *You thought I'd forgot, didn't you.*

''Yohn! Get up here.''

The fox looked back again, flicked her ears, and after that ignored all noise from the van.

Piri chuckled. "Looks like we've got us a new companion." He took out his flute and played a travel song as the van creaked deeper into the moor.

About Rebecca Lyons and "The Erin Cory"

Rebecca received her degree in chemistry, with supporting work in physics and biology, from Roosevelt University in Chicago, although they probably did not expect that her main use for her scientific training would be as background for her science fiction. She currently lives ''on a postcard in Colorado'' with two feline roommates.

There are many variations (Cerridwn's Cauldron, the Holy Grail, etc.) on the story of a vessel that never runs out of food or drink, but Rebecca has given this old tale a new setting with an interesting twist, as well as making a good point regarding the proper uses of magic.

The Erin Cory

Rebecca Lyons

Outside her fourth-floor door, Maddy juggled her grocery bag to her other arm and fumbled for her keys. The elevator door whooshed open and with a shriek of excitement Vanessa, dreadlocks flying, burst out. Maddy jumped and dropped the keys.

"Vanessa! If you don't sound like a banshee. Look, you made me drop my keys."

"We having pot supper tonight, Mama?" The girl's dark, smiling face looked not a bit remorseful.

"No. Sale chicken tonight. Don't want to push our welcome with the pot."

"No more beans and barley?"

"Not till we finish the chicken. Your brother will be happy. Now are you going to take this bag or pick up the keys you made me drop?"

Vanessa stooped down to pick them up. "Oh, Mom. Look. Our door's coming apart."

Wooden splinters stuck out of the door frame and the door was just slightly ajar. "What the—" Maddy set the groceries on the floor as Vanessa turned a worried, frightened look to her. "Vanessa, I want you to go to your grandmother's house for a while. I'll call you there."

"But, Mom—" Rustling noises from inside the apartment made them turn.

"Don't argue with me! Go!" Vanessa turned and quietly made for the stairs. Heart pumping, Maddy eased the door open. She saw no one inside, but—

"Oh, my God." She had meant to stay silent, but the quiet exclamation came out unbidden. She opened the door farther.

The apartment was a mess—drawers upended over the floor, books and newspapers askew, one bookcase overturned. More rustling noises came from her son's bedroom. She gasped and started, as if to run, but the figure that came into view was her son Michael, his portable radio hugged close.

"They didn't take it, Ma."

"Michael! Honey, how long you been here?"

He shrugged. "Five minutes, maybe."

"Come over here by me." He obediently trotted over to her.

She took his hand and guided him into the hall. "Stay here. Was anyone here when you got here?"

"No."

"Did you hear anything?"

"No. Nobody else is here. I looked through the whole house." He still cradled the radio close.

Her face crumpled in dismay. "You did what? Oh, Michael, you should never— Oh, I'll talk to you later. You stay here. Hear me? Stay here."

He nodded, and she cautiously reentered the apartment. Her feet trod on crumpled paper. She reached down and picked up some hard copy from her latest project. Her eyes immediately snapped to her desk.

The computer was still there, and the printer beside it, though her chair was overturned. She walked into the room, paper still in hand. The TV was still there, and Michael's radio, obviously. As she absently put her hand on the desk, the clink of metal distracted her. She looked down to see a pile of coins, silver ones. A couple fell to the floor as she watched.

The coin she picked up was silver and about the size of a half dollar, but it wasn't Kennedy staring out at her, and she couldn't read the words. For some reason they reminded her of—

"Finn."

"Finn? Finn O'Neil?" It had been a couple days earlier; she had opened the door a crack at his knock.

"Maddy Prudence Jackson?"

"You've got the right place. Come in." She closed the door to take off the chain, then opened it again. "So, you're the folklorist, Professor Eason's friend. Please, come in. Excuse the place. It's kind of a mess. Sit down."

"Thank you." He nodded politely, almost a bow, and took a seat. The front room was both living and dining room, with a small table where Vanessa sat and squirmed and a desk where Maddy's computer sat.

"Vanessa, don't you play with those pencils." Maddy's daughter stopped with a giggle. Maddy sneaked looks at the stranger as she finished drying her hands on a dish towel—pale skin set off by black hair and ice-blue eyes. Not bad-looking for a white man. "Finn O'Neil, you said?" she confirmed as the man took out pencil and paper.

"Fin? Like in a fish?" Vanessa asked with another giggle.

"Girl, you shush. Shouldn't you be getting out some dishes for us to eat on? Supper will be ready soon."

"Oh, Mama."

"You go on now." She turned to Finn. "I'm cooking supper in that same old pot you were asking about. You're welcome to stay to supper if you like."

His angular face brightened measurably. "Yes. Thank you."

"Now what do you want to know about that old cooking pot of mine?" She sat down on the couch opposite him.

"Old. Yes. You had said it was very old."

"Been in my family for, oh, four generations at least. It goes to Vanessa next, then to her daughter."

Vanessa smiled and glanced shyly at Finn as she set four places around the table.

Finn was writing all this down. "Yes. Can you tell me where the pot was found?"

"Found? I don't know. My mother gave it to me. Her mother—I was the oldest daughter—her mother gave it to her. She was the oldest daughter, too. Her mother, my great-grandmother, was a slave on a plantation in South Carolina." Finn nodded. "I don't know where she got it. My grandma used to call it the Erin Cory, but I don't know why."

"Iarinn Coire." Finn had paused in his writing, his eyes alight. "Iron cauldron." She arched an eyebrow at him. "Gaelge. Irish."

"I didn't know that. Irish, hm? You didn't look like you knew Swahili." She'd certainly never heard an accent like his in her North Chicago neighborhood.

He didn't get the joke. "And this iron cooking pot, it is strange and wondrous?" He stared down at his notes.

Maddy gave him a sideways glance, then nodded cautiously. "I wouldn't say that. But it's about the only heirloom I have, and it's been a big help in ways I can't begin to explain." Her eyes drifted over to where her daughter was laying out forks and napkins. "My work pays well enough, but trying to raise two kids, both in private school—it ain't easy. It—" She grimaced as rock music suddenly blared from another room. "Michael! You turn that thing down! Right now! You hear me?"

"But, Mom! It's U2!" A young kid appeared in the doorway hugging a radio.

"I don't care if it's me and you both. That thing goes down or it goes off."

"Awww."

"Use those headphones! That's what your uncle bought them for."

More protests followed, but the music diminished. Maddy turned back to Finn. "Sorry. I tell him over and over, but . . . you were asking?"

"This pot. You say it has wondrous powers, and feeds you from nothing."

Maddy gave him another narrow glance. "Now when did I say that?" she asked quietly after several seconds of silence.

"I . . . uh, I've been studying."

"Studying? My pot's in books?"

"Perhaps. If it's the same one. It does feed you?"

"Beans and barley, beans and barley." Vanessa started a singsong chant.

"Vanessa, hush, girl. You mean other people know about this? I've rarely told anyone about this except family that's grown up with it. I figured no one would believe me."

With great sincerity, Finn said, "I believe you."

Maddy stared at him openmouthed for a moment. "Well, I'll be—I'll be—" She broke off and laughed. "Well, if you'd told me this and I hadn't grown up with it, I'd think you were crazy. It's a relief to find someone who doesn't think I am."

"It does feed you, then?"

"Yes. It's been a godsend, let me tell you."

"What does it feed you? How much?" Finn leaned forward.

"Beans and barley—"

"Vanessa, hush! Well, it feeds us about as much as we need." Maddy leaned back. "We don't always use it, but we've never gone hungry. It's always there when we need it. All you do is put the pot on the stove—"

"With water? How long does it take?"

"No, you don't even need water. You can smell it when it's cooked, then you can take the top off, and it's done. It's potluck." She chuckled. "Literally. Sometimes you get soup or stew, sometimes bread. Once I took the top off and there were two little game hens surrounded by carrots and onions. Good, too."

"Beans and barley, Mom," Vanessa interrupted shyly.

"Oh, yes. Beans and barley. Sometimes it gets a run on something and we'll eat that for days, sometimes weeks at a time. There were times, well, after my husband left, we ate out of the pot every night in the week."

Finn looked very excited. "Yes. This is miraculous."

Maddy shrugged. "It's just an old iron pot. You see, what you do is—"

"Mama," Vanessa interrupted again. "I think it's ready."

Maddy sniffed the air. "You're right." She moved to the kitchen. "The top came off, so I guess it is done. Beans and barley, Vanessa, beans and barley. We've had a run on beans and barley for a couple weeks now," she said to Finn.

"I like it," Vanessa said.

"I know you do, girl, but your brother isn't terribly fond of it. Me, I'm getting a little bored with it myself. Not that I'm complaining, pot," she said to her supper. "Finn? Where are you going? Aren't you going to stay to supper?"

Finn had risen, and bowed slightly in her direction. "I must go. I have the information I sought."

"But there's more. I haven't finished telling you—"

"I have all the information I need. Thank you."

"But—well . . ." Maddy replaced the pot lid and went to open the door for him, since he seemed quite adamant about leaving. "Well, I hope I was able to be of some help in your research."

"Yes, much help. More than you realize. Thank you!"

"Uh, Finn. You're not going to tell everybody about this, are you?"

"No. I promise. I will tell no one. Thank you so much, Maddy Jackson." He left, leaving Maddy staring after him.

"He was kind of a strange man, Mama."

"Yes, he was. But I guess it takes all kinds. Wish he'd let me finish, though. Vanessa, give your brother the bad news and then finish setting the table. All this talking is making me hungry."

* * *

"Mom? Mama?" Maddy's focus drifted away from the silver coin. Her son stood in the doorway, his eyes large and wary. "Can I come in now, Mama?"

"What? I—oh—"

"I checked the whole place. Ain't no one else here."

"Oh, I suppose so, Michael." Clutching the coin in her hand, she reached for the phone.

In a small sleeping room a neighborhood away, Finn reverently examined the old cook pot. It seemed nothing special, just a three-legged pot with a lid and a handle to hang it over the fire, but Finn had no doubt that it was the treasure he sought. Carefully he set it down, kicked off his Reeboks, and struggled out of his jeans.

Soon he was attired in a red tunic, embroidered knotwork on the edges, over a white undertunic. His feet were clad in fine leather boots, and a sword hung from his belt. He slipped a golden torc around his neck and opened the door to the closet. A rectangular patch in back flickered like a broken TV.

Only one more thing left. He picked up the phone and punched out numbers, smiling in satisfaction.

"Maddy Jackson?" The voice on the other end sounded tinny and distracted.

"Yes? Who—"

"This is Finn. We talked about your Erin Cory?"

"Finn! What—what do you want? Oh, you have to call back; I have to call—"

"Do not be afraid. Nothing was hurt. I took only what I needed."

Alarm made the voice on the other end shrill. "What? What are you talking about?"

"I had to make you think it was an ordinary theft until I was away. I took only the Erin Cory, and I left you a goodly sum of silver for it."

"You? You left the silver? Broke into my apartment?"

"I did not take your electronic things. I took only what I came for, the cauldron."

"My cooking pot? Just a second. You just wait." After a couple moments she was back. "My pot! You stole it!"

"Did you find the silver?"

"I don't want your silver, damn it! I want my Erin Cory!"

"I am a champion of my people, and they have great need. You have children. I'm sure you can understand."

"No, I don't understand. You scared me and my two babies half to death to steal an old cooking pot, and you want me to understand? You're deranged. You're crazy."

"I am not deranged," Finn said patiently. "I am a hero of the Gael. My people need the food the pot can provide. I have paid you for it."

"Four generations of heirloom can't be bought for thirty pieces of silver."

"Only ten . . ."

"I want my Erin Cory back. I'm calling the police." With a sigh of consternation, Finn put down the receiver and turned to the closet where shadows flickered and played.

"We cannot raid the Sidhe for supplies," the sorceress-queen, Ailin, had said to him before he left. "Their magic is too strong. Be successful, Finn. Find the Iarinn Coire, else we die."

But the proud eyes that had bored into his seemed to say more. *Prove me wrong*, they had seemed to challenge. Beneath the hope and hunger and despair—*prove you're more like your brother than I think.*

That is what he had read in them as he turned from her and vanished into the doorway, the same doorway that he now faced from the other side. He held the handle of the cauldron casually but reverently by two fingers. Yes, he would prove to her, prove to them all, of what mettle was their new champion made.

In spite of his hero status, fear clutched him just a little as he stepped through the shadowy patterns in the back of the closet. The air that met him smelled different, a little musty, but smelled of home. Finn smiled.

He was within the dark passage of the mound; before him was a rectangular patch of blue sky. A white cloud scudded across it, and a bird appeared briefly. He took it as a good omen.

As Finn stepped from the mound, a grey-haired warrior, half nodding with sleep, looked up, gasped, and jumped to his feet.

"Finn! My lord!" In back of him Finn saw a multitude, the army of the Gael ranged around the cooking fires. The grey-haired warrior turned and called. Faces turned to him, and when they saw Finn, several came running.

"I thank the Dagda that I am not too late," Finn murmured, and lifted the cauldron above his head for all to see. A gasp and a sigh took the whole crowd. Soon, Finn was surrounded by his people, surrounded by expressions of awe, relief, thanks, and from all of them the underlying expression of hopelessness stalled.

The aging Queen Ailin, one of the first to approach him, smiled with relief, and the army surrounding him raised their swords and spears in a cheer so loud the Sidhe must have heard it over their own cookfires.

"Finn," Lady Ailin said. "You have brought us hope."

"I have brought you food." Finn gave the cauldron to one of the squires. "Put it over the fire, and put the lid on. There is no need of water. Now go." The boy smiled and bowed his head, taking the cauldron reverently, and took off at a dead run. Finn turned to Ailin. "It took longer than I'd hoped in that strange Otherworld. Are my men still well?"

Ailin and her nephew, Lord Marc, exchanged puzzled but amused glances. "My lord," Marc said. "You were gone but three days and three nights. This is but the morn of the fourth day."

Finn glanced at him, honestly surprised. "Was I?" He turned to Ailin. "Strange are the ways of your magic, Ailin."

"Never mind." They began walking toward the cookfire where a crowd had gathered around the pot. Marc walked ahead. "You are here and safe, and you have brought the cauldron. You are sure it is the cauldron?"

Finn smiled indulgently. "I have seen it work. I have no doubt."

"You must have many strange adventures to tell of your time in the Otherworld."

"Indeed I do."

"I would hear them."

"And I will gladly tell them, though it will take many nights."

Ailin's weary face creased into a smile, and she leaned closer. No one else was near. "I must admit to you, Finn, I had misgivings when you were declared champion after the Sidhe killed your brother."

"You had doubts as to my ability?" Finn was patient and forgiving, as befits a hero.

"Not your ability, no. You are as strong as your brother. But you have always seemed rash and hasty. Wisdom and patience also befit a warrior."

Finn arched an eyebrow and changed the subject. "You worry about the Sidhe."

"As I should. We had agreed to surrender if your brother was defeated by their champion. We broke faith."

"I will not suffer my people to be destroyed because of the failings of one man, even my brother."

Ailin smiled again and dropped the subject. "You will be wanting a bath and fresh clothing. My servants can see to this."

"I will indeed, my queen, but not till my men have eaten." He sat down at the queen's cookfire and accepted a cup of watered ale from a servant. As they waited for the wondrous pot to fill with food for the army of the Gael, Finn began to tell them of his wondrous adventures, of silver towers that reached into the sky, of chariots that puffed smoke and had invisible horses inside, of lamps that glowed without fire. He had easily captivated his audience's attention when one of his men came over and waited for his attention.

The man seemed hesitant, even embarrassed. "My lord," he said when Finn glanced up at him. "My lord, the pot still gives nothing."

"Nothing? What do you mean?"

"Nothing. We have waited two hours and more. There is still nothing inside." His puzzled expression was overcast with the same despair Finn had seen before leaving for the Otherworld.

"How have you used it?"

"We did as you instructed. We put it over the fire, put the top on, and waited."

"You did not put water in it?"

"You instructed us not to."

Finn rose. "Let me see this."

It was as the man had said. The iron pot radiated heat from the fire below, yet when they lifted the lid with a hook, they saw nothing within.

"Perhaps," the druidess-queen said behind him. "Perhaps it does need water."

"Perhaps," Finn agreed, puzzled himself. "Very well. Fill it with water."

Water was poured in and immediately began to steam. "Not so much. Not so much," the queen directed. "Leave it only half full." The men did as she commanded and replaced the lid. Their haggard hungry looks were leaning again toward despair. Finn and the queen walked away.

"Are you sure," asked the queen quietly, when they were well out of earshot, "are you sure you have the right cauldron?"

He stopped and faced her. "My Lady Ailin, your magic put me within a league of the cauldron, though even then it took me months to find it. The people there live as thickly as sacrifices within a wicker; they crowd out the trees and grass. But I spoke to the dark woman, who told me she only had to put the pot over her fire, put the lid on, and wait."

"Did she say how long it took?"

"She said it took different times. I assumed it took no longer than a usual meal. Sometimes it gave her barley stew, sometimes game—"

Queen Ailin was shaking her head. "But you did not see this for yourself? You did not see an empty cauldron give forth food?"

"I had no reason to doubt her, my lady."

"Those of low birth may say anything if they wish to sell you something, if she is interested in your silver rather than the truth."

"I did not . . . exactly buy it from her, my lady."

Queen Ailin paused to look up at him. "What? Did she then give it to you?"

For the first time, Finn looked uncomfortable. "No. I took it."

"Took it?" The queen frowned, and her voice became harsher. "How do you mean? Took it by force?"

"No, my lady. No one was hurt. I would not hurt a woman. I took it from the house when there was no one there and left a goodly sum of silver in return."

"But you stole it."

"The lives of my men, my clan, were at stake. She and her children would not starve without it, and my people would."

"You stole the cauldron from a woman and her children?" Her voice was louder now, and people nearby had begun to stare.

"They had no need of it! They would not starve. Look!" He flung his arm out. "The cookfires of the Sidhe are still out there! The smoke from their meals drifts up to our nostrils. They need not attack. They need only wait. And they know it!"

Her face as she looked at him was as stony as her hair was grey.

From a little ways away, one of the men called out. "Finn, my lady. The pot has boiled dry."

She glanced away from Finn and strode to where the

men stood with the cauldron. "It is said"—she turned back to face Finn—"that the cauldron will not boil the food of cowards."

Finn's jaw worked as he tried to keep back anger. "I am no coward, lady," he said slowly. "I entered your magic Door into a strange country of folk darker than night. Your magic with languages was incomplete. Oh, I could understand the language of birds, but they spoke of no cauldron. I only half understood the language of the people. I braved many dangers to bring back this cauldron. I am no coward!"

"You stole it from a woman and her babes. This is not the action of a hero." Around her the listening army began murmuring among themselves.

"My clan is starving! The Sidhe will destroy us soon!" Around him, his men's faces were as hard as the druidess's. "The woman will never miss it. I left silver for it."

The queen walked to the pot and with a hook turned it to show the empty interior.

"I don't understand." Finn strode to it. "I did as she said."

"It is obvious the magic fails us." She let go of the pot, and it swung over the blazing fire. "You have shamed us."

"No."

"It is you who have brought destruction on us."

The men around them now began to grumble. "We are doomed!" one whispered.

"No!" Finn began to back up.

The men began to speak. "The Sidhe will have our heads," one said. "Our women and children will be slaves."

"No," said Marc, drawing his sword and advancing on Finn. "Perhaps only one head will suffice."

"I have brought you the cauldron you seek. Obviously we are not using it properly. Lady Ailin! Stop this nonsense!"

"The gods will forsake us while we have a coward as champion." She did not look at him.

"I am no coward!" He backed up as Marc approached. "I went through the Door—" He looked behind him. "The Door." The mound was not far away. He broke and ran for it. The voices of his men roared behind him in anger and anguish. He reached the mound. "The Door. It's here somewhere." Something poked him painfully in the ribs. "Ow!"

"Will you die like a champion or like a coward? Draw your sword."

"There is no need to fight. The cauldron will work. I swear it."

"Life in the Otherworld has made you soft. I will take your head without a fight if I have to, coward." He drew back his sword to strike.

Finn drew his own and blocked the blow. "Stand back! I am champion and can outfight you. You have no chance."

Perhaps he was right. He was their best, save for his dead brother, and Marc was weak with hunger. But Finn had not touched a sword in many months. He had become soft, he realized. And Marc had anger behind him—and many men. Finn could not outfight them all.

Though Finn had nicked Marc's arm, Marc's return scored a strike against his leg. Finn cried out and stumbled backward against the mound. To one side, Queen Ailin was chanting, arms upraised. Chanting a curse, Finn realized. The next blow he blocked rammed vibrations all the way up his arm, and he almost lost his weapon. He only half blocked the next blow, and it scored a deep gash against his upper chest and left arm.

He could not hold out, he realized, and broke away, trying to circle the mound, trying to find the Door. A score across his back made him fall. Queen Ailin's spell reached a climax, and the mound began to buckle beneath him.

"Let you live your curse all the hours of your life. Let you wander until you have found your honor. Let us be rid of you!" The dirt of the mound crumbled in on itself. The fall, though only a few feet, seemed to last for a long time. He landed heavily, his injured arm trapped beneath him, on a hardwood floor. Something lay beneath his head—his Reeboks. The back of his closet shimmered with magic. Briefly he saw the images of Marc and Ailin. He rested his head against the Reeboks, feeling the blood seeping out of him.

A metal clang sounded, and the pot came hurling out of the closet at him. He tried to fend it off with his good arm, but the pot was still hot and burned him. He cried out in pain as the cauldron and its lid went bouncing into the interior of the room. Ailin's image reappeared once more, mouthing silently at him, then the flickering at the back of his closet collapsed into a shining point at the center before disappearing altogether. He stared at empty shelving.

He had no idea how long he had been away from the Otherworld. He hoped the phone still worked. Crawling to it, he lifted the receiver, heard a dial tone, and punched 911.

"Please help me," he said into the receiver. "I'm bleeding." He gave them the address. "Hurry." He dropped the receiver and rested his head against the floor, sobbing from injuries and shame.

"Mrs. Maddy Prudence Jackson?" The woman's voice on the phone sounded hesitant.

"Yes. This is she." Maddy was working at home on the computer that day and was a little annoyed at being disturbed. It was nearly impossible to work in the evening with the kids around.

"Yes, my name is Anne Woloszyk. I'm a nurse at Rush-Presbyterian—"

"Rush-Presby? Oh, my God. The kids. My babies! Are they all right?"

"The kids? Oh, no, Mrs. Jackson. I'm not calling about your children. I didn't even know you had children."

Annoyance returned. "Well, then—I don't understand."

"Let me explain. Do you know someone named Finn O'Neil?"

Annoyance increased. "Yes, I do. Or did."

"He's a patient here at the hospital—"

"Patient? What happened to him?"

"He was in some kind of a fight, apparently. Came in with several knife wounds. I've been assigned to him. He told me that he had something of yours, an iron cooking pot?"

"My pot! It's been found?"

"He said he borrowed it and wanted to make sure it got back to you."

"Borrowed it? Hmph! That's not my word for it."

"Would you like me to come by with it? I've just gone off shift, and he was very adamant that it be returned to you."

"Yes, I would like that very much, Mrs. Wo— Wal—"

"Woloszyk. Ms. I can be by in about an hour and a half."

"Thank you very much, Ms. Wo— Wolosh—"

The other laughed. "Anne. Just call me Anne."

Later, Maddy opened the door almost before Anne Woloszyk knocked. "I was looking out the window for you. Come in."

A pretty white girl with glasses stepped in. Her wavy hair was caught back in a barrette, and she was dressed in nurse's whites and sensible shoes. A Jewel shopping bag hung from her arm.

Maddy closed the door behind her. "It was good of you to come over, Anne. It must have been out of your way."

"Oh, not that far. I just live in Rogers Park."

"Let me take your cloak. Is it a bit chilly?"

"Just a little. Thank you." Maddy put the cloak on a hook and turned back with open curiosity.

"Mr. O'Neil," Anne began, "was very concerned that I give this back to you as soon as possible." She took the pot and its lid out of the shopping bag.

"Hmph," Maddy said in response to Mr. O'Neil. "Yes, there it is. My old cooking pot. My Erin Cory. I sure am glad to have it back."

"It's very unusual. Sort of like the cauldron in *Macbeth*." She handed it to Maddy and found herself a seat.

"Mm?" Maddy was inspecting the pot.

"*Macbeth*. Shakespeare. It's a play. There are these three witches around an old cauldron, and Macbeth comes by—"

With an indulgent smile, Maddy interrupted her. "Yes, I have been to college. I do know about Shakespeare."

Anne stammered and subsided as Maddy walked into the kitchen with the pot.

"Now you tell me what this Mr. Finn O'Neil has gotten himself into."

"Oh, yes. He came in with several severe gashes that required quite a few stitches."

Maddy reentered the front room and sat down across from Anne. "Is he going to be okay?"

"He lost a lot of blood, but he wasn't critical." She hesitated for a moment. "They were talking about moving him to the psychiatric section." Maddy sat back. "He was talking . . . strange. Odd things. Did he seem strange to you?"

Maddy nodded, with a wry smile. "Very strange. What kind of things was he saying?"

"He was very . . . concerned that you get that cauldron back. Gave me the keys to his place and insisted. That's what he called it. A cauldron. He said that, uh, that it might save his honor and let the gods favor him again."

"Gods! He some kind of heathen?"

"I don't know, Maddy. Perhaps he thought he was."

"Maybe I should visit him. Poor boy. Show him there are no hard feelings."

Anne lowered her eyes. "That'll be a little difficult, Maddy. When I came on shift this morning, I found out he'd disappeared."

"Disappeared?"

"Gone. Without a trace."

"How could he disappear, as injured as he was?"

"I don't know. Though perhaps he heard talk of the psychiatric wing, and it scared him."

Maddy sighed and leaned back. "You know, it makes me wonder. You think you can trust people, and I let him into my house. Me alone with two children. Perhaps I was crazy to let him in."

Anne was fishing in her purse. "He left this." She held out a piece of paper. "It has your name on it. It doesn't make a lot of sense."

Maddy took it. " 'May the dag—dagda? bless you and me,' " she read. " 'I am a hero and cannot live in shame. I go to salve my honor. There might still be time to save my people.' You're right. It doesn't make much sense."

"At least you've got your stew pot back."

"That's right, at least." She rose and entered the kitchen.

"Why don't you stay to supper? Make up some for all your trouble," she called into the other room.

"Oh, I don't want to be any bother."

"No bother at all. My kids'll be home soon. I'd have to get supper for them in any case. Besides, around here there's always plenty." She laughed, as if at a private joke. "You know, that Finn—one of his problems was that he was just too damn hasty. He never did let me finish telling him about my cooking pot."

"He seemed to think there was something unusual about it."

"Oh, there is, though no one believes me." She paused, musing. "Maybe that's why I let him in. He believed me."

Anne came in to stand beside her. "Can I help? Cut vegetables or something?"

"No need. The pot does everything."

"Sort of a medieval crockpot."

Maddy laughed. "It's been in my family a long time, but it ain't that old. But I never got a chance to tell that Finn." She fished around in the cupboard above the stove. "Ah, here it is. This old pot ain't worth nothing without its stone." To Anne's puzzled look, she brought out a flattened stone, about as big as her hand, variegated like agate or marble, and worn smooth. "You ever heard of stone soup?"

Anne nodded, smiling. "Soup from nothing."

"Well, that's what this is. You put the stone in the bottom," she explained as she did so, "put the lid on, and start the fire under it. That's all you gotta do, and you get supper. Stone soup. Soup from nothing." She smiled at Anne's doubtful look. "Sometimes it's a microwave, sometimes it's a slow cooker. You're looking at me kind of funny, Anne."

Anne smiled. "If you heat that pot up, you'll get a hot rock, nothing more."

"I suppose if someone had told it to me, I'd find it hard to believe, too. But I learned about this pot standing in front of my mother's stove when I wasn't even big enough to see the stove top. She learned it from her mother the same way. And her mother's mother was a slave on a plantation, and she didn't even have a stove. There are some things you just have to accept." She turned to look at the iron pot. "Sometimes I'm afraid that if I stop believing, it'll stop happening."

Anne's look was doubtful, kind, and a little pitying.

"It was Shakespeare who said, 'There are more things in heaven and earth, Horatio—'" Maddy stopped to sniff the air.

"'Than are dreamt of in your philosophy.' Yes, I know the quote.

"Why, I do believe it's going to be a microwave today," Maddy said. "Maybe it knows there's an unbeliever in the room."

Anne was sniffing the air in astonishment. She smelled food, coming from the pot.

With a wooden spoon, Maddy lifted the lid and set it aside, then spooned some of the brimming stew out and tasted it. "Mm. Excellent. As usual." She offered some of it to Anne, who tasted.

"Unbelievable! and I was standing right here." She looked at Maddy as if she might be a sleight-of-hand artist.

Maddy laughed and tasted again. "Beans and barley. I guess it was good I didn't tell that Finn about the stone, or he would've taken it, too. This old pot has fed us well for four generations, but I do wish it would get off this kick of beans and barley."

About Barbara Rosen and "The Griffin"

According to the scribbled biographical information she sent, Barbara is "cosily married to my Griffin" (I'm fairly sure I'm deciphering her handwriting correctly. . . .) and rescues abandoned animals. She says that Hawk was one of her strays, now placed in a loving home, and she thinks her characters' bios are more interesting than hers.

The Griffin

Barbara Rosen

The birds hadn't awakened yet. Mariellen fumbled for her key, her breath drifting away in white clouds on the cold air. In a month it would be daylight when she got off the subway; in a month she wouldn't be half-frozen by the time she got to work. She pushed open the door and flicked on the lights, blinking in the sudden fluorescent glare.

Inside it was comfortably warm. A racket of excited barking met her ears before she was halfway down the stairs.

"All right, all right, take it easy."

She unlatched the door leading to the backyard and turned to survey the kennels. The Jefferson dog was crowding the front of his cage, eyes pleading. Too well housebroken for his own good, poor thing.

"Okay, you first." She released the catch and the cage door swung wide. The dog bolted into the yard, stopped outside the door, and cocked his leg against the fence.

Mariellen watched until he was finished. Then she filled her bucket, pulled the paper lining out of his cage, and began her morning cleaning.

* * *

By the time Dr. Saunders arrived all the boarding animals had been taken care of and Mariellen was halfway through the hospital ward. The doctor didn't usually disturb her when she was working, but today he came downstairs, pacing restlessly and peering into the cages.

"The Roth cat had diarrhea again," she reported. "Should I run another fecal?"

"Might as well."

"And the Feingold dog still won't eat."

He nodded. "Let's wait another day; that one can afford to lose a little weight."

"That's for sure. Okay, oh, yes, the Johnson dog. Do you want to keep her on fluids?"

"Yes."

"I need to start another bag, then."

"Fine." The vet hesitated. "Anything else?"

"Not so far."

"Let me know." And he left.

That was odd, Mariellen thought. *Why didn't he wait for me to come up today? Wonder if there's some animal he's especially concerned about. No, he'd've mentioned it.* She leaned down to open the next cage.

"What the hell—!?" Her hand jerked back involuntarily and she dropped the sponge. There was something really disgusting here. She squatted on her heels and took a good look.

Pink. Pink and—stubbly? Was that stubble? Or ... Mariellen leaned closer. No, not stubble. Pin feathers, maybe. Yes, there was the head: it was a bird, all right. But enormous, ungainly ... A huge hooked beak, dark eyes showing through translucent lids ... The skin was translucent too, with branching blue veins beneath the pink. Whatever it was, it was awfully young.

Mariellen opened the cage and extended her hand.

The eyes opened slowly, obsidian eyes rimmed with blue. For a long moment the bird studied Mariellen's hand, turning its head to look first with one eye and then the other. Mariellen held still. The head came closer, bobbing a little on the scrawny neck. Huge, taloned feet shuffled as it stood upright; naked wings flailed for balance. And then the head came to rest in Mariellen's outstretched palm and the shining eyes closed contentedly.

She flexed her fingers, stroking the hot skin at the huge bird's throat. It snuggled closer.

"What happened to *you*?" she crooned. "Why aren't you with your mama?"

She slowly withdrew her hand and the nestling, disappointed, opened its eyes again and got up on all fours to follow her.

All fours?!?

Mariellen blinked. It *couldn't* be! There must be two animals in that cage. But Dr. Saunders wouldn't put a cat in with a baby bird and besides—besides, it wasn't exactly a cat.

The—the *thing*—had come all the way to the front by now. And behind the wings it wasn't a bird at all, it was fuzzy and golden and flecked with brown. It had sturdy hind legs and a tasseled tail.

Mariellen felt as if she were going to vomit. For a moment she was so angry that her vision blurred.

To do this! To stitch together two unrelated species, to put animals through this kind of agony so some damned arrogant scientist could play God!

The monster teetered at the edge of its cage and squalled at her.

Mariellen sat down on the floor, gathered it into her lap, and wept.

She didn't hear Dr. Saunders on the stairs.

"Mariellen?"

She lifted her head and glared at him. "What sonofabitch did this?"

"Did what?"

"This! This—graft, this obscenity!"

"Oh. Nobody."

"*No*body?" *Don't give me that,* her tone said.

Dr. Saunders sighed. "The Tsantes family brought it in last night. They found it when they were vacationing in Greece. That is, they found an egg."

"An *egg*?"

The doctor nodded. "They thought it was an ostrich egg," he continued. "They took it home for a souvenir."

"There aren't any ostriches in Greece," Mariellen protested.

"*I* know that, *you* know that . . ." He shrugged. "They found this enormous egg, they figured it had to've come from an ostrich. So they took it."

Mariellen was silent. She could just picture it: the careless tourists on their holiday, the thoughtlessness with which they would rob a nest, break off chunks of living coral, carve their initials in the skin of a cactus that would still be quietly bleeding to death when they were safely and ignorantly home. . . . She held the creature in her lap more closely.

"They had it in a suitcase," Dr. Saunders was saying, "with a lot of underwear piled up around it so it wouldn't break. But it broke, all right." He smiled. "When they opened the suitcase there was nothing left of it but bloody bits of shell and wet membrane. And that." He pointed. "Mrs. Tsantes was hysterical."

"Serves her right," muttered Mariellen.

"Well, at least they didn't toss it into the nearest Dumpster." Dr. Saunders was grinning now. "Do you have any idea what kind of animal that is?"

Mariellen shook her head.

"Unless I'm very much mistaken, it's a griffin."

"A—but that's mythology!" She squinted at him suspiciously. "Are you making this up?"

"See for yourself."

It was true. There was no scar where the naked bird body ended and the fuzzy lion body began. The golden down began almost imperceptibly just behind the wings and gradually grew denser until the whole back of the body was covered with fur.

"What does it eat?" she asked.

"That's a good question. If it were a lion cub I'd put it on kitten formula. But raptors need raw meat, roughage. . . ."

Mariellen considered. "I'll try it on formula first. If it won't accept that we can always switch over to meat."

"Sounds good to me," said the vet.

The griffin eyed Mariellen curiously.

"Think I'm your mother, do you?" she asked. "All right. Here comes breakfast." *Now how on earth am I supposed to get a nipple into that beak*? she wondered. *Do griffins nurse their young? Well, it must eat something.* She sat cross-legged on the floor again and took the little griffin into her lap. "All right, now . . ." She nudged the nipple against the corner of the oversize beak. "Aren't you going to open? Come on . . ." She squeezed a few drops of formula out, hoping against hope that some of it would penetrate. "You don't have to look at me like that. Here, I'll wipe it off, okay?" She decided against trying to force the beak open; all *that* would accomplish, she suspected, would be the donation of a couple of fingers toward this infant's first meal.

She set the bottle down. "A bottle baby you are not," she muttered. "Let's try you on some meat."

By the time she got back with the meat Mariellen imagined the griffin was beginning to weaken. How long had it been without food? Since last night, at least. There would have been some residual nourishment from the yolk sac, but surely that must be gone by now. She cut the beef into narrow strips and went back downstairs.

As soon as the griffin saw the meat it began to squall. "Got the right stuff this time, did I?" she asked it. "Okay, open wide." She unlatched the cage and the griffin came scrambling out, not waiting to be lifted. She dangled a strip of meat. It gulped it down without hesitation, gaped for more. Mariellen laughed. "Call you anything, but don't call you late for lunch, huh?" The griffin paid no attention; it was too busy eating. It ate three pounds of stewing beef before it was satisfied.

"Success!"

"Hm?"

"The griffin. He ate for me."

"Wonderful!" The vet smiled. "You'd better call the Tsanteses, let them know."

"All right."

"What's the matter?"

"It's just—they don't really *want* him, do they? I mean, he was an accident. . . ."

"They're the ones who brought him in."

"Well, yes, I know. But—"

"Give them a call."

"All right," Mariellen said again. Dr. Saunders was right, of course; the griffin belonged to the Tsantes family. But they didn't want him. All *they* wanted was an ostrich egg to put on their damned mantelpiece. Just because they'd brought him to the vet didn't mean they wanted him back. It was going to be like the time those bastards brought the ocelot in. She just knew it.

The ocelot had been a beloved exotic pet until it grew up and began wrecking the house. The owners had had it declawed—not by Dr. Saunders—and the wounds had become infected, gangrenous. The only way to save the animal's life had been to amputate some of its toes.

And when Mariellen had called to tell the owners that their ocelot would live, all that had mattered to them was that it wasn't beautiful anymore. It had been Mariellen's lot to hold the warm, breathing body in her arms as Dr. Saunders put it to death.

Now there was this griffin. Hell, the Tsanteses hadn't wanted a pet to *begin* with! And—Mariellen had to admit it—the griffin was far from beautiful.

She sighed. Might as well make the call and get it over with.

"Manny?" Mariellen could hear Mrs. Tsantes faintly in the distance. "Would you take this call? It's the vet."

In a moment Mr. Tsantes was on the line. "Yes?"

"I'm just calling to let you know that the—uh—animal you brought in last night is doing fine." Mariellen tried to sound enthusiastic. "We've got him eating."

"Oh, Jesus," said Mr. Tsantes.

"Pardon?"

"I thought the thing would die."

"He didn't," said Mariellen succinctly.

"Oh, Jesus." There was a pause. "Listen, can't you find somebody else to take that thing? We don't want it."

"I see." Mariellen thought, *Why the hell didn't you think of that before you brought it home?* "We'll do what we can," she said.

The griffin was huddled in the back of its cage, sleeping off its meal. Mariellen squatted to peer in at it, but it didn't move. She wondered how it would sleep when it grew up. Would it put its head behind its wing like a bird? Or sleep tail over nose like a big cat? She wondered if it would be allowed to live long enough for anybody to find out. Damn those people anyway.

She got slowly to her feet and went to give the bad news to Dr. Saunders.

The vet nodded. "Well, we expected this," he said.

"Are you—? I mean, you're not going to—?"

"I certainly *hope* not."

Mariellen didn't pursue it; she knew the answers as well as he did. A veterinarian's office was not a shelter or a free boarding facility. Every charity case took up cage space that was intended for use by paying clients. But Dr. Saunders was speaking.

"What?"

"I said, I don't suppose *you'd* want to take him."

"Me?"

"He'd have to stay here for a while, of course. Until we're sure he's stable. But after that—" He shrugged and looked at her hopefully. "Take a few days. Think it over."

"I—" Mariellen was silent. She was thinking of how helpless the griffin was, how dependent on their mercy. She was remembering its deep, glowing eyes, the trusting weight of its head in her open hand. "It's a wild animal," she said. "It ate three pounds of meat this morning and it's only a baby. It's going to be enormous, isn't it?"

"I would think so."

It trusts me, thought Mariellen. *In this whole world, I'm all it's got.*

"Do you suppose it could be trained? Housebroken?"

"I don't know."

It trusts me, but can I trust it? she was thinking. *What will it do to my house? What will it do to my life?*

"What about Hawk?" she said.

"Oh, I don't think Hawk would hurt him, do you?"

"That wasn't what I meant. Hawk may be a humongous Doberman, but *you* know what he's like. I could come home someday and find this cute little griffin picnicking on my dog."

The vet snorted. "If I know Hawk, he'll have it following him around like a puppy."

"Well, maybe."

"You don't have to decide right away," he reminded her.

"I know." But on some level that had nothing to do with reason, Mariellen knew that her decision had already been made.

For the rest of that week Mariellen's mood swung wildly from excited anticipation to horrified dread. Assuming responsibility for a large, carnivorous wild animal of unknown propensities was utterly insane. Whenever she allowed herself to imagine what the griffin might be like when it was full grown, she knew that she couldn't possibly go through with it. But when the griffin squalled at the sound of her voice, when it scrambled into her lap and nestled there, she felt a wave of protective love that overcame all reason. At those times she positively looked forward to bringing the little thing home, to giving it the comparative freedom of her small apartment. She pictured it basking in the sunlight and playing with Hawk.

After all, she assured herself, *he's perfectly gentle now. Look how carefully he takes his meat from my hand.*

At the beginning of the second week Mariellen took the griffin home.

By this time the tips of the pin feathers had burst and the naked pink bird body was covered with a fine golden down. The griffin's front half looked ridiculously like an oversize Easter chick. On a diet of raw meat sprinkled with bone meal and powdered vitamins it had grown alarmingly. When Mariellen held it in her lap now, the lion half spilled over onto the floor.

Dr. Saunders had lent her a large airline carrier to take the griffin home in. Now he helped her load it into the back seat of a cab. Mariellen was barely able to squeeze in beside it.

The cabbie glanced over his shoulder. "Big dog, huh?"

"No." Mariellen smiled. "It's a griffin."

The cabbie maintained an offended silence for the rest of the trip. When they arrived Mariellen had to wrestle the carrier out of the cab by herself.

"Well, here we are," she said.

The griffin didn't respond. It was turning its head from side to side, blinking in the sunlight.

"I don't know how I'm supposed to get you up the stairs." She stooped and began to drag the carrier toward her building. Once inside she stopped to consider.

"Three flights ... can you climb?" She opened the carrier. "Come on, then."

The griffin stepped out slowly. Its eyes were huge and its tail twitched.

"It's all right," Mariellen soothed.

The griffin looked up at her and made a twittering sound she hadn't heard before.

She laughed. "That's right. We're home." She lifted the empty carrier into her arms. "Follow me, now."

For a moment the griffin stood watching Mariellen ascend. Then it humped itself along behind her, wings flailing uselessly. By the time they reached the top of the first flight both were panting.

"A fine pair *we* make," Mariellen said. "Tell you what. If I join the gym, will you come too?"

The griffin gulped and shut its beak.

"Rested already, are you? All right, let's go. Two more flights."

Hawk was whining softly on the other side of the door.

The griffin was familiar with dogs, of course, but he'd never met one face-to-face without bars in between. If Hawk came bounding out on top of him now, Mariellen was afraid he might try to run away.

"Let's put you in your carrier, all right?" But it wasn't all right; there was no way the griffin was going back into that thing. When Mariellen persisted it ruffled up its feathers and clacked its beak at her.

"Oh, hell." She put her hands on her hips. "What am I going to do with you? Hawk has to go out." Maybe she could get hold of Hawk's collar as she opened the door. . . . "Well, here goes."

She turned the key, cracked the door open, and made a wild grab for Hawk as he hurtled by. She missed, but the griffin didn't. Before she could react, it had fastened its beak in Hawk's shoulder. Hawk screamed.

"Dammit!" Mariellen managed to lock her hands around the griffin's throat and pull it away from Hawk before it could do any more damage. She was glad to see that the dog was sensibly keeping his distance.

She loosened her hold slowly, keeping one wary hand on the griffin's neck. It seemed calmer now that Hawk had retreated, but she didn't dare let go. She maneuvered it through the open door, reached in for Hawk's leash, and shut the door in the griffin's face.

With his enemy out of sight Hawk came to Mariellen to be leashed. But he kept looking nervously at the door and his flanks were quivering.

"You poor thing," she said, stroking his head. "What did that nasty griffin do to you, hmm?" She checked him over briefly. There was an ugly gash on his shoulder, but aside from that he seemed to be all right. "Let's get you out first. Then we'll clean you up, okay?"

Hawk looked up at her and wagged his tail once. *I hear you*, the wag said, *but I'm not happy.*

He favored his left foreleg all the way down the stairs.

As she walked her dog, Mariellen had ample time to regret her decision to bring the griffin home. What had poor Hawk done to deserve this?

Well, yes, he *had* come rushing out the door. But he hadn't been heading for the griffin, he'd been coming straight toward— Mariellen stopped in her tracks, causing Hawk to turn and look questioningly back. Could it be? Was it possible that the griffin had been *protecting* her?

After all, it had never reacted one way or the other to the dogs it had seen at work. Maybe she was being too hasty. In any case, the office would be closed by now; she wouldn't be able to bring it back until morning anyway.

"All finished, Hawk? Come on, let's go home."

Mariellen opened the door a crack and peered inside. The griffin was nowhere in sight. As she stepped over the threshold Hawk braced his legs and pulled back against the leash.

"Come *on*, Hawk! It's all right, fella, he's not here."

Where *was* he, anyway? She hauled Hawk inside and shut the door. The dog pressed against her, quivering. No point in keeping him leashed; he'd only be at a disadvantage if the griffin attacked him again. When she turned him loose he shrank back against the door, looking at her pleadingly. "Don't worry, sweetheart," she said. "I won't let him get you." *At least I hope I won't.*

She tiptoed through her apartment, looking into corners and underneath furniture. Was it always so quiet in here? Mariellen could hear herself breathe. Behind her, at the door, Hawk whined once and was silent. She entered the bedroom.

And there, curled up on the bed, was the griffin. It was such an anticlimax that she almost laughed.

Griffins *did* sleep with their tails wrapped around them, she noted, but they put their heads behind their wings like birds too.

Hawk didn't meet the griffin again until evening. The griffin, rested and fed, was enthroned on Mariellen's bed like a pasha. When Mariellen called Hawk in, all it did was look at him with each eye in turn and ruffle its feathers contentedly, clucking like a whole barnyard full of chickens. Hawk advanced a step, sniffing audibly. When nothing happened he rested his big head on the bed.

"*Good* Hawk," Mariellen crooned. "What a good *boy!*" The griffin edged closer to Hawk, stretched out its long neck, and began to nibble around his ears with its hooded, yellow beak. Hawk closed his eyes.

Mariellen let out the breath she'd been holding. This was going to work. It was actually going to work!

"Hawk," she said, "allow me to introduce you to our new griffin."

Before she went to bed Mariellen shut Hawk out of the room, lifted the griffin onto the newspapers she'd spread in a corner, and waited until it had used them. So *that* was all right.

As she went out with the soiled papers Hawk came trotting back in, went straight to his bed, and curled up with a sigh. The griffin had clearly chosen to sleep on Mariellen's bed; it was already climbing back up, using its beak as well as its claws.

When Mariellen got under the covers it snuggled close, draping its neck around hers like a feather boa. In the middle of the night she half awoke to find the griffin preening her as it had Hawk; dozing off again she dreamed that her mother's careful hands were combing and braiding her hair, strand by strand.

In no time at all it seemed as if Mariellen had always lived with the griffin. After the first couple of weeks she left the bedroom door open when she went to work. Her two pets had become such good friends that she no longer worried that they might hurt each other in her absence.

The griffin had, of course, continued to grow. In a month's time it was taller and longer than Hawk. When it got up on the bed now it no longer climbed, but sprang, half spreading its wings. Mariellen wondered how much longer her bed was going to take it.

Its appetite had grown too. Mariellen tried to interest it in Hawk's kibble, but all it would eat was meat—pounds and pounds of stewing beef, liver, and kidneys. "I spend more on you than I do on myself," Mariellen told it. "Do you know that?" But the griffin just came closer and ruffled its head feathers. "Oh, all right, I'll scratch you."

Even in its first plumage the griffin was a beautiful beast. Mariellen's fingers almost disappeared in the dense golden crest that crowned its head. Its eyes, half-closed with pleasure, were the color of honey bathed in sunlight. They could outstare the sun and see in the dark. At night they glowed like a cat's.

The wing feathers were chocolate brown with a fringe of gold. Behind the wings the lion body had grown long and angular, with claws to rival the talons up front.

Mariellen hadn't dared to take the griffin outside. Her landlord had never made any trouble about Hawk, but she had an idea that he might not be too happy if he found out he had a griffin on his premises. Besides, there were laws about keeping exotic pets in the city—and the griffin was certainly exotic.

Nevertheless, Mariellen knew that she couldn't keep such a large animal cooped up forever. Somehow she was going to have to let it get out and exercise.

The solution occurred to her one morning as she was walking Hawk. Even now, with the season so far advanced, it was just beginning to get light when she left for work. What if she set the alarm for an hour earlier and gave Hawk and the griffin a good romp in the park? Nobody was on the streets at that hour. Well, almost nobody. Mariellen did not permit herself to think about the muggers and rapists that kept nice people from going into the park when it was dark outside. Presumably the sight of Hawk would keep them at bay. And if it didn't . . . "Would you protect me?" she asked the griffin. "Would you understand if somebody threatened me?" With any luck she wouldn't have to find out.

The following morning Mariellen leashed Hawk, stepped out into the hall with him, and held the door open for the griffin to follow. It came as far as the threshold and stopped.

"*Come* on," Mariellen invited. The griffin took a step back. "Do I have to put a leash on you?" Hawk was whining, wondering why she was taking so long. "This is ridiculous," Mariellen muttered. And she stepped behind the griffin, pushed it over the threshold, and slammed the door.

Immediately all hell broke loose. The griffin, turning to retreat from the big scary world outside, found its way blocked. Panic-stricken, it flung itself against the door, squalling loudly and leaving long scratch marks on the paint. Mariellen was afraid it would break its neck.

She reached for the doorknob just as it leapt again. Its talons closed on her forearm and sank in like daggers. "Oh, shit!" With one desperate heave she got the door open and stumbled inside, almost falling over the griffin as it streaked in ahead of her.

Clutching her bleeding arm she made her way to the bathroom. The arm looked pretty bad and it was starting to hurt like hell, but she could flex her fingers all right. She didn't think any nerves or tendons had been damaged.

In all the excitement Hawk had been forgotten in the hall. When Mariellen got around to looking for him she discovered that in his anxiety he had deposited a large, smelly load on the landing.

Evidently, she thought as she went back in for paper towels, *this is not going to be my day.*

It was several days before all three of them were recovered enough to experiment with the great outdoors again.

This time Mariellen was less ambitious. She reasoned that it might be easier and safer to take the griffin out onto the fire escape first.

On Sunday morning, after Hawk had been walked, Mariellen opened the fire escape window, climbed out, and called to the griffin. As she'd hoped, the streets were relatively empty. Few people bothered to get up this early on Sundays.

The griffin came to the window willingly enough. Resting its head on the sill, it cocked one bright eye at the sky and the other at the sunlit sidewalk below. Mariellen patted the bars beneath her and kept calling. The griffin's head lifted and craned outward and finally one taloned foot advanced to the windowsill and clung there. "What a brave fellow! Come on, then!" There was a flutter of wings and the whole enormous eagle body stood framed in Mariellen's window.

It was fascinating to watch the griffin look around. Mariellen was used to Hawk's superior senses of hearing and scent, but she'd never been around an animal that was *visually* superior to her before. Not only could the griffin look directly at the sun without discomfort, it was clearly watching things that Mariellen couldn't see. Its head snapped around, now this way, now that, following—what? a bird? a plane? Mariellen giggled. With a griffin in her life, anything seemed possible.

"So? Are you going to come out?" As if it had understood, the griffin stepped forward, bringing the remainder of its improbable body into view. Bathed in sunlight it ruffled its feathers, half spread its wings, and basked.

Now that the griffin had discovered the joys of the fire escape it wanted to be out there all the time. Mariellen would go about her housework with the window open, the griffin's long, tasseled tail hanging over the sill like a bellpull.

Once she heard a child's voice from below: "Mommy! Look at that big bird on that fire escape!"

And the mother's bored response: "It's stone; they put it there for decoration."

"It *moved*, Mommy! I *saw* it!"

"Don't be silly. Come on. You're going to make us late."

"But I *saw* it, Mommy!" The child's wails of protest faded out, presumably as its mother dragged it off.

Mariellen grinned. *A good thing*, she reflected, *that adults don't usually look at anything above their own eye level*. But this couldn't go on forever. Sooner or later the griffin was going to be discovered, and then what?

It was time to have another try at bringing the griffin to the park.

Mariellen didn't make the mistake of trying to rush the griffin again. After Hawk's walk she shut him in the bedroom, propped open the hall door, and encouraged the griffin to venture out.

It was a slow business. Here there was no expanse of bright sky to entice the griffin, only a long, shadowy hallway with an abyss at the end where the stairs began. In the space of a half hour it had advanced no farther than the welcome mat.

Mariellen persisted. On subsequent mornings she fed

the griffin out in the hall, moving closer and closer to the stairs until she finally had it going down a full flight to get its meat.

Now that the hall was familiar territory the griffin began, quite literally, to spread its wings. Mariellen's apartment, with its small, cluttered rooms, wasn't big enough to accommodate its full wingspan, but the hallway was. It began by stretching, went on to flapping, and eventually startled both Mariellen and itself by taking momentarily to the air. It made such a ruckus over this accomplishment that Mariellen had to hustle it back into her apartment before it woke up all the neighbors.

The very next morning it launched itself halfway down the stairs and glided to the landing below, never touching down once.

"So you really can fly," Mariellen said. "What's going to happen when we go to the park? Are you going to come back to me?" It was something to think about. A griffin wasn't the sort of animal one could walk on a leash. Even if she could improvise a harness, Mariellen suspected that the griffin could overpower her with no trouble at all. Either it would stay with her of its own free will—or it wouldn't.

That night she dreamed that she had the griffin out in the park. It sailed up into the sky, shedding golden sparkles from its wings, higher and higher until it melted into the clouds and was gone. She reached futilely after it and it was there after all, a warm conglomeration of feathers and fur. Mariellen smiled in her sleep, her happy arms full of griffin.

It was still shadowy outside when they arrived at the park. The griffin, reveling in its newfound powers, had sailed down all three flights of stairs without hesitation and followed Mariellen out onto the street.

Once they reached the park, however, it hung back, squalling and jittering.

"You're not much for novelty, are you?" Mariellen

asked it. "All right, you can look from there." She returned to where the griffin had stopped and stood beside it, gently scratching around its head. After a while its eyes glazed contentedly and it began to make clucking noises in its throat. "See? Nothing's going to hurt you here." She advanced again and this time the griffin followed.

It was strange to see it picking its way over the dewy grass. *I've never seen him in a natural setting before*, Mariellen thought; *only against a backdrop of man-made things. And even this isn't right for him, all this green. . . .*

Except for the tip of its tail the griffin stood perfectly still. In the first rays of the rising sun it shimmered like a figure picked out in gold thread on a medieval tapestry.

Mariellen looked at her watch. "Come on," she said, "it's time we were getting back." The griffin twittered, staring up into the distance. "I have to bribe you, huh? That's what I like about you. You're so docile and obedient." She pulled a plastic bag of meat strips out of her pocket. "How does breakfast sound? Ah, *now* I have your attention, do I?" She fed the griffin a piece of meat. "No, you don't get any more till we're moving. *That's* a good griffin. What a good boy!"

It was a great relief to Mariellen to have assured herself that the griffin would follow if she lured it with meat. Apart from assuaging her fear that she might lose her pet, it meant that now she could consolidate both her morning outings. Long before sunup the next day she clipped a leash on Hawk, put the griffin's breakfast in her pocket, and headed for the park.

Afterward Mariellen was to remember that summer as a sort of honeymoon with the griffin. The dark untenanted streets, the early morning hush, breathed magic.

When they got to the park she would let Hawk run loose. The big dog would race in joyous circles as the griffin scurried along behind flapping its wings to keep up. Then, panting, sides heaving, they would collapse together onto the cool grass. Sitting there with them Mariellen would hear the dawn chorus of the birds. It was like being in the center of a crystal cup: a vibration of silvery chirps beginning at the rim of the world and swelling until it filled the sky.

Then the sun would rise. All the silver and black would dissolve into color, the flat silhouettes of trees solidifying into shifting masses of green. In the low, slanting light the grass glowed in multiple transparencies, crisscrossed by its own shadows.

And Hawk's amber eyes, the griffin's golden ones, would be looking into Mariellen's with love.

Little by little the griffin learned to fly. It had been half spreading its wings to sail down the stairs for some time now, but that was more like parachuting or hang gliding than real flying; Mariellen had never seen it even attempt to take off from level ground. She was beginning to doubt that it could.

But in these morning romps with Hawk the griffin kept extending its wings as it ran and one day it achieved just the right combination of angle and groundspeed to take to the air. It was only up for a moment, so astonished at itself that its legs kept running as it flew. Mariellen laughed aloud. It looked like a cartoon character that hadn't yet realized that it had run over the brink of a cliff.

When it landed in a tangled heap of wings and claws, she lavished praise and reassurance in equal measure as she helped it get its mismatched parts reorganized. "What a *good* griffin! What an *exceptional* griffin! Here, that's your foot holding your wing down. Let me just—*that's* the way! Better now?" The griffin picked up a strand of her hair and preened it absently, as if returning the favor. But its eyes had a distant look and it kept turning its head, now this way and now that, to look up at the sky.

Sure enough, the next morning it began practicing in earnest. As soon as it began to run its wings were in motion, angling against the wind for the magical combination of speed and thrust that would bear it aloft again. Every now and then it would spring straight up from its muscular hindquarters, wings flapping futilely.

Not until it had reduced itself to a state of panting, glassy-eyed exhaustion was Mariellen able to approach. "You're trying too hard," she told it. "We all know you can fly." The griffin bowed its golden head, ruffling its crest to ask for petting. Its wings stood out from its body as it tried to cool itself; Mariellen could feel the heat rising from its breast.

What must it be like, she wondered, *to have a gift and not know how to use it? To be defeated by the very arduousness of your attempts?*

She stood for a long time stroking and soothing the griffin before she called Hawk to be leashed and started back home.

It said a lot for the griffin's intelligence, Mariellen thought, that it seemed to pace itself after that. It still tried to fly, but there was no frenzy now. Watching it was like watching an athlete in training. It put itself through a sort of exercise routine, stretching, flexing, and beating its great wings before it tried to get off the ground. Sometimes it succeeded, sometimes it didn't. But it always left time to play with Hawk before the sun got too high and they had to go home.

The sun was rising later now. In no time at all it was going to be too cold in the mornings to stay out very long. But as the darkness gradually closed in, Mariellen was able to prolong the griffin's outings in the park without too much worry about being seen.

They had been incredibly lucky so far, she realized. On the few occasions on which someone had actually seen the griffin the reaction had been one of startled disbelief. No curiosity, no overtures of friendship, no panic: just a quick double take followed by a casual saunter across the street. *As if*, Mariellen thought with amusement, *putting a double*

*line of parked cars between you and the big, wild beast
would do any good.*

But no one had screamed, no one had alerted the police
. . . no one had made trouble.

In fact, the nearest thing there had been to "trouble"
had been Mariellen's friends, who couldn't understand why
she never wanted to go out and do things with them anymore. "What do you *mean*, you're going to bed? It's only
eight-thirty, for God's sake! Are you sick? Do you want
me to come over? I *know* you have to be at work early,
but you never *used* to go to bed at—oh, all right. I'll talk
to you Saturday, okay?"

Sometimes Mariellen thought she should just tell them
about the griffin and get it over with, but somehow she
never did. Working with animals, that was okay, that was
her livelihood. Owning Hawk—well, that was okay too:
Hawk was, theoretically at least, her protector. But sharing
her home with a griffin . . . *What do you need it for*? she
imagined them asking. *It's big, it's expensive, it's damned
inconvenient—hell, it's probably illegal*! Mariellen smiled.
It was all true, no question about it. But they'd have it
backward if they put it like that. The real question, the
only one that mattered, was not whether she needed a
griffin but whether this particular griffin needed her.

Besides, Mariellen happened to love her particular griffin. But she was quite certain that her friends wouldn't
understand that either.

Four-thirty. They had almost two hours before the sky
grew light. Mariellen turned Hawk loose, watching his
breath stream behind him in misty banners as he ran. The
griffin skimmed along in pursuit. He was getting pretty
good at this, Mariellen noted. His air time was longer every
day. He still lost altitude from time to time, but all he
needed to do was kick off with his strong lion's legs to be
aloft again. Now and then he'd make a playful dive, talons
reaching for Hawk's hindquarters, and Hawk would yelp

and put on more speed. *He's not really frightened,* Mariellen thought. *He knows the griffin would never hurt him.* And indeed, the next time the griffin dove, Hawk flung himself to the ground and allowed his friend to "catch" him, striking up with his forelegs and snapping at the air as the griffin parried with its beak.

Mariellen felt as if she could watch them forever.

They were resting when the sun rose. The summer chorus of birds had been silent for some time now: without young to rear and territories to defend, the birds no longer heralded the dawn. Against the slowly lightening sky the trees took on form and color, shaggy clumps of yellow and scarlet now instead of green. The wind picked up, blowing leaves like confetti.

It was going to rain again. The gulls had assembled on the lake as they always did before a storm. As Mariellen watched, one detached itself from the flock and winged toward them, keening.

Suddenly she felt the griffin tense under her hand. She glanced down just as it sprang away, eyes fixed on the gull. It leapt once, twice; then the huge wings beat down against the solid air and carried it out over the lake.

Hawk was on his feet, whining excitedly.

In slow motion the griffin rose, wheeled, hovered over the gull, and plummeted to strike.

A flurry of feathers exploded from the griffin's talons and was carried away by the wind: white leaves flecked with red.

"Griffin!" Mariellen called. "Griffin! Come back!"

But this time there was no awakening, no warm griffin snuggled in her arms to comfort her. She screamed again, her throat tight with unshed tears.

The griffin flapped heavily to the shore. There it crouched, oblivious of Mariellen, mantling over its prey. When she tried to approach, it turned to face her, hissing like a cat. Its eyes were wild.

Oh, God, what am I going to do? She pulled her bag of

meat strips out of her pocket and waved it temptingly, but the griffin showed no interest. It had the gull torn open now and was ravaging it with its hooked beak, tearing and gulping. When it lifted its head its cheeks were sticky with blood. *The sun is up*, Mariellen thought. *The sun is up and people will be coming.*

"Griffin," she pleaded. "Please!" The griffin paid no attention.

The first spectators arrived.

"All right, calm down. Where is he now?"

Mariellen blew her nose and clutched the receiver as if it were a lifeline. "Here," she said, "with me. They wanted to shoot him, but I wouldn't get out of the way and when they grabbed hold of me, Hawk—" she choked.

"I know," Dr. Saunders said, "they had it on the news. He'll be all right; it was only a tranquilizer dart."

"But they took him away!" Mariellen wailed. "He's waking up somewhere in a cage, all alone—!" She started sobbing again.

"He'll be all right," the vet repeated. "He's licensed, isn't he?"

"Yes."

"Good. Then they can't keep him when you come to claim him. Anybody can see he's not a vicious dog."

"He was trying to protect me."

"And he did. He did a great job. Was that when you got the griffin away?"

"Uh-huh. He—after they sh-shot Hawk they picked him up to put him in a cage and while they were busy I took the gull away. He was almost finished. He didn't care anymore."

"And then he followed you?"

Mariellen nodded. "Yes. He was still hungry. I showed him the meat. . . ."

"Right through all those people, huh?"

"Yes." To her surprise, Mariellen giggled. "They got out of the way."

"I'll bet they did."

"But it's no good," Mariellen said, suddenly tearful again. "They know now. They followed us. Everybody *knows*."

"I know." There was a long pause. "Look, I can't stay on now. People will be coming in."

"Who's going to clean all the—?"

"I will. Don't worry about it, you've got enough to deal with over there. I'll call you back at eleven, okay?"

"Okay. Thanks."

"Sit tight." And he hung up.

Mariellen moved over to the window and pulled a corner of the curtain aside. They were still out there, all those people. *What's the matter with them?* Mariellen asked herself angrily. *Don't any of them have jobs to go to?*

She missed Hawk, missed his solid dependability, the way he would suddenly be at her side waiting humbly for her to notice him. She missed the feel of his warm, flat forehead under her hand.

She let the curtain fall, turned, and nearly fell over the griffin.

"This is all your fault," she told it, "do you know that?"

The griffin chirred and stood on tiptoe, stretching its long neck to put its head on her shoulder.

"Oh, leave me alone." She turned her back on it and went to sit on the bed. *What am I going to do?* she wondered. *How am I going to get Hawk back? What if the police come with a warrant and break down the door? How am I going to keep them from taking the griffin away? What's going to become of us all?*

There was a shuffling sound from the living room, followed by a thud. Mariellen went to look. The griffin had squeezed behind an armchair and was huddled in the corner, moaning to itself. Mariellen had thought the morning could hold no further misery, but in that first instant of utter panic she knew how wrong she had been. Was the griffin sick? Had the gull somehow poisoned him? Pushing the chair aside, she knelt beside the griffin, lifting its head in her hands. It looked up at her with one golden eye and a tear slid down its beak onto her wrist.

"So that's it," she whispered. "You miss him too." And she pulled the griffin close and held it in her arms until it slept.

The ringing of the telephone awakened them both. Untangling herself from the griffin, Mariellen made her way groggily across the room and lifted the receiver.

"Dr. Saunders here. Sorry I'm late."

Mariellen yawned. "That's okay."

"I've been making some calls. How would you like to work for an animal shelter? In the country?"

"I don't *want* to put him in a shelter!"

"What?"

"The griffin. I'm not putting him in a shelter."

"No, no. The griffin will live with you and Hawk. In a trailer."

"Oh." Mariellen came fully awake. "Would you mind starting over, please?"

"There's a no-kill shelter in Pennsylvania looking for a full-time caretaker. They only pay minimum wage, but you'd get a trailer, free utilities, a big garden. . . ."

"Do they know about the griffin?"

"Their consulting veterinarian is an old classmate of mine. A very good vet, by the way. I've told him everything. He feels you're exactly the sort of person they've been looking for. Overqualified, of course . . ."

"Would the griffin be able to—to run free there?"

"Not during adoption hours. But the rest of the time—yes. The nearest town is about ten miles away."

"I'll take it," said Mariellen.

The vet laughed. "So fast? Don't you want to know how big the shelter is? What you'll have to do?"

Mariellen shook her head impatiently. "It doesn't matter. It's the only way, don't you see?"

"Yes. You're right, of course. If you stay here, they

won't let you live. I—you *do* have other options, you know. I'm sure any zoo would be delighted to—"

"You know damned well that I wouldn't put the griffin in a zoo."

"I didn't think you would." The vet's voice was warm. "I'll tell the shelter manager to call you and make all the arrangements, then?"

"Yes. Please." Mariellen took a deep breath to steady her voice. "I'm going to miss working for you, Dr. Saunders."

"I'll miss you too. Those people in Pennsylvania don't know how lucky they're about to get."

"Thanks," said Mariellen. And then she hung up because she was afraid she was going to start crying again.

The trees had already lost their leaves up here and it was cold. Mariellen swung open the trailer door, breathing deeply of the forest-scented air. Hawk bounded down the steps, cocked his leg against the nearest clump of weeds, and danced back to her, barking excitedly.

"Yes, yes, we're coming." She glanced into the dim interior of the trailer. "Well, lazybones?" The griffin's head appeared in the doorway. "Spoiled rotten, that's your problem. What do I have to do, start waking you up at four o'clock in the morning again?" The griffin shook itself, ruffling its feathers. Its long tail trailed behind as it descended the steps. "Disgraceful, that's what you are." Mariellen moved the griffin's tail out of the way so she could close the door. She had to admit, it was nice not to have to get up in the middle of the night anymore. Nice to be able to sleep until a reasonable hour, like a normal person. Not, she thought ruefully, that her life was ever likely to approximate what anybody would call "normal" again.

By now the griffin had relieved itself on the same clump of weeds Hawk had used and was starting to perk up. Hawk barked in its face and tore away, inviting it to chase him. The griffin stretched, first one wing, then the other, shook itself again, and galloped clumsily after the big dog.

Mariellen settled herself on the trailer's steps to watch.

Twice they circled, three times, and then the griffin took to the air, spiraling upward. Into the brilliant morning sky it rose, golden in the sunlight. And even when it was visible only as a bright speck against the blue, the sound of its voice came faintly back to them, crying out its joy.

About Elisabeth Waters and "Weather Witch"

I like to end my anthologies with something short and amusing, and since Elisabeth has been my live-in secretary for the past fifteen years, she's right there when I need a story in a hurry. This one, however, was already on hand, having been part of the short-short issue (9). Elisabeth is currently working on another story about Jan, who grew up to become a stage magician.

Elisabeth, in addition to writing, ice skates and takes flying trapeze lessons. (Maybe she's suicidal. . . .) Her first novel, *Changing Fate*, came out in April 1994, and she is just starting her second one.

Weather Witch

Elisabeth Waters

It was all Peter's fault. If he hadn't given me *How to Become a Witch in Twelve Easy Lessons* for my birthday, none of this would have happened. And he didn't want to weed the vegetable garden yesterday.

Well, maybe some of it was my fault, too. I didn't want to weed the garden either; it's really not a fun way to spend a beautiful Saturday morning. And I am nearly two years older than Peter, and Dad is always saying that a big sister should set a good example for her little brother. And I was the one who looked up at a sky with only a couple of puffy little clouds high up in it and remarked, "Gee, if it were raining, we wouldn't be able to weed the garden."

Peter's face lit up, the way it always does when he gets one of his bright ideas. His "bright" ideas always get us into trouble we could never have imagined when he came up with them, and if I'd had any sense at all I'd have run for the garden and started weeding. "Jan, I'm pretty sure there's a rain-making spell in that book I gave you."

I guess I don't have much sense, because I followed Peter up to my room and helped him look for the book

He was the one who found it, shoved under my bed with eight other books I'm supposedly reading, including my history textbook and two library books—one overdue, one miraculously not.

As advertised, the book was divided into twelve lessons, and it did say on the first page to do them in order. But Weather Magic was lesson seven, and we didn't have time to do lessons one through six and still make it start raining before Dad found us goofing off.

So we took the book and went outside to our favorite place down by the stream where we hide when we don't want to do chores. Bruce, our collie, followed us, but he just lay down and went to sleep, so he wasn't in our way. Peter held the book and told me what to say and I cast the spell. I think I did just what the book said to, and Peter says I did, too. And at least part of it must have been right, because it did rain. But, honest, the book said "rain," not "tornado"!

I was standing there with my eyes scrunched closed, concentrating on making it rain, when Bruce started whimpering and scrambled to his feet. I opened my eyes to see what was bothering him, and saw all those dark grey clouds piling up. I yelped, Peter looked up from the book, and the wind hit the tops of the trees with a great rushing roar. We ran for the storm shelter under the barn as fast as we possibly could and made it just as the storm hit. I got pretty wet during the last few seconds before Dad, who had been watching anxiously for us, got the door closed behind me.

Peter was smart enough to hide the book under his shirt before Dad saw it, and Dad was so relieved we were safe that he didn't ask too many questions about where we had been and what we'd been doing that we didn't notice the storm coming sooner.

It was a pretty bad storm, but at least nobody got killed or badly hurt, and most of the crops are okay. But it went straight through the place where we cast the spell, and it only missed our house by about ten yards!

Today is a beautiful day, with not a single cloud in a brilliant blue sky. And as soon as I finish cleaning up the vegetable garden and weeding what's left of it, I'm going to take that book, starting with lesson one, and read it very, *very* carefully.